Peanut, Butter, & Crackers

Fetch!

PAIGE BRADDOCK
Coloring by Kat Efird

VIKING

To Mom and Dad, for instilling in me
a love and respect for animals. –P. B.

VIKING

An imprint of Penguin Random House LLC, New York

First published in the United States of America by Viking,
an imprint of Penguin Random House LLC, 2021

Visit us online at penguinrandomhouse.com.

Library of Congress Cataloging-in-Publication Data is available.

Manufactured in China

ISBN 9780593117460

1 3 5 7 9 10 8 6 4 2

Book design by Paige Braddock, Jim Hoover, and Lucia Baez.

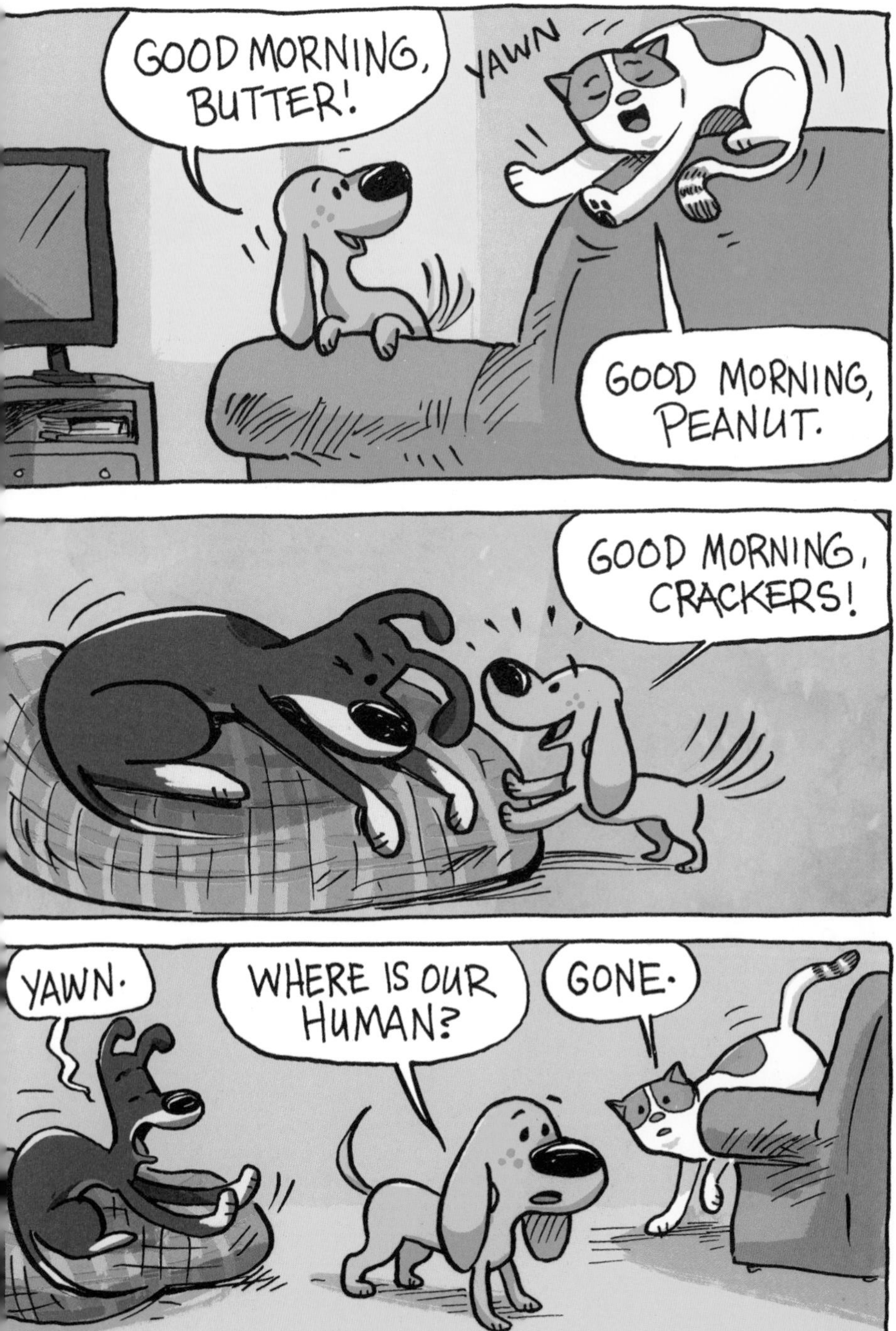
GOOD MORNING, BUTTER!
YAWN
GOOD MORNING, PEANUT.
GOOD MORNING, CRACKERS!
YAWN.
WHERE IS OUR HUMAN?
GONE.

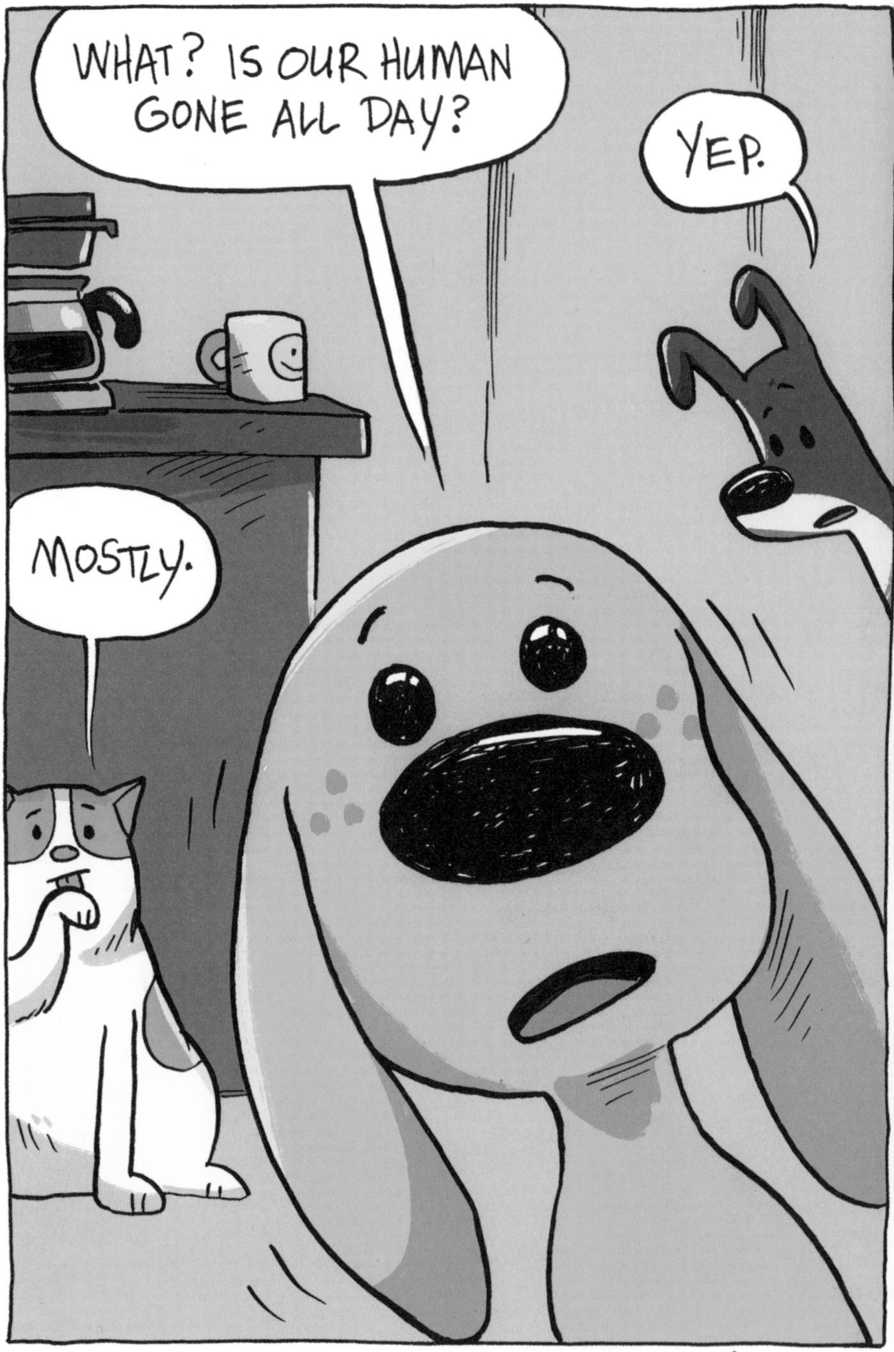
WHAT? IS OUR HUMAN GONE ALL DAY?
YEP.
MOSTLY.

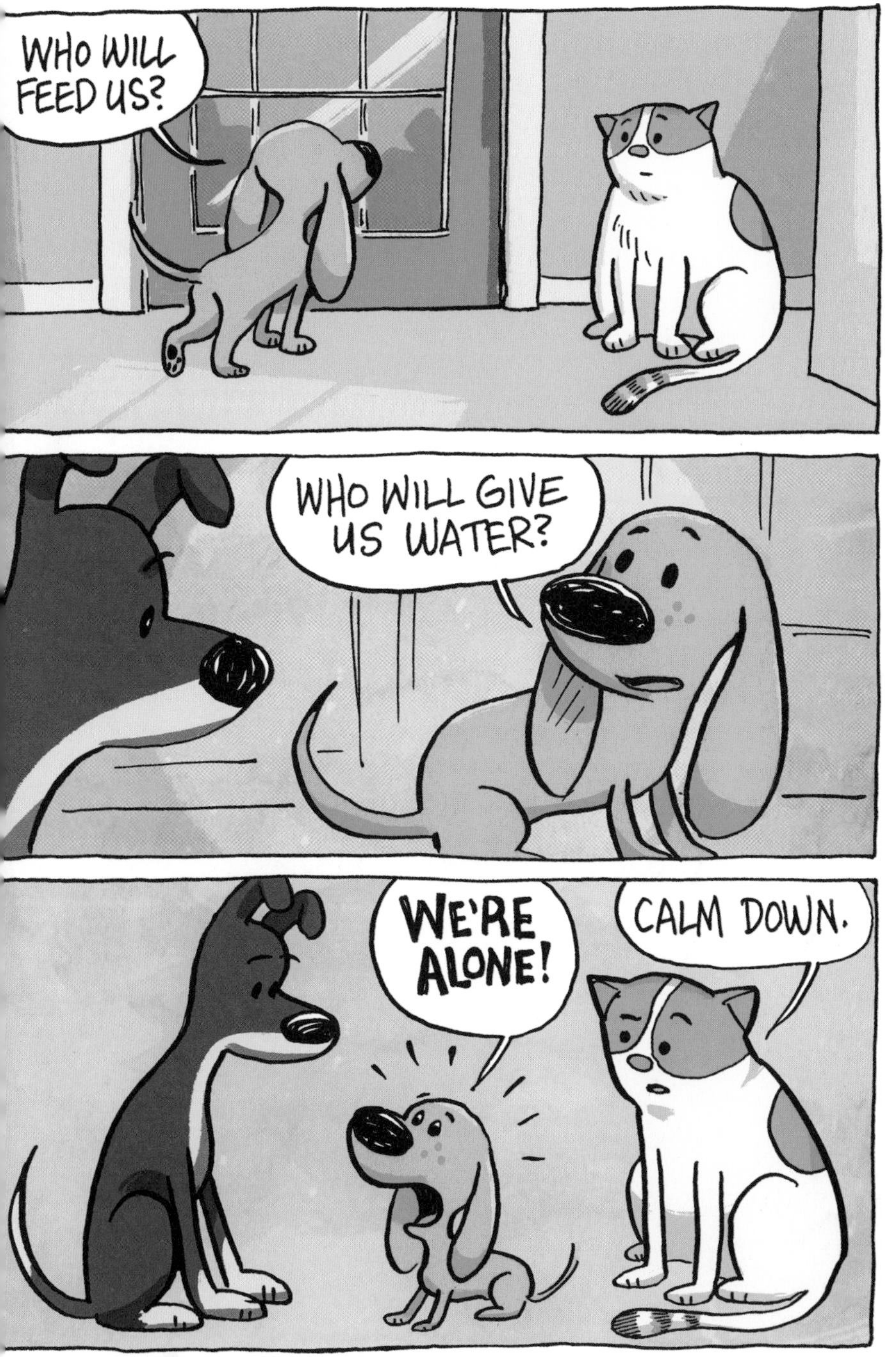
WHO WILL FEED US?
WHO WILL GIVE US WATER?
WE'RE ALONE!
CALM DOWN.

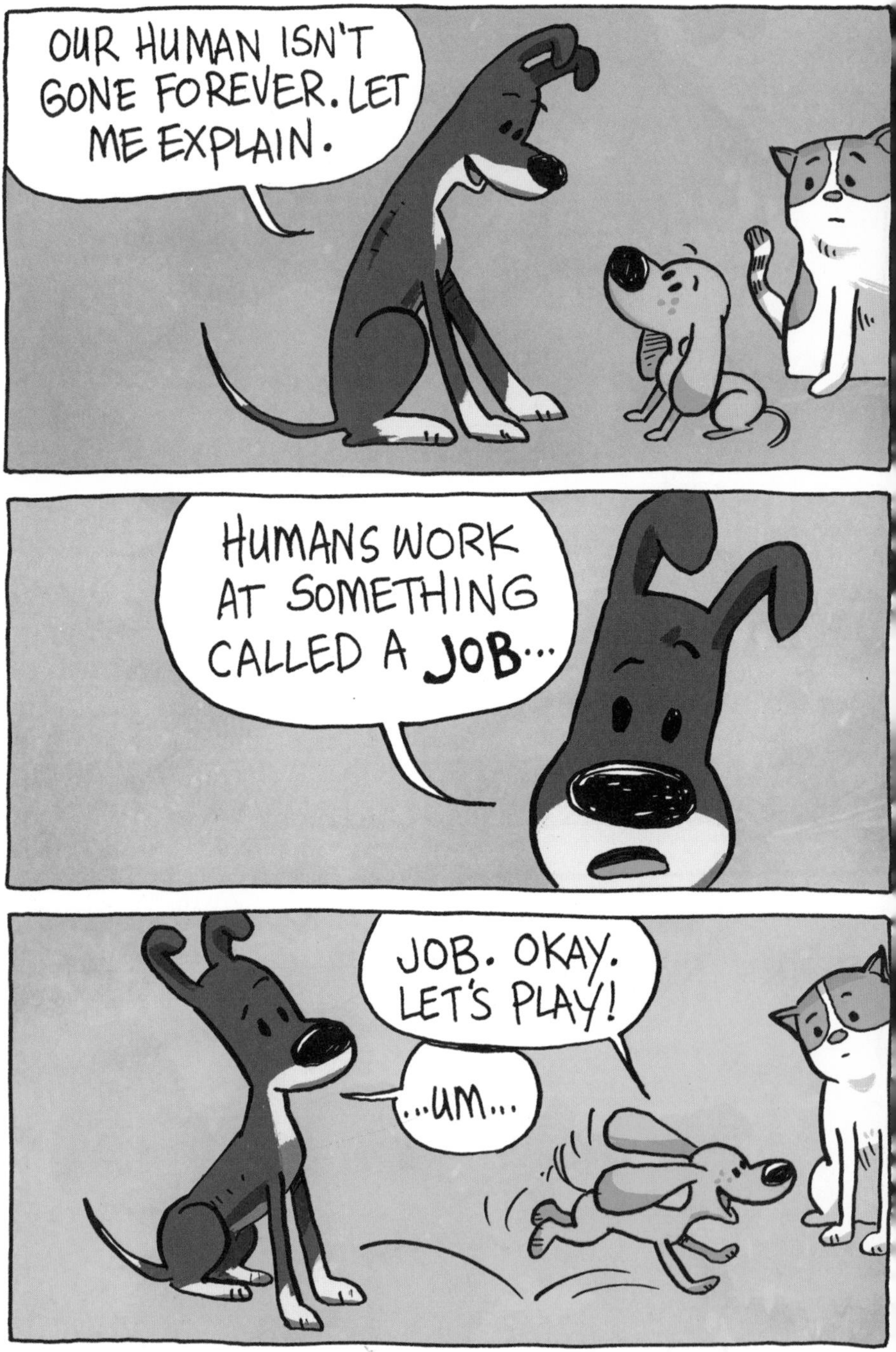
OUR HUMAN ISN'T GONE FOREVER. LET ME EXPLAIN.
HUMANS WORK AT SOMETHING CALLED A **JOB**...
JOB. OKAY. LET'S PLAY!
...UM...

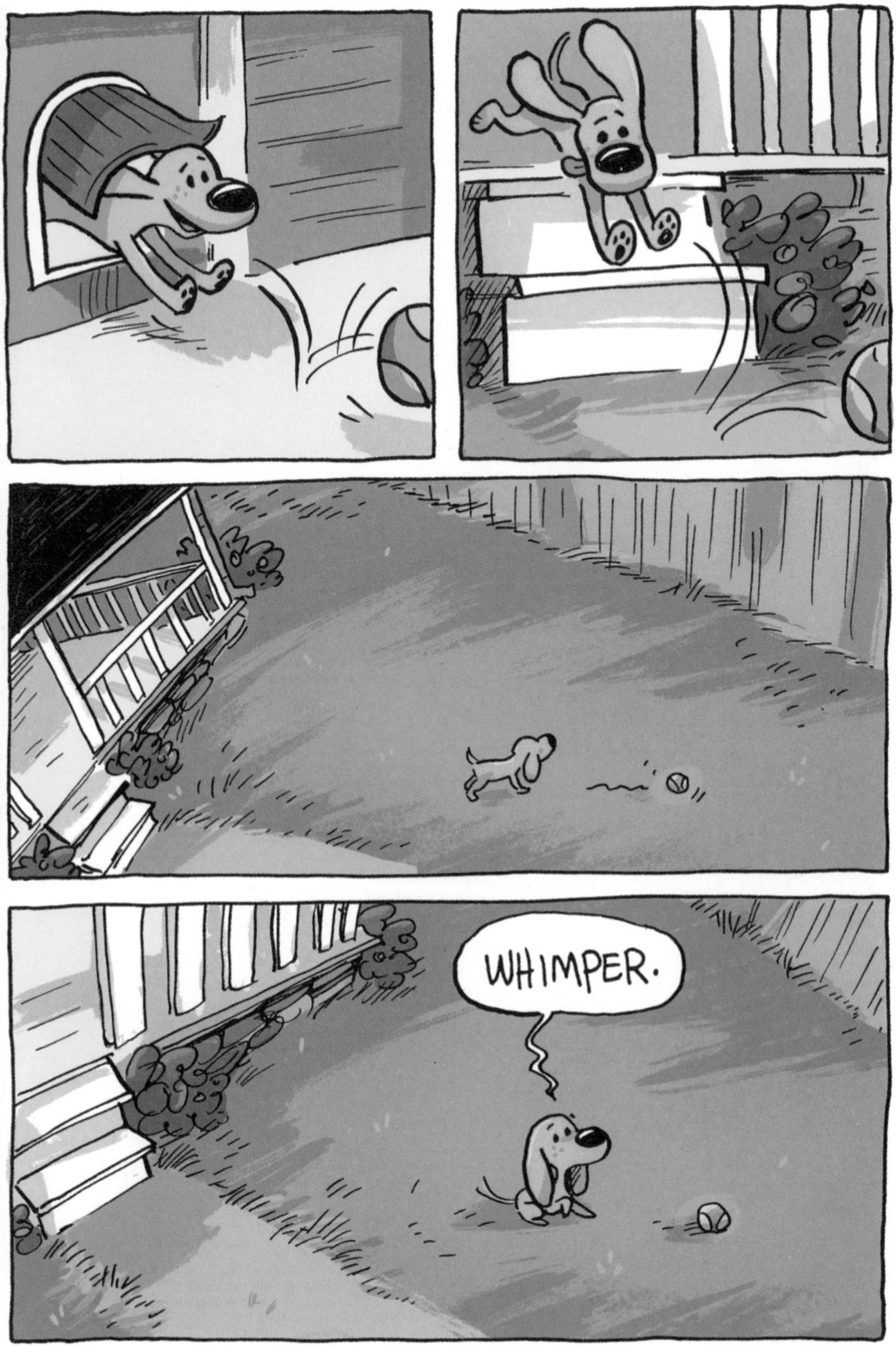
WHIMPER.

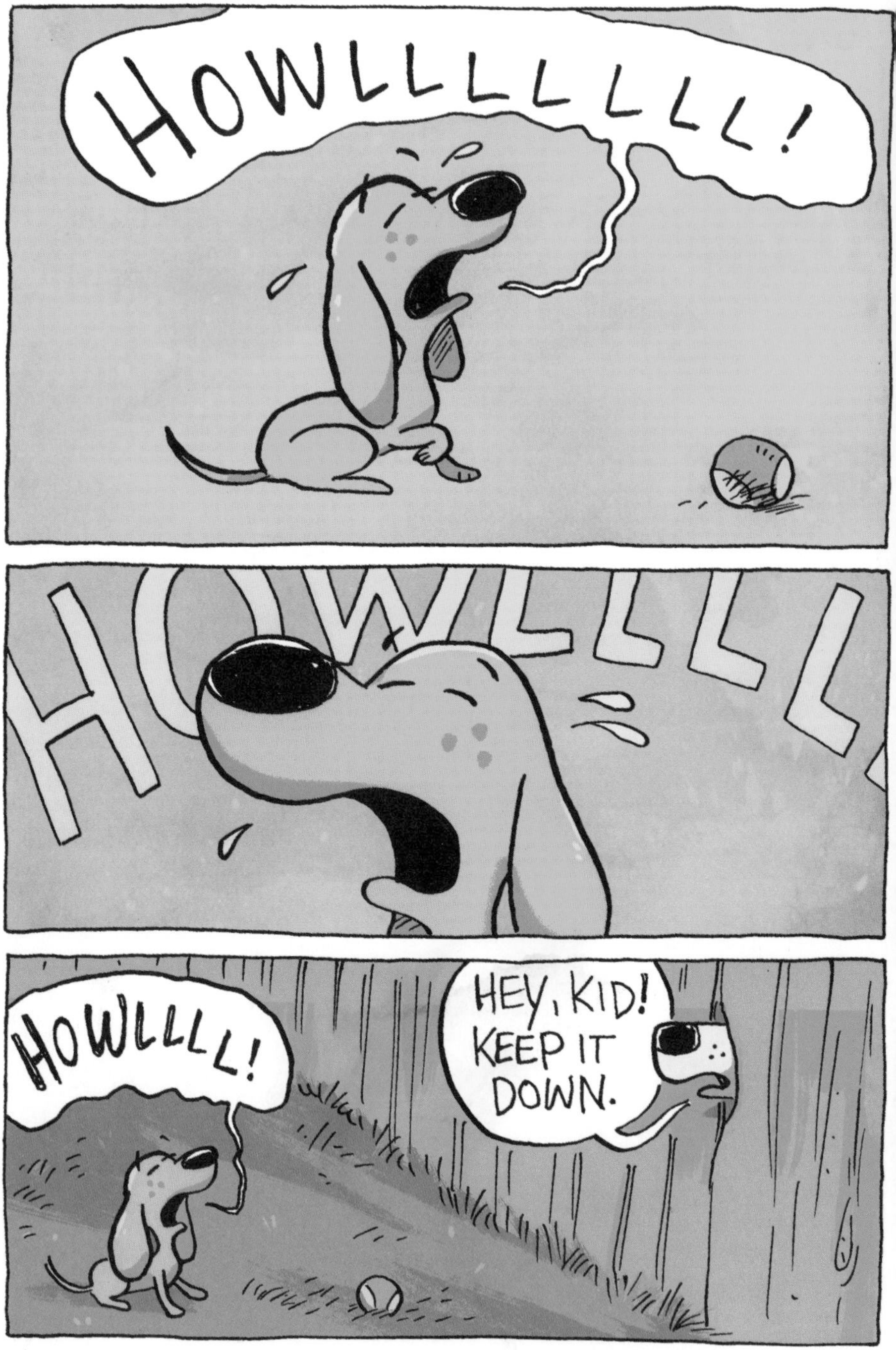
HOWLLLLLLLL!
HOWLLLL
HOWLLLL!
HEY, KID! KEEP IT DOWN.

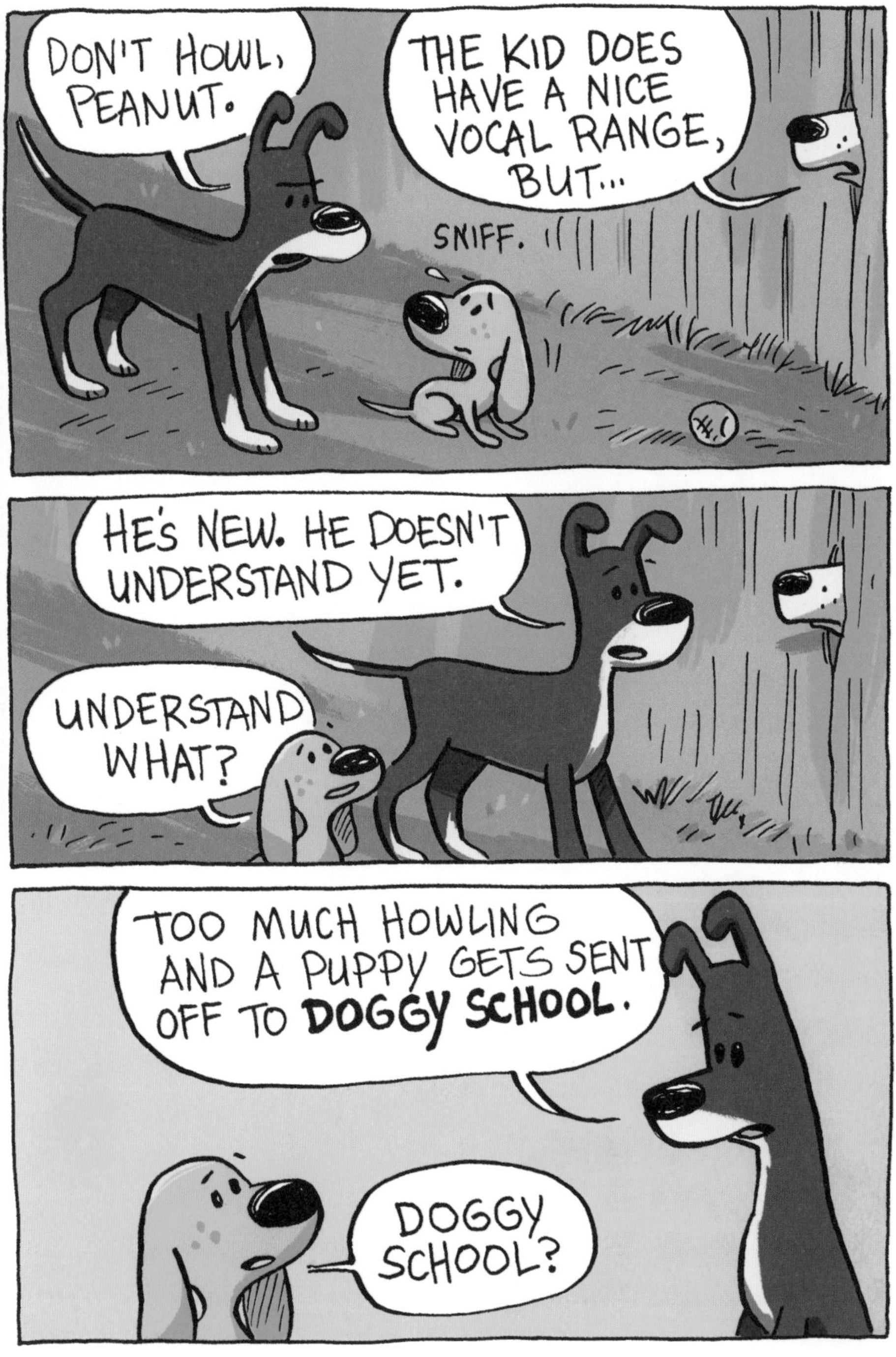
DON'T HOWL, PEANUT.
THE KID DOES HAVE A NICE VOCAL RANGE, BUT...
SNIFF.
HE'S NEW. HE DOESN'T UNDERSTAND YET.
UNDERSTAND WHAT?
TOO MUCH HOWLING AND A PUPPY GETS SENT OFF TO **DOGGY SCHOOL**.
DOGGY SCHOOL?

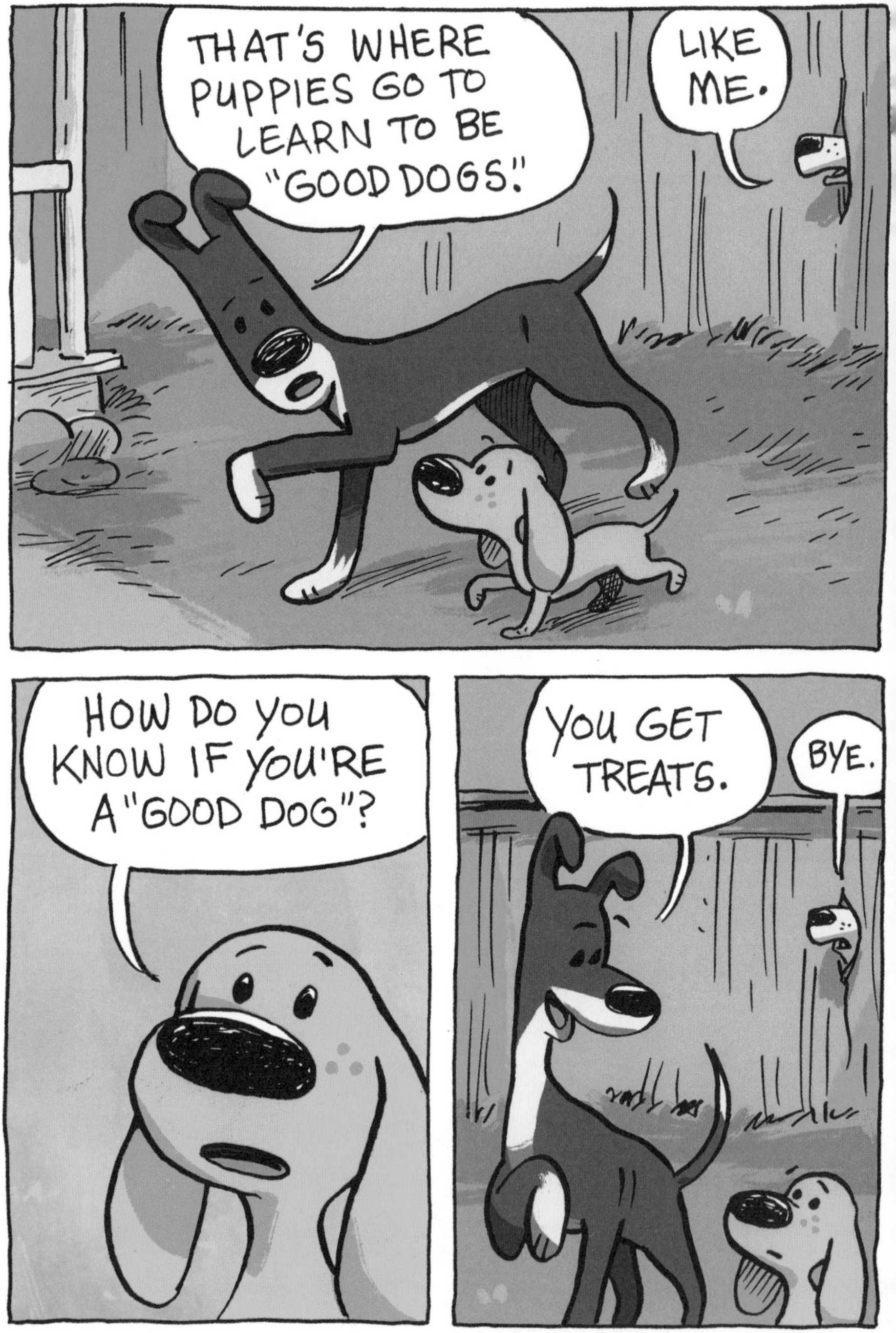

THAT'S WHERE PUPPIES GO TO LEARN TO BE "GOOD DOGS."
LIKE ME.
HOW DO YOU KNOW IF YOU'RE A "GOOD DOG"?
YOU GET TREATS.
BYE.

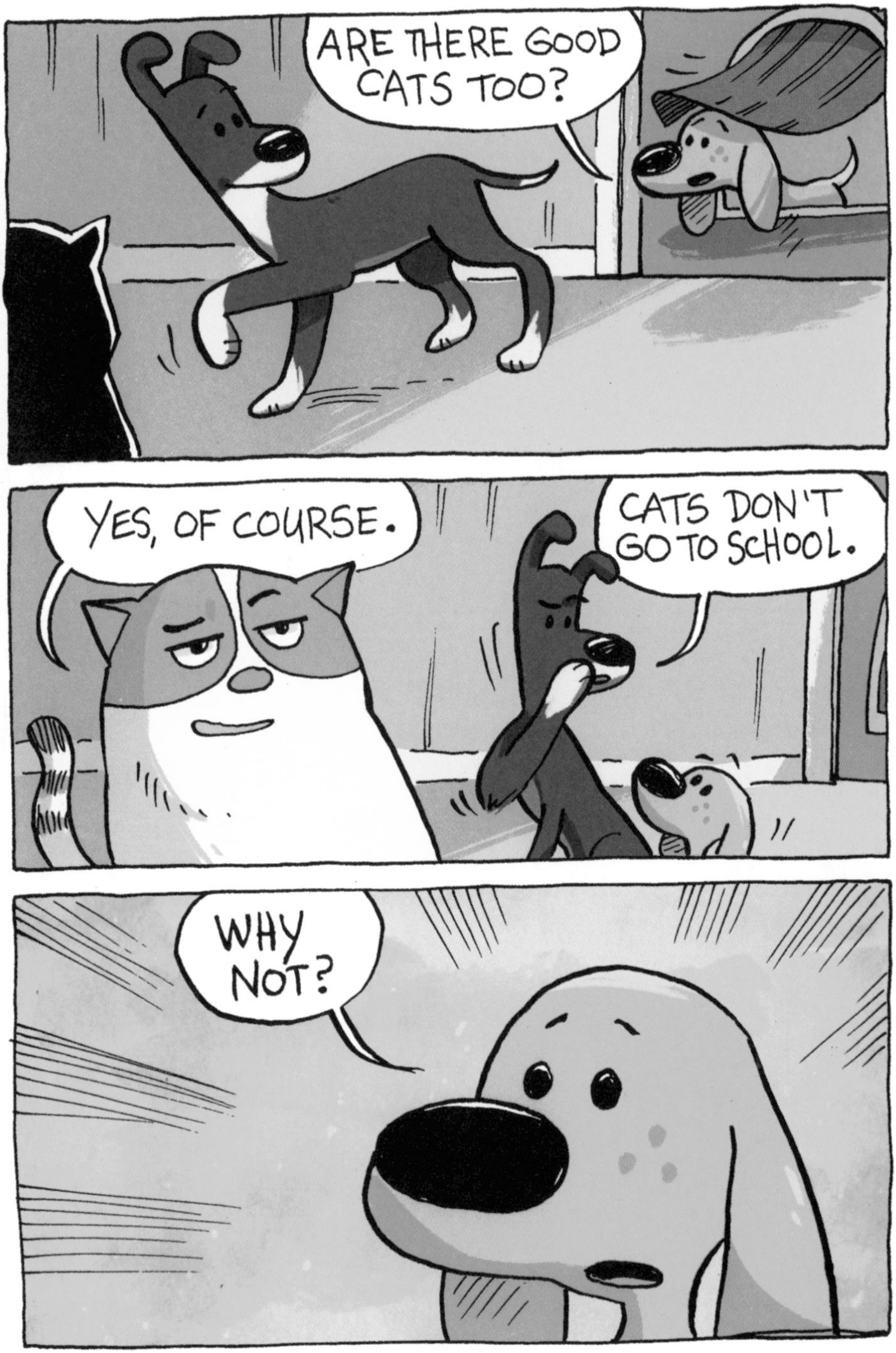
ARE THERE GOOD CATS TOO?
YES, OF COURSE.
CATS DON'T GO TO SCHOOL.
WHY NOT?

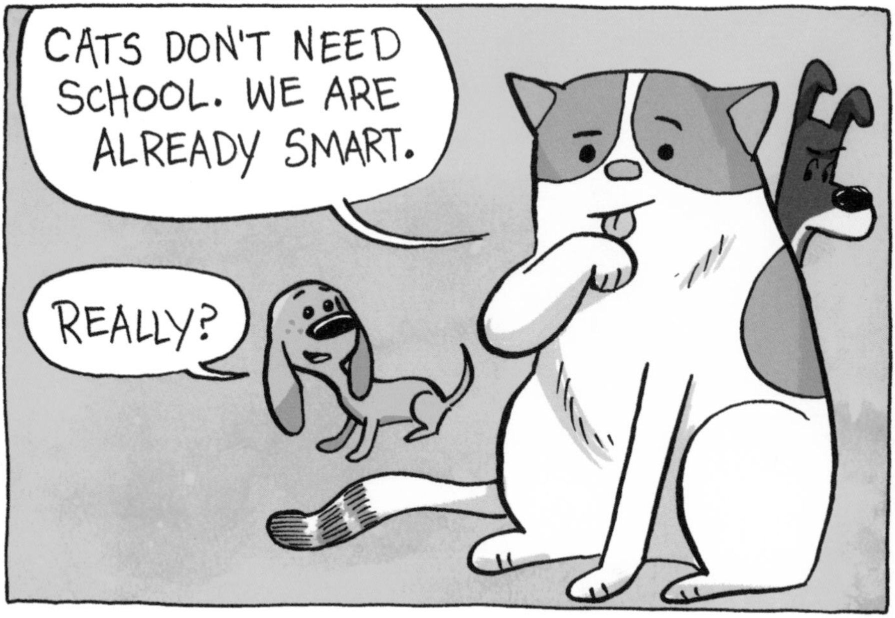
CATS DON'T NEED SCHOOL. WE ARE ALREADY SMART.
REALLY?

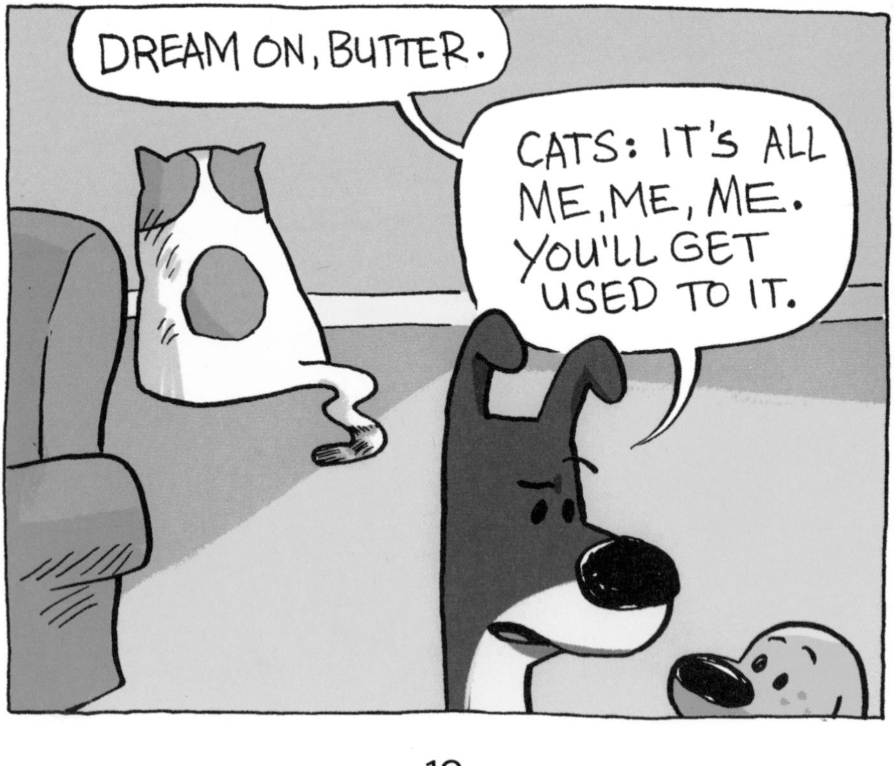
DREAM ON, BUTTER.
CATS: IT'S ALL ME, ME, ME. YOU'LL GET USED TO IT.

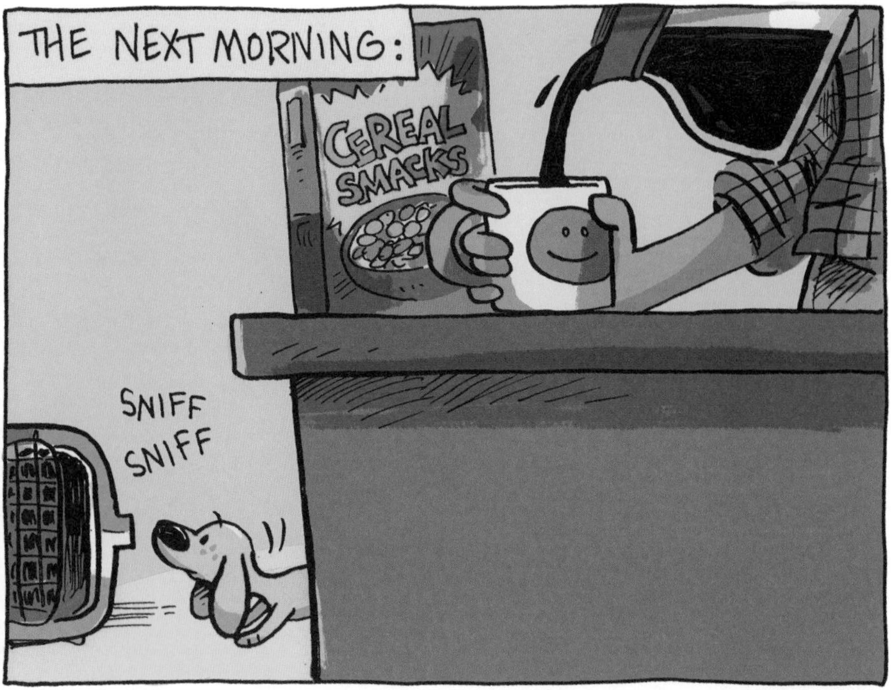
THE NEXT MORNING:
CEREAL SMACKS
SNIFF SNIFF

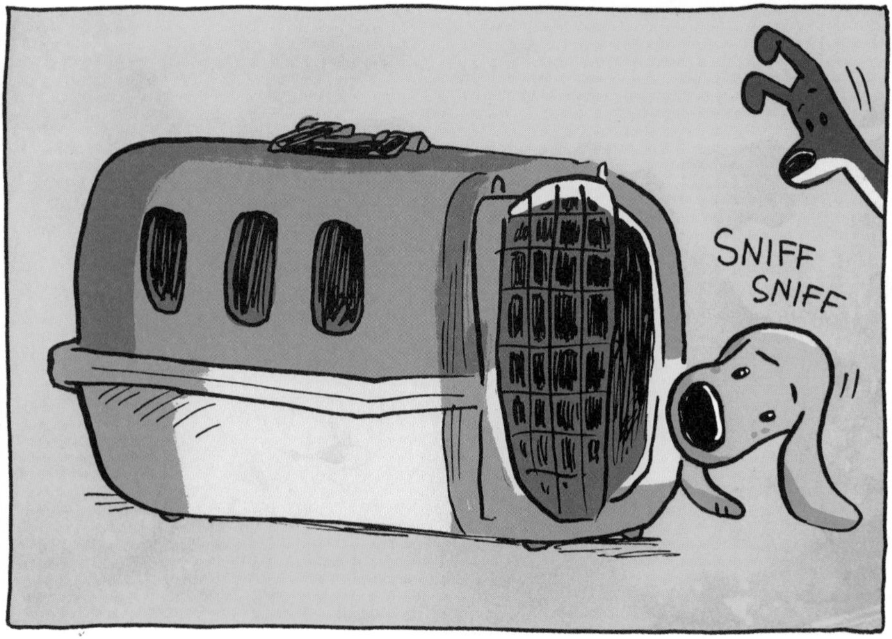
SNIFF SNIFF

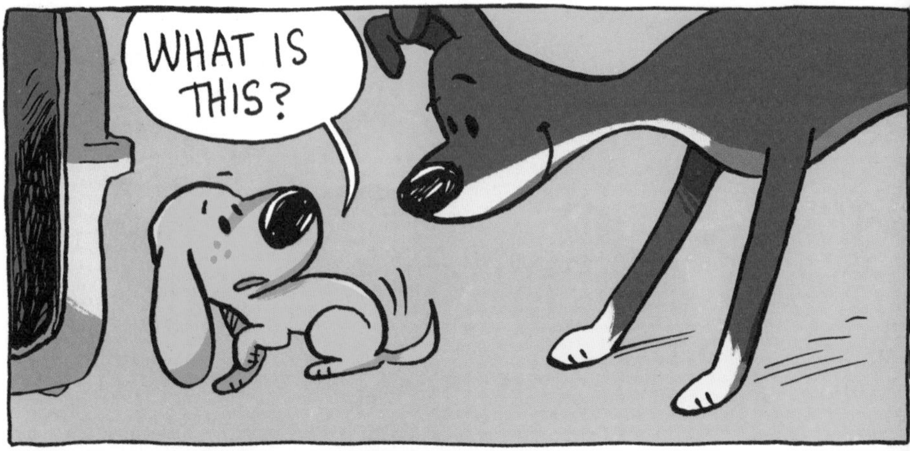
WHAT IS THIS?

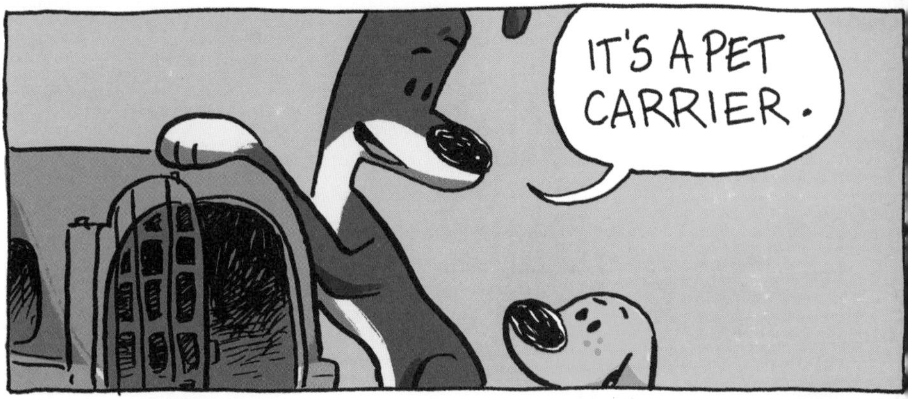
IT'S A PET CARRIER.

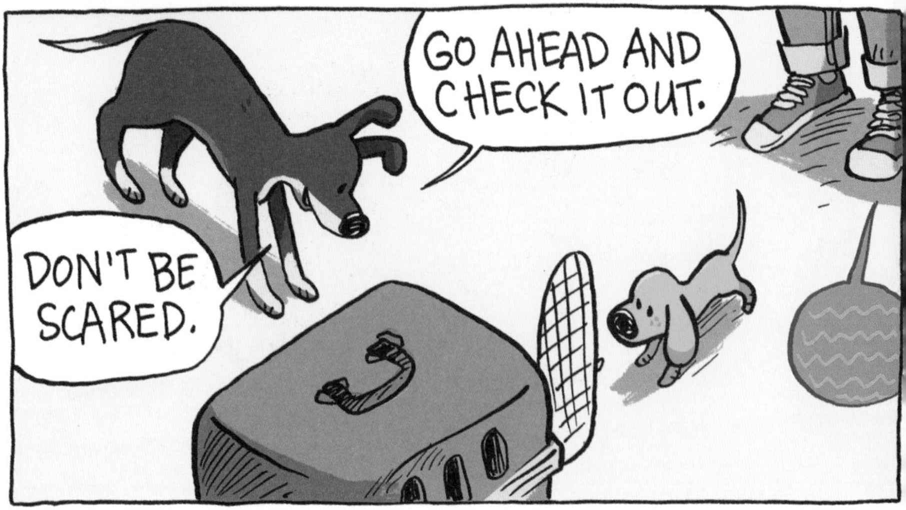
GO AHEAD AND CHECK IT OUT.
DON'T BE SCARED.

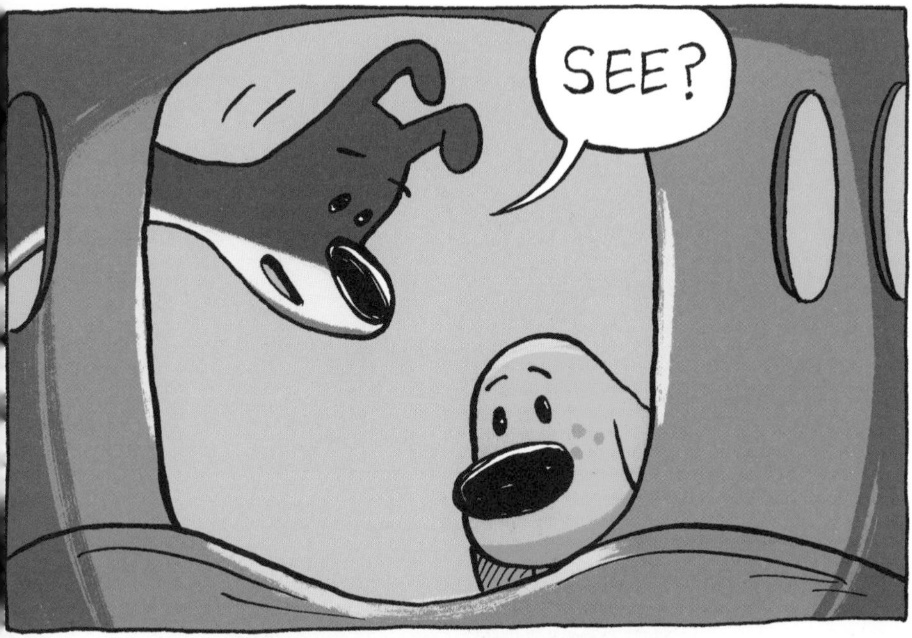
SEE?

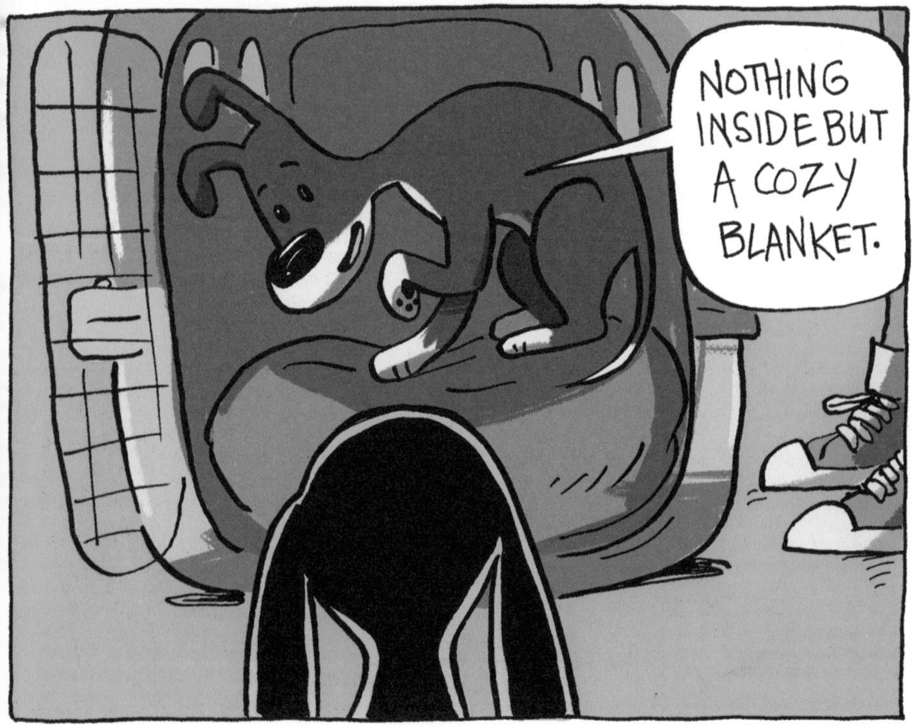
NOTHING INSIDE BUT A COZY BLANKET.

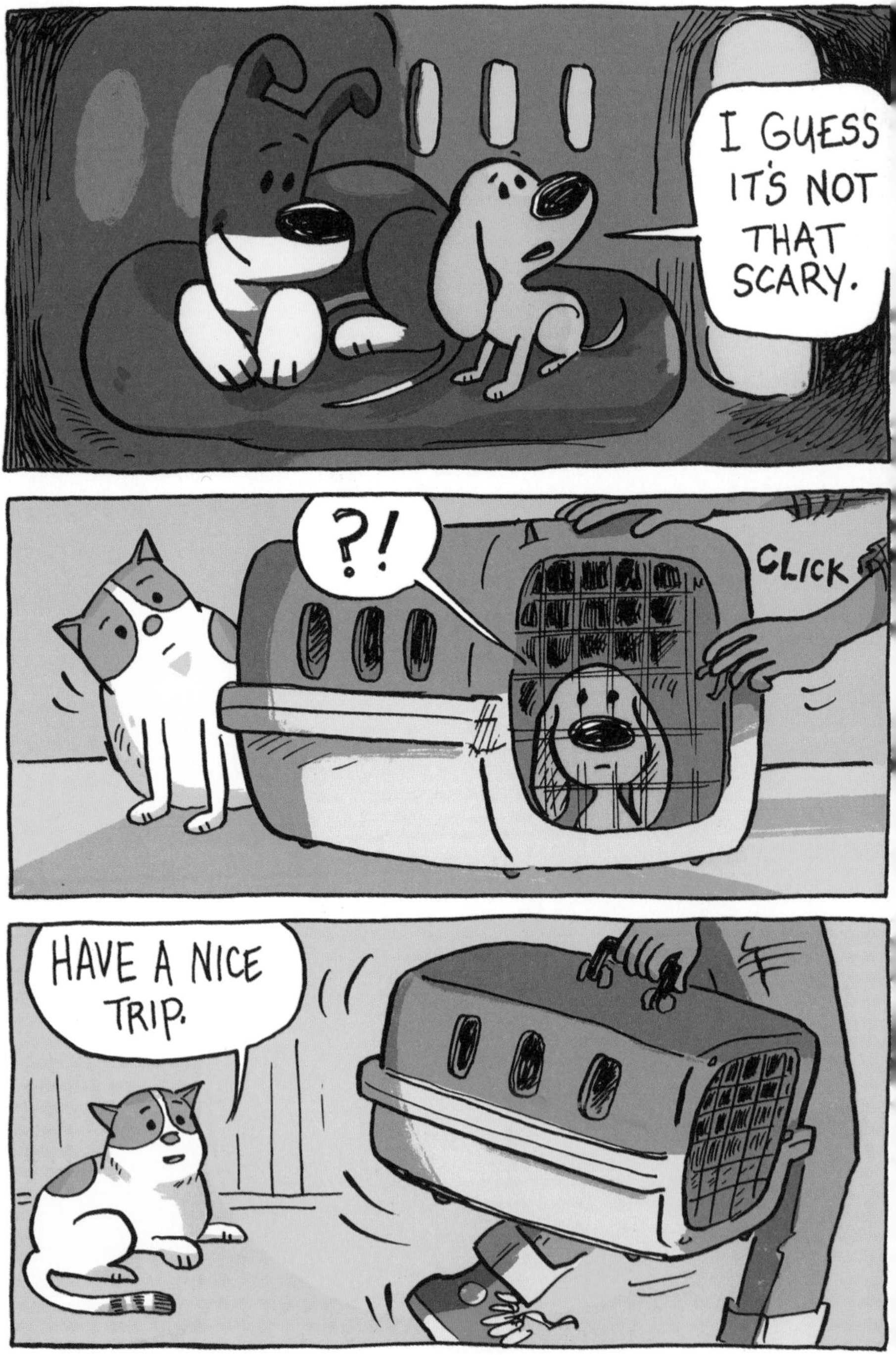
I GUESS IT'S NOT THAT SCARY.
?!
CLICK
HAVE A NICE TRIP.

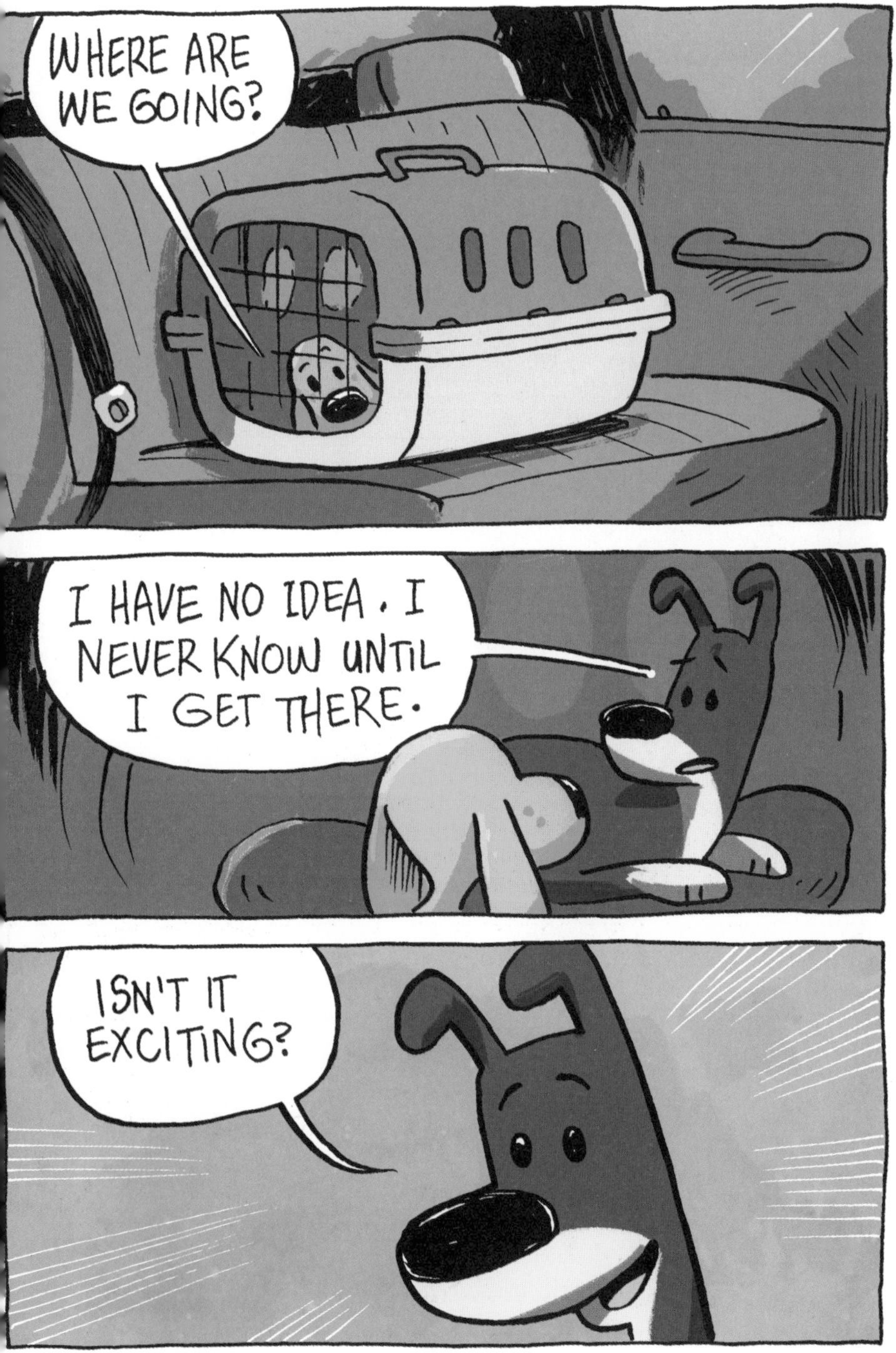
WHERE ARE WE GOING?
I HAVE NO IDEA. I NEVER KNOW UNTIL I GET THERE.
ISN'T IT EXCITING?

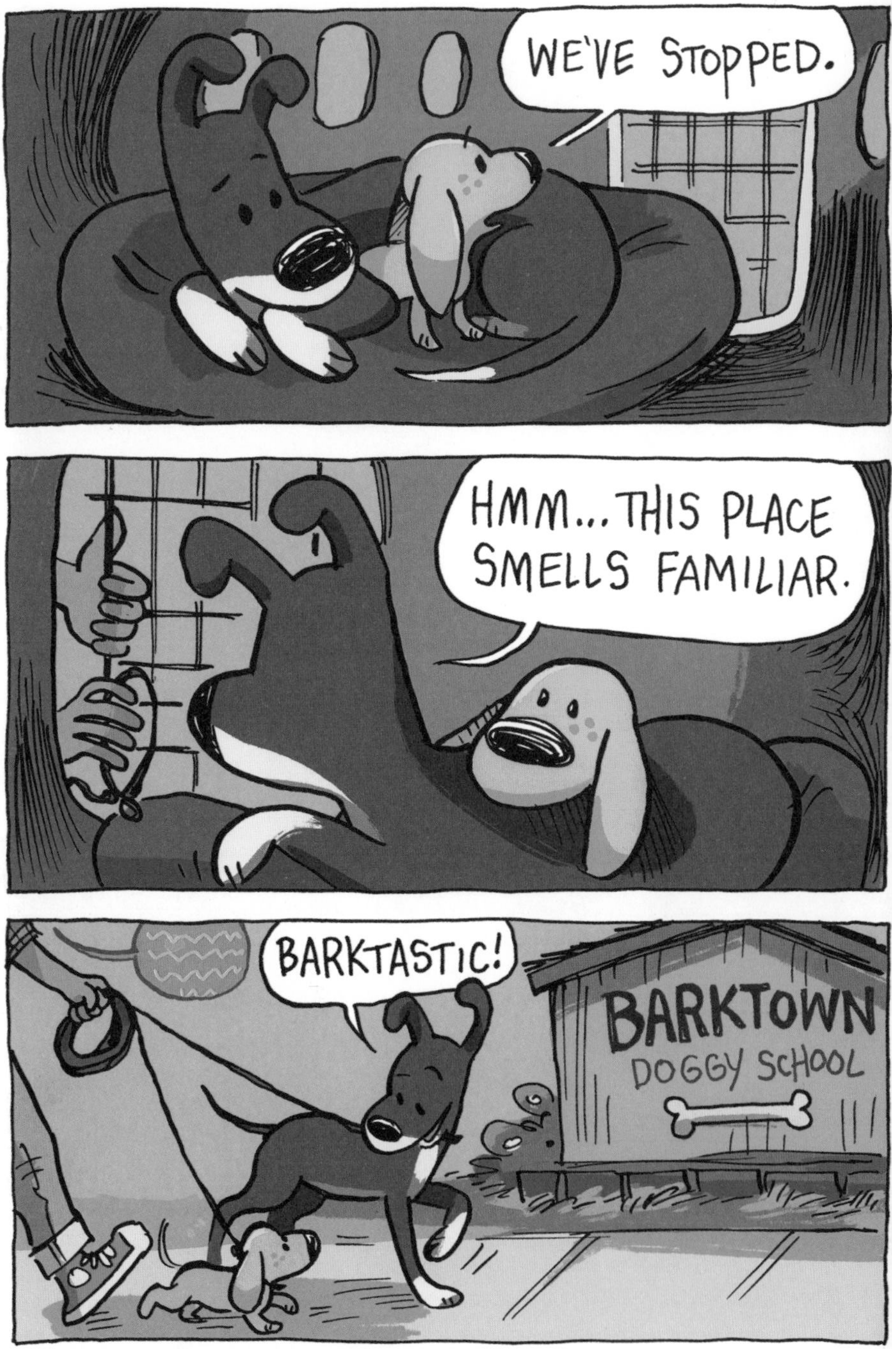
WE'VE STOPPED.
HMM... THIS PLACE SMELLS FAMILIAR.
BARKTASTIC!
BARKTOWN
DOGGY SCHOOL

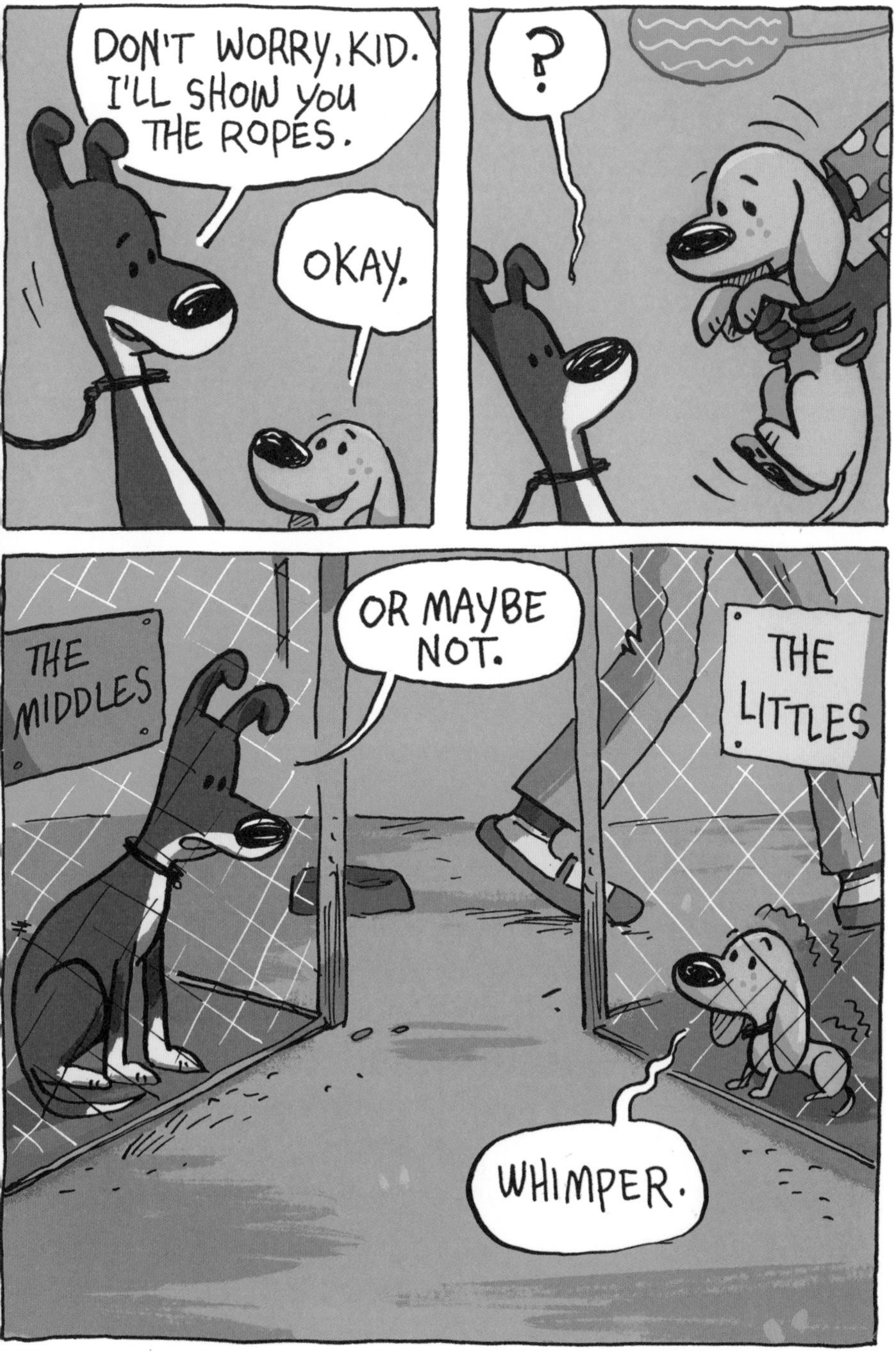
DON'T WORRY, KID. I'LL SHOW YOU THE ROPES.
OKAY.
?
THE MIDDLES
OR MAYBE NOT.
THE LITTLES
WHIMPER.

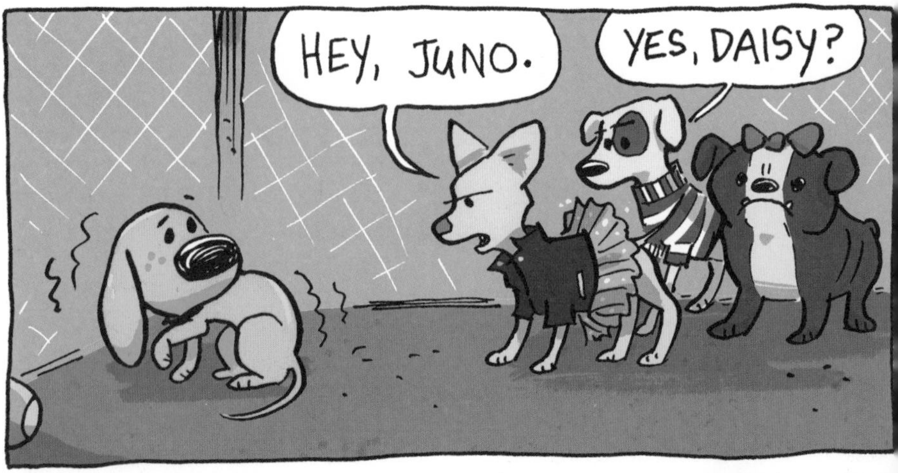
HEY, JUNO.
YES, DAISY?

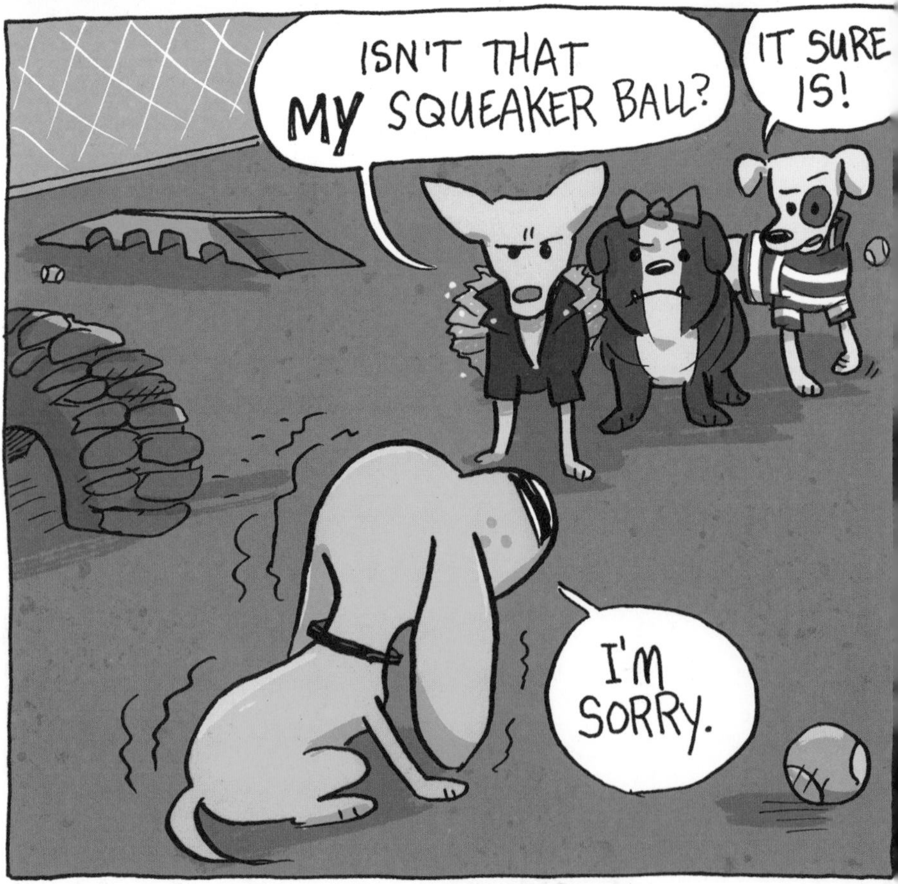
ISN'T THAT MY SQUEAKER BALL?
IT SURE IS!
I'M SORRY.

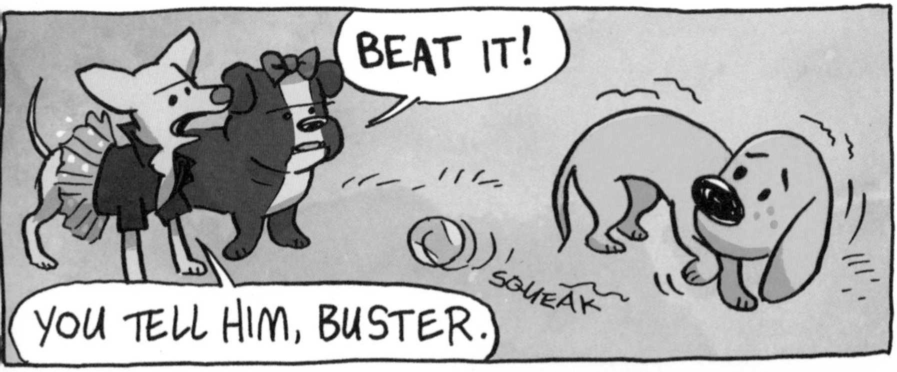
BEAT IT!
YOU TELL HIM, BUSTER.
SQUEAK

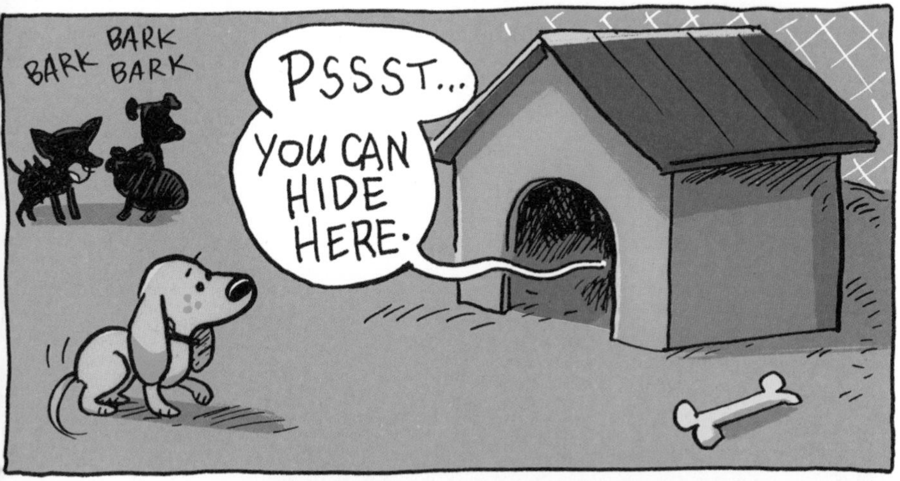
BARK
BARK
BARK
PSSST...
YOU CAN HIDE HERE.

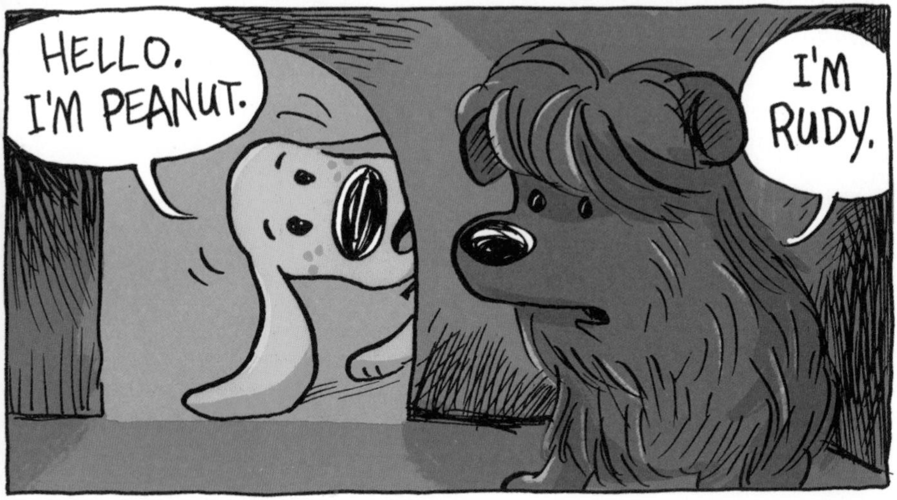
HELLO. I'M PEANUT.
I'M RUDY.

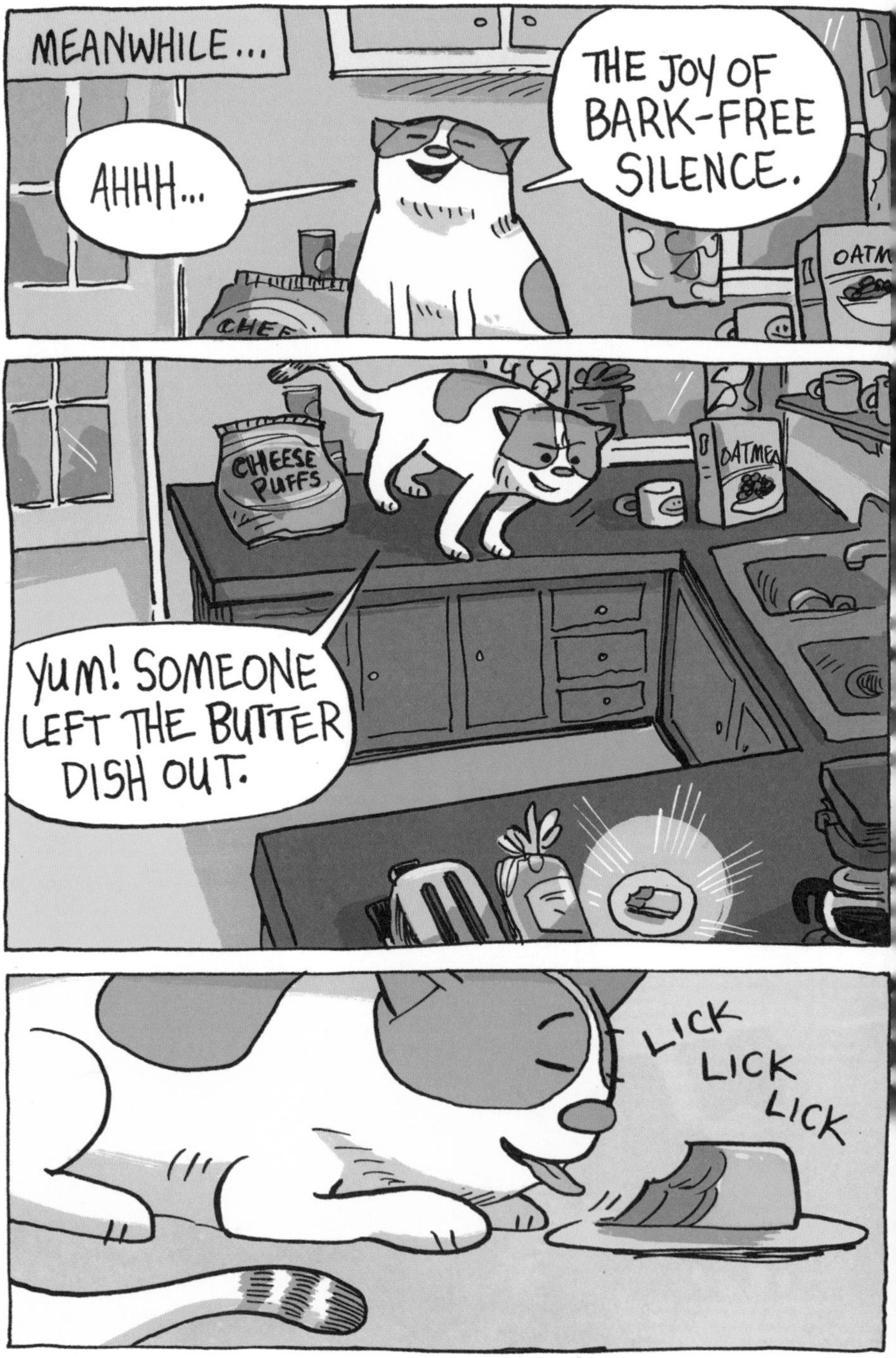
MEANWHILE...
AHHH...
THE JOY OF BARK-FREE SILENCE.
CHEESE PUFFS
YUM! SOMEONE LEFT THE BUTTER DISH OUT.
LICK
LICK
LICK

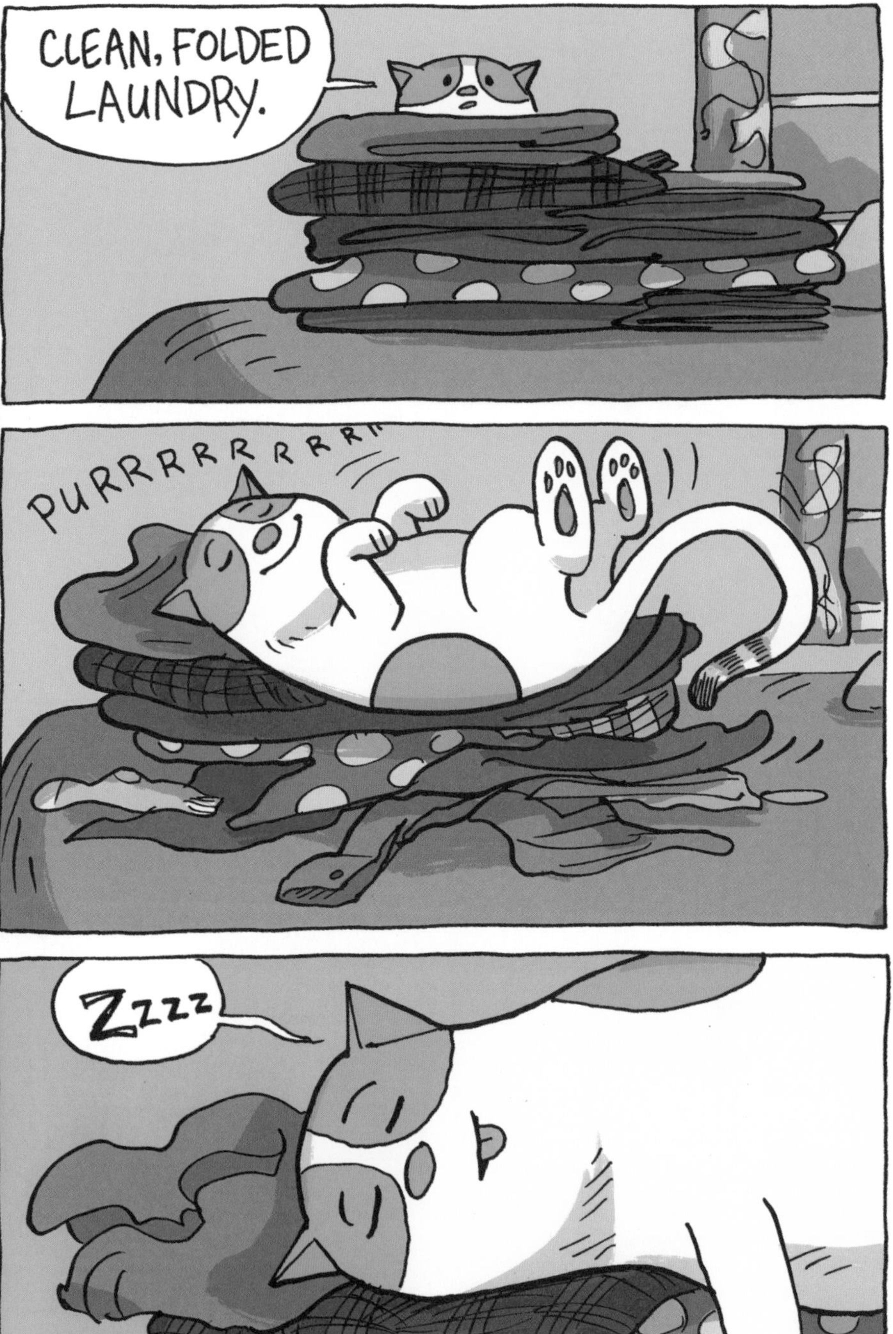
CLEAN, FOLDED LAUNDRY.
PURRRRRRRRR
Zzzz

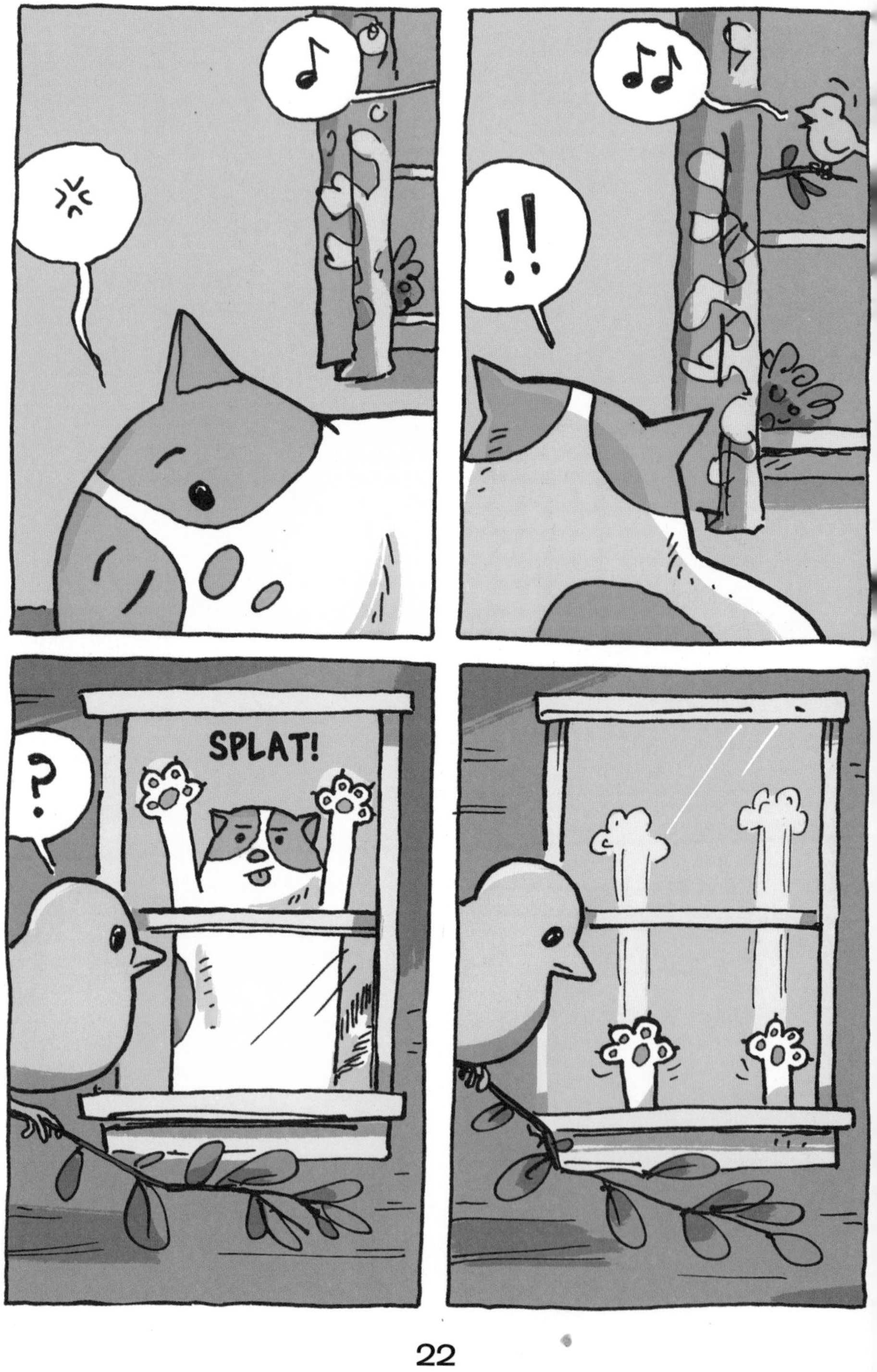
♪
♪♪
!!
?
SPLAT!

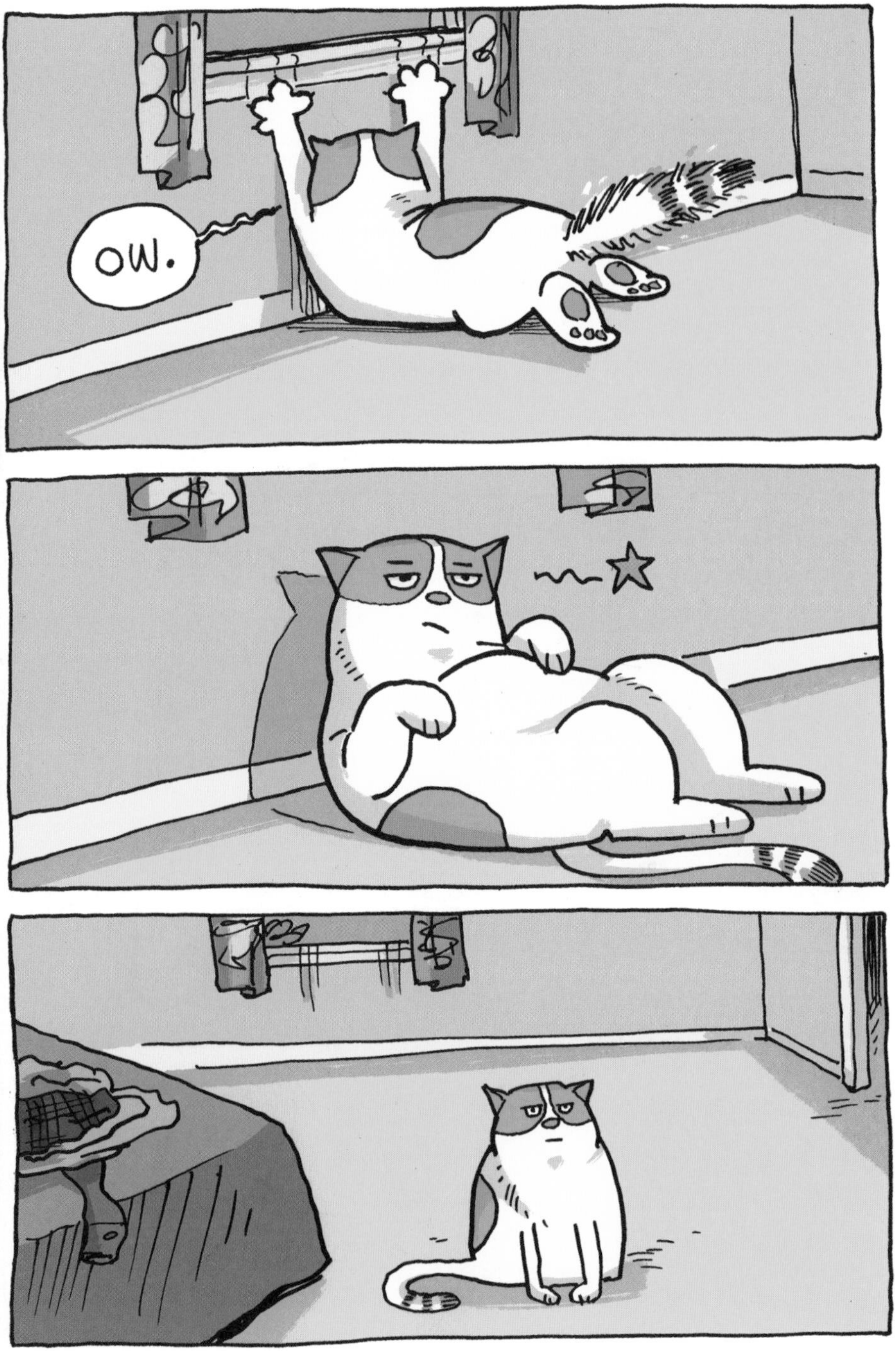
OW.

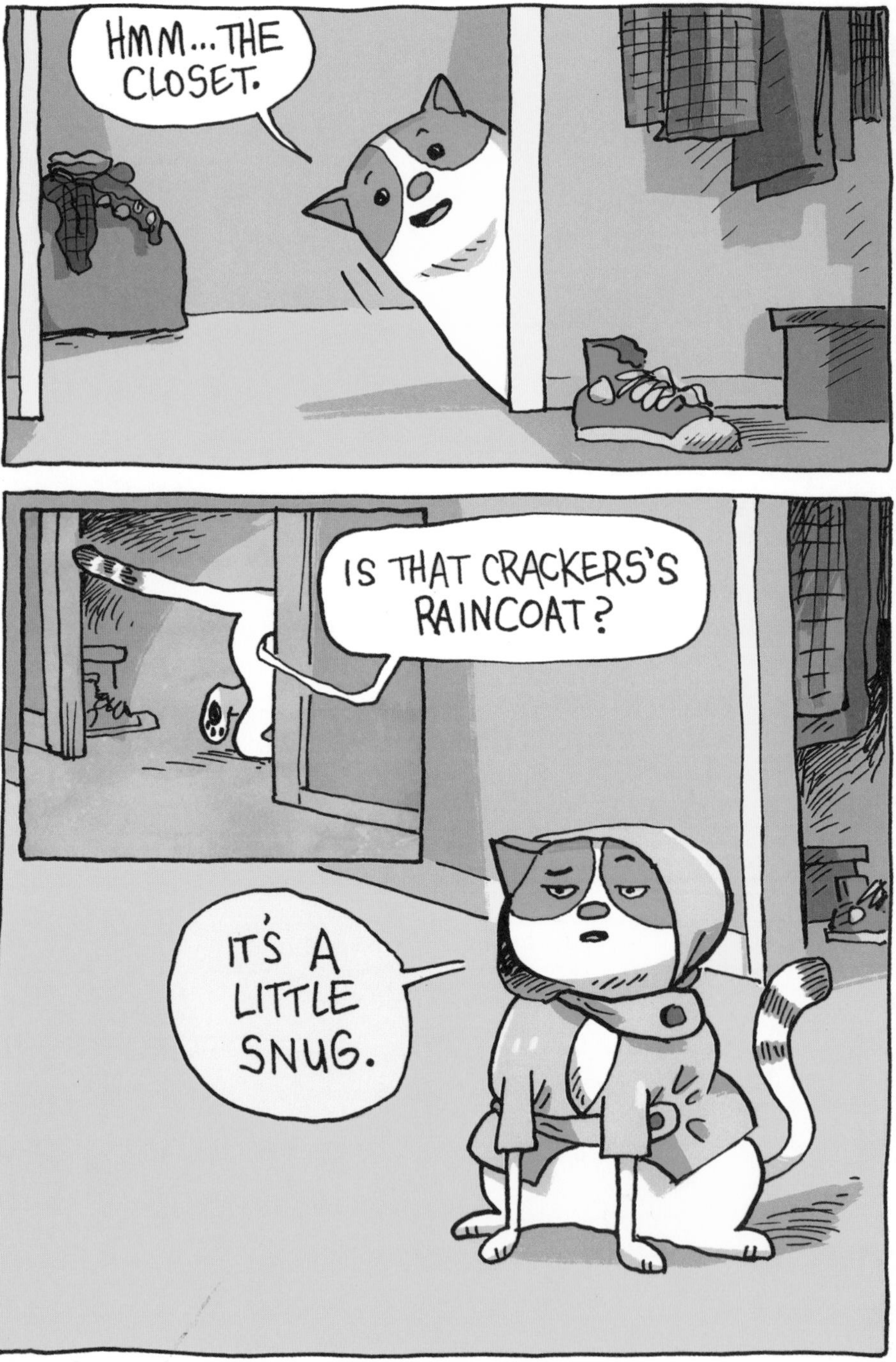
HMM... THE CLOSET.
IS THAT CRACKERS'S RAINCOAT?
IT'S A LITTLE SNUG.

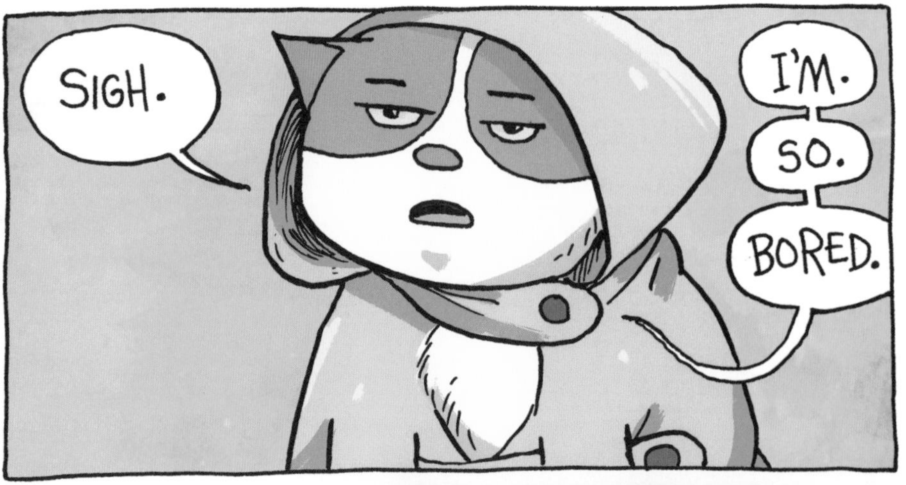
SIGH.
I'M. SO. BORED.

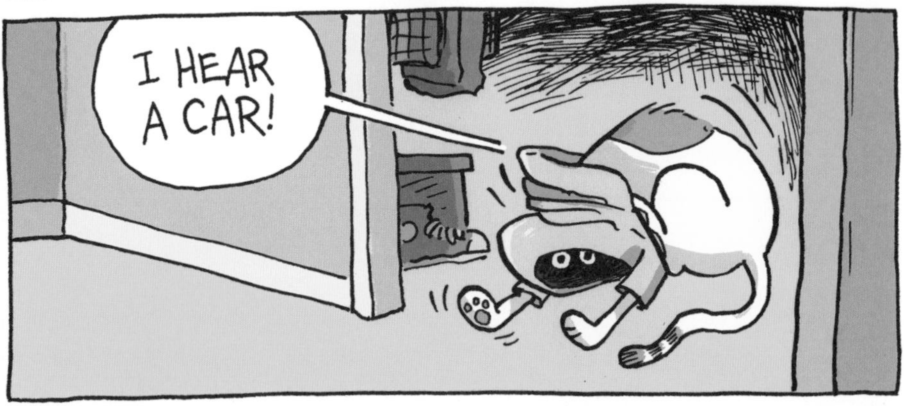
I HEAR A CAR!

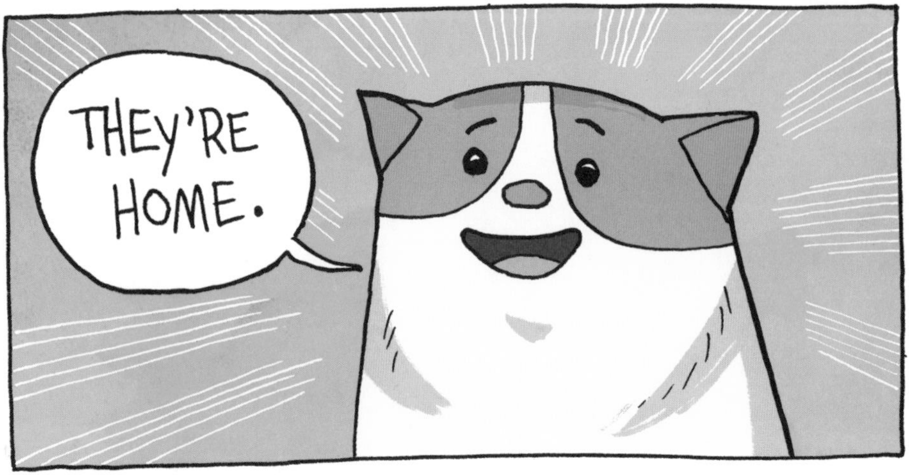
THEY'RE HOME.

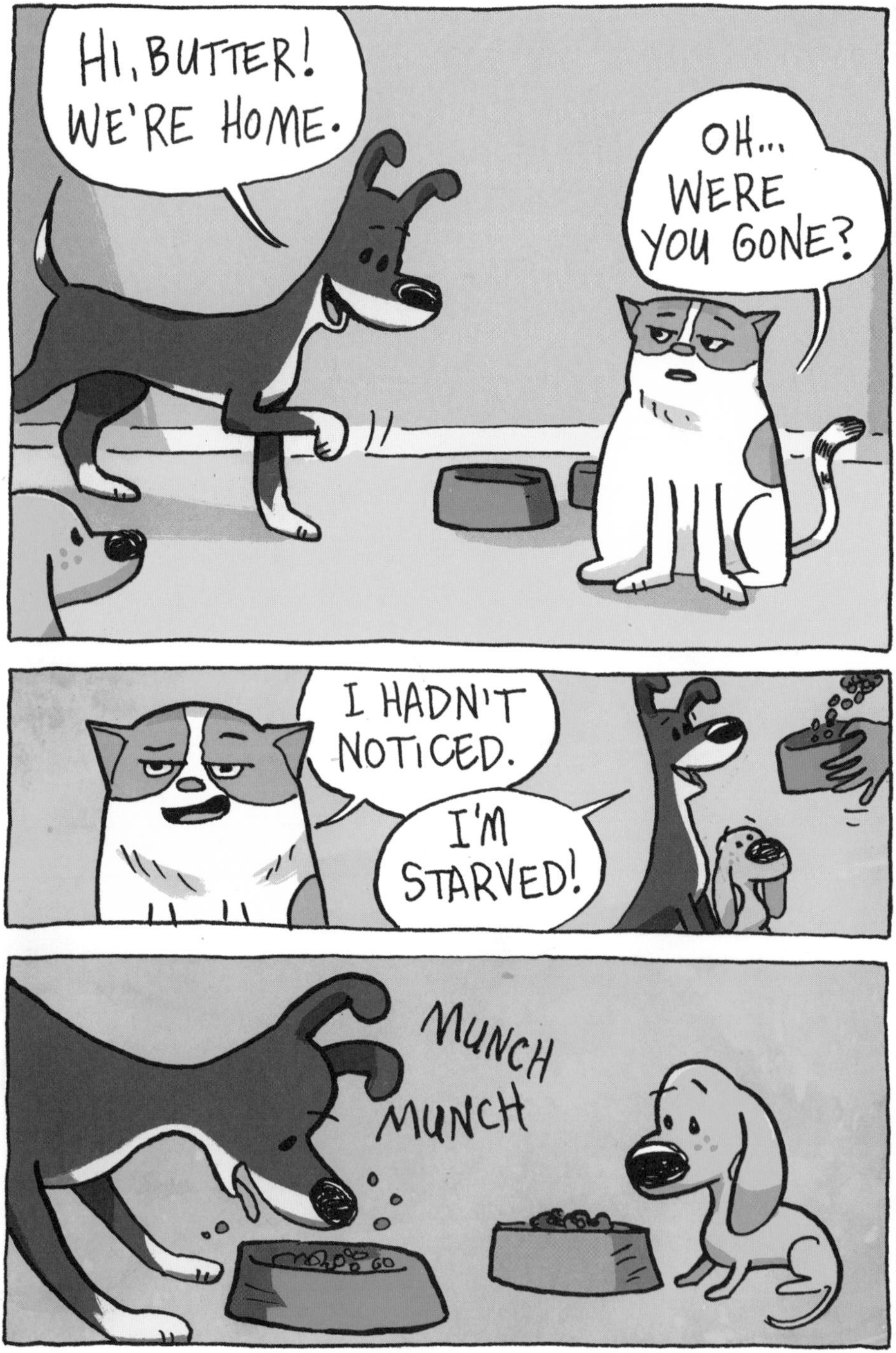
HI, BUTTER! WE'RE HOME.
OH... WERE YOU GONE?
I HADN'T NOTICED.
I'M STARVED!
MUNCH
MUNCH

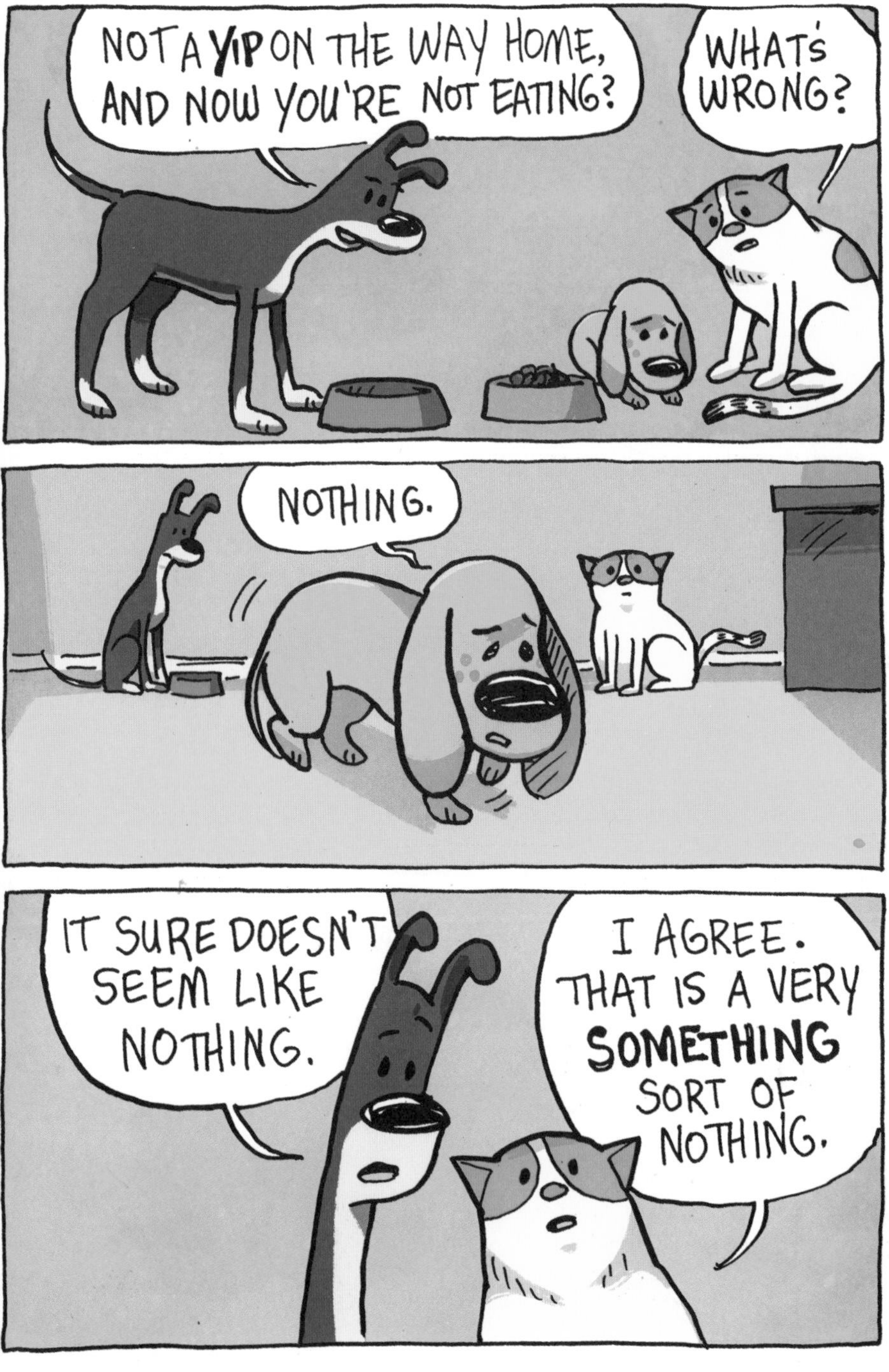
NOT A YIP ON THE WAY HOME, AND NOW YOU'RE NOT EATING?
WHAT'S WRONG?
NOTHING.
IT SURE DOESN'T SEEM LIKE NOTHING.
I AGREE. THAT IS A VERY SOMETHING SORT OF NOTHING.

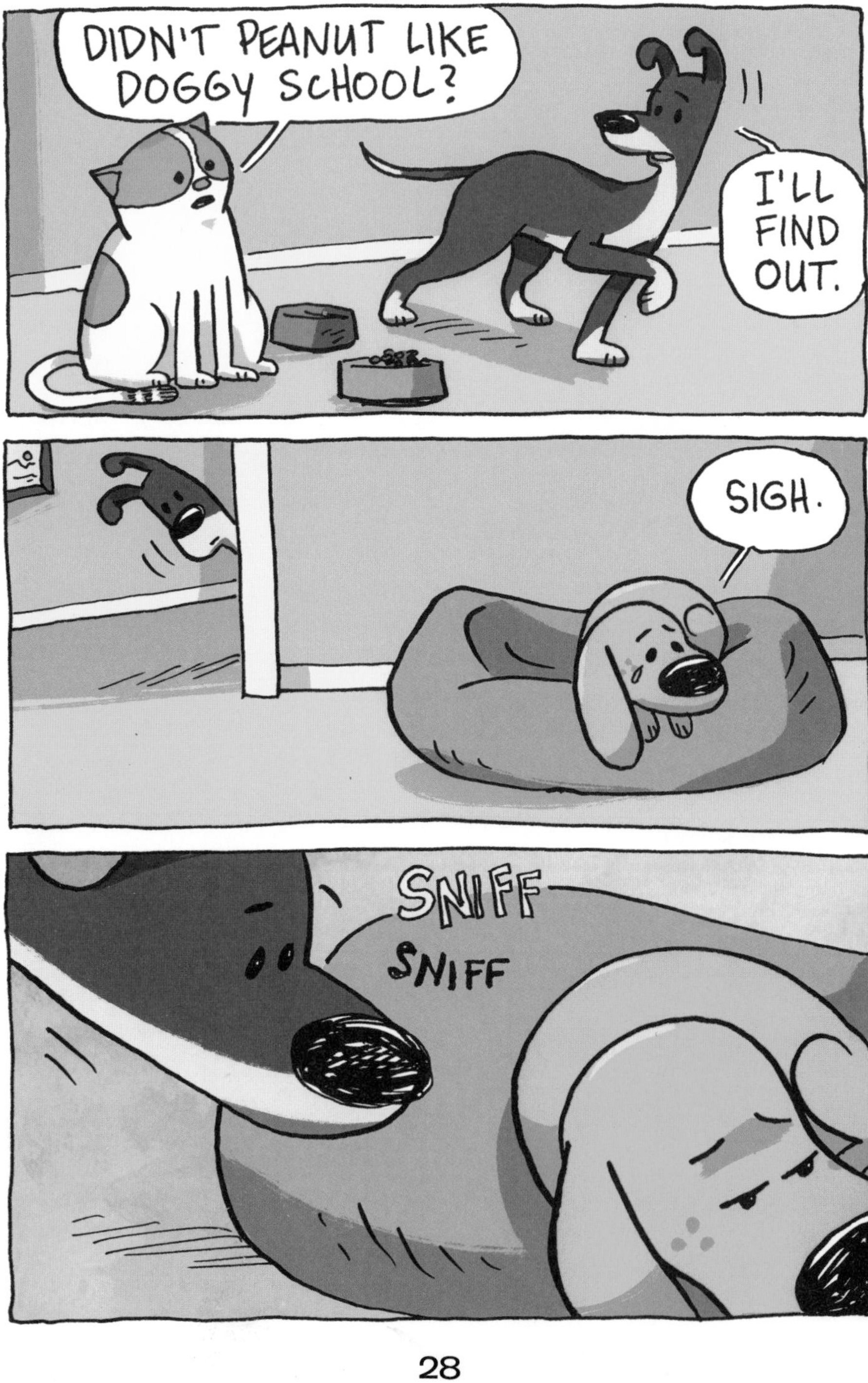
DIDN'T PEANUT LIKE DOGGY SCHOOL?
I'LL FIND OUT.
SIGH.
SNIFF
SNIFF

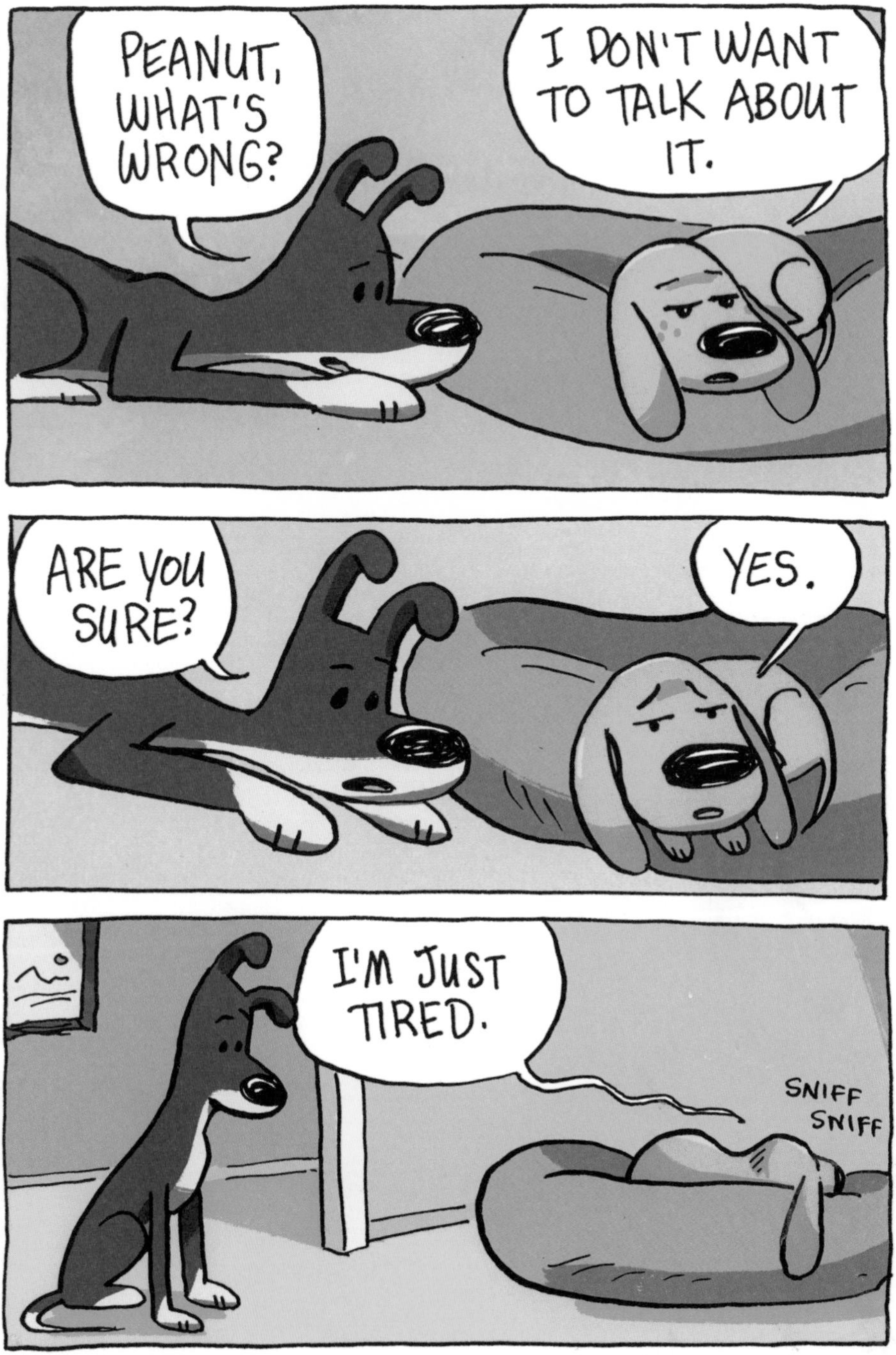
PEANUT, WHAT'S WRONG?
I DON'T WANT TO TALK ABOUT IT.
ARE YOU SURE?
YES.
I'M JUST TIRED.
SNIFF SNIFF

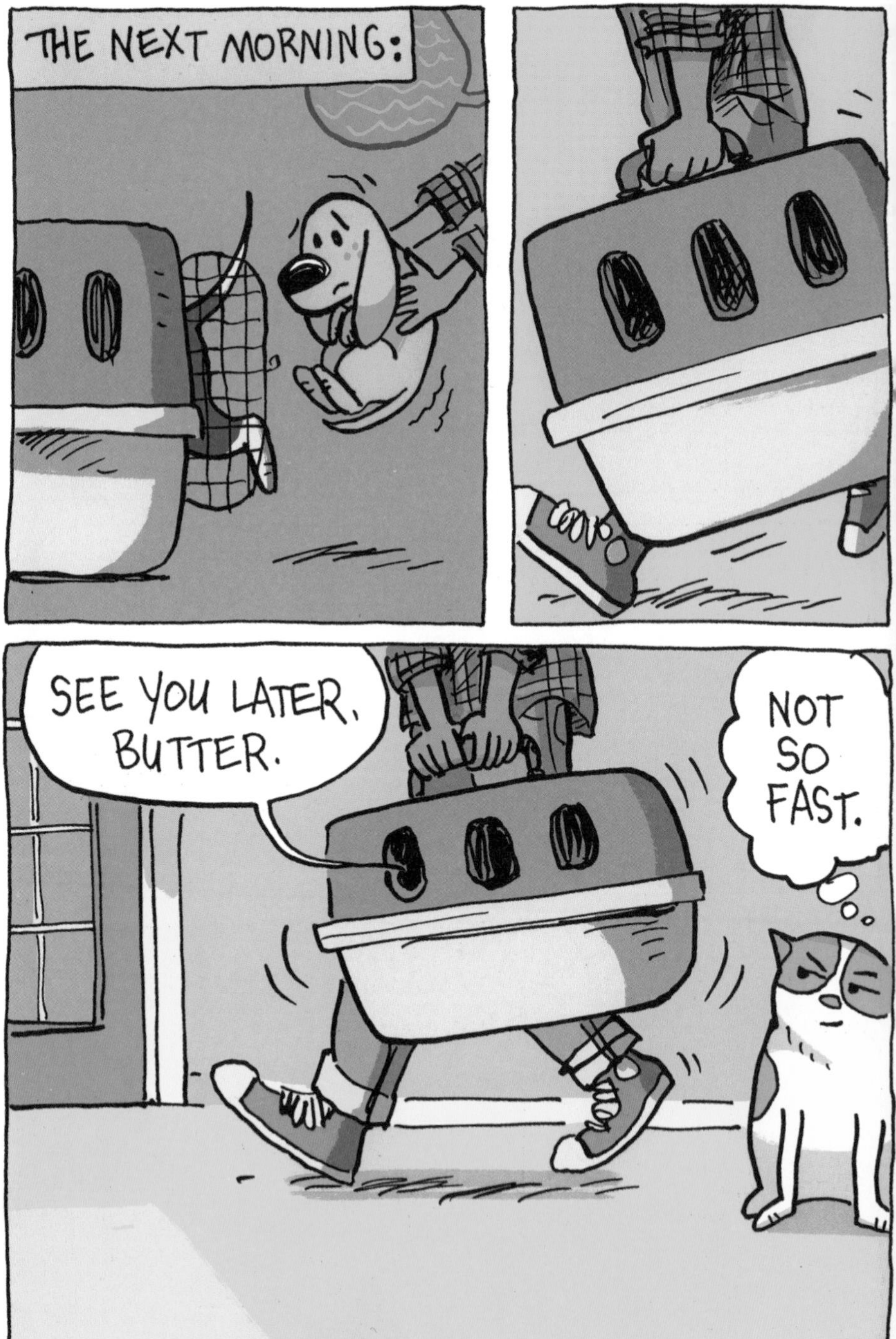
THE NEXT MORNING:
SEE YOU LATER, BUTTER.
NOT SO FAST.

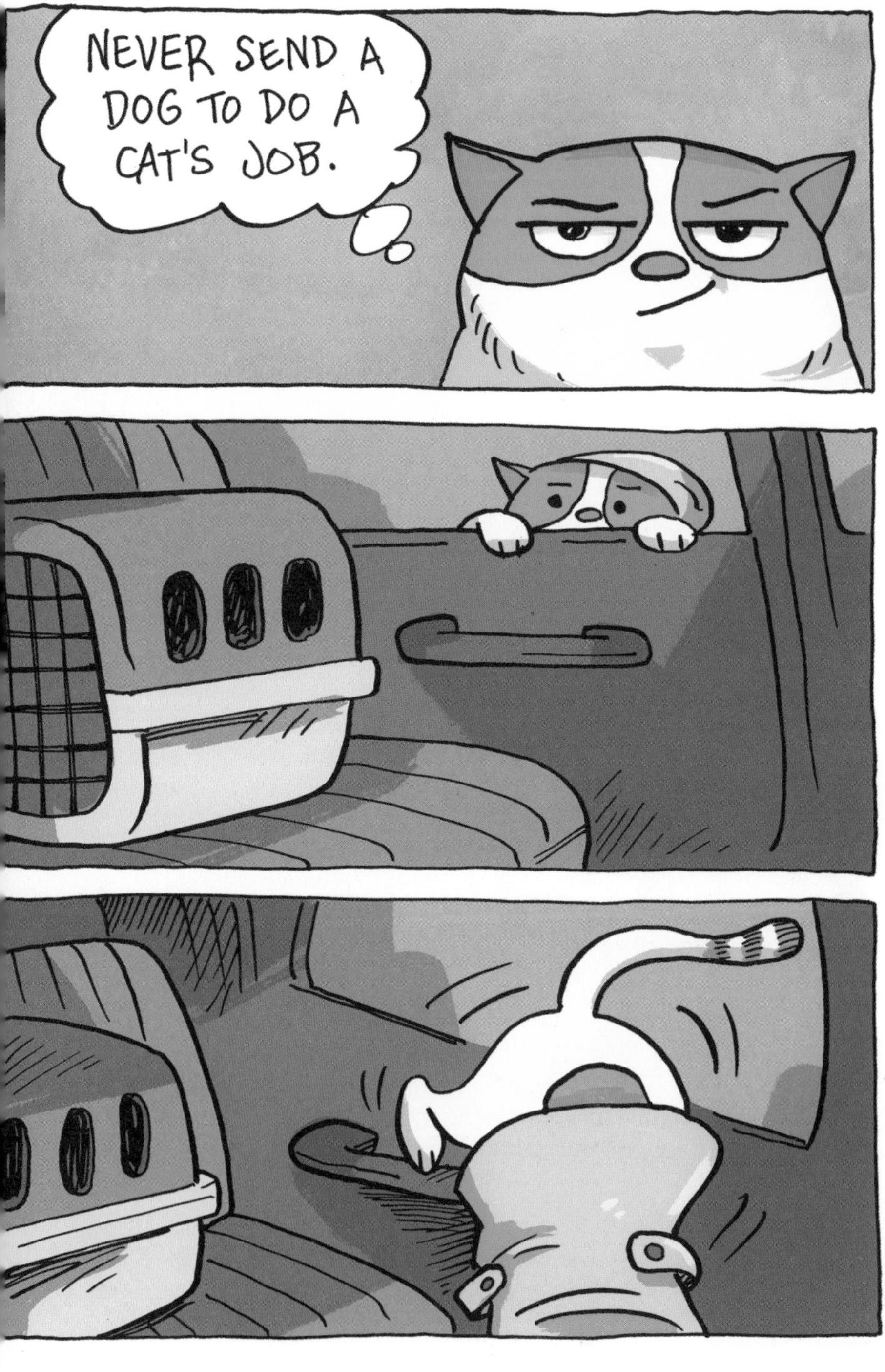
NEVER SEND A DOG TO DO A CAT'S JOB.

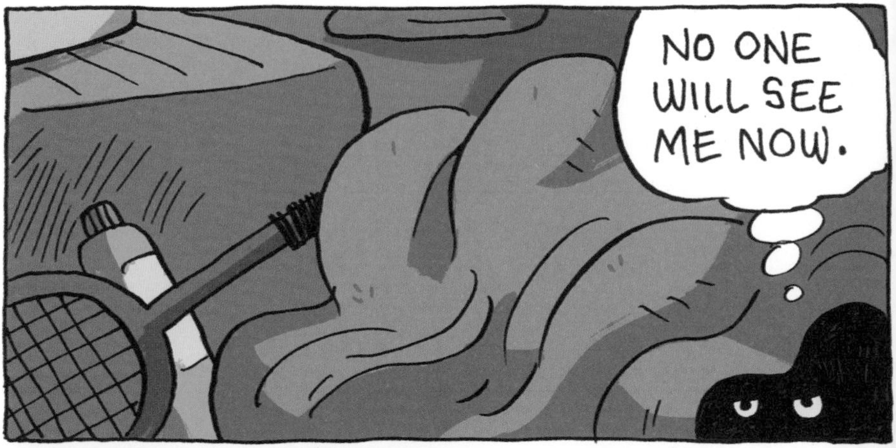
NO ONE
WILL SEE
ME NOW.

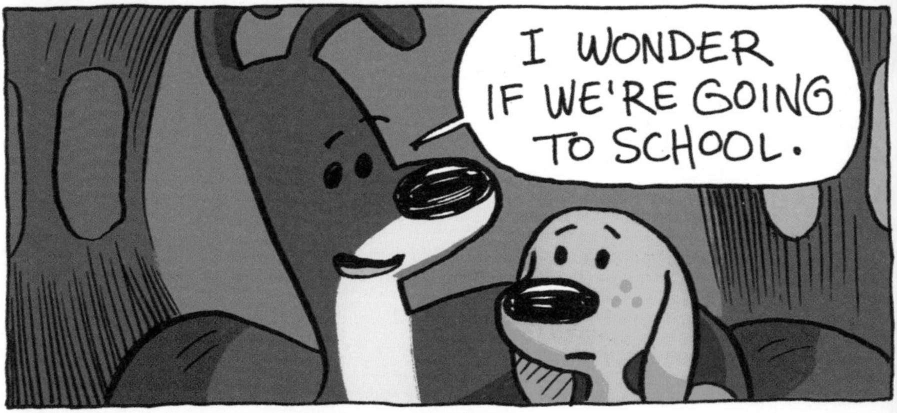
I WONDER
IF WE'RE GOING
TO SCHOOL.

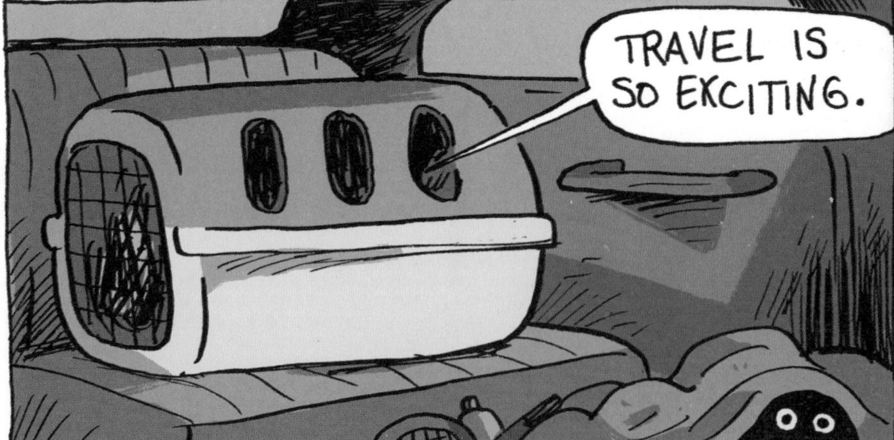
TRAVEL IS
SO EXCITING.

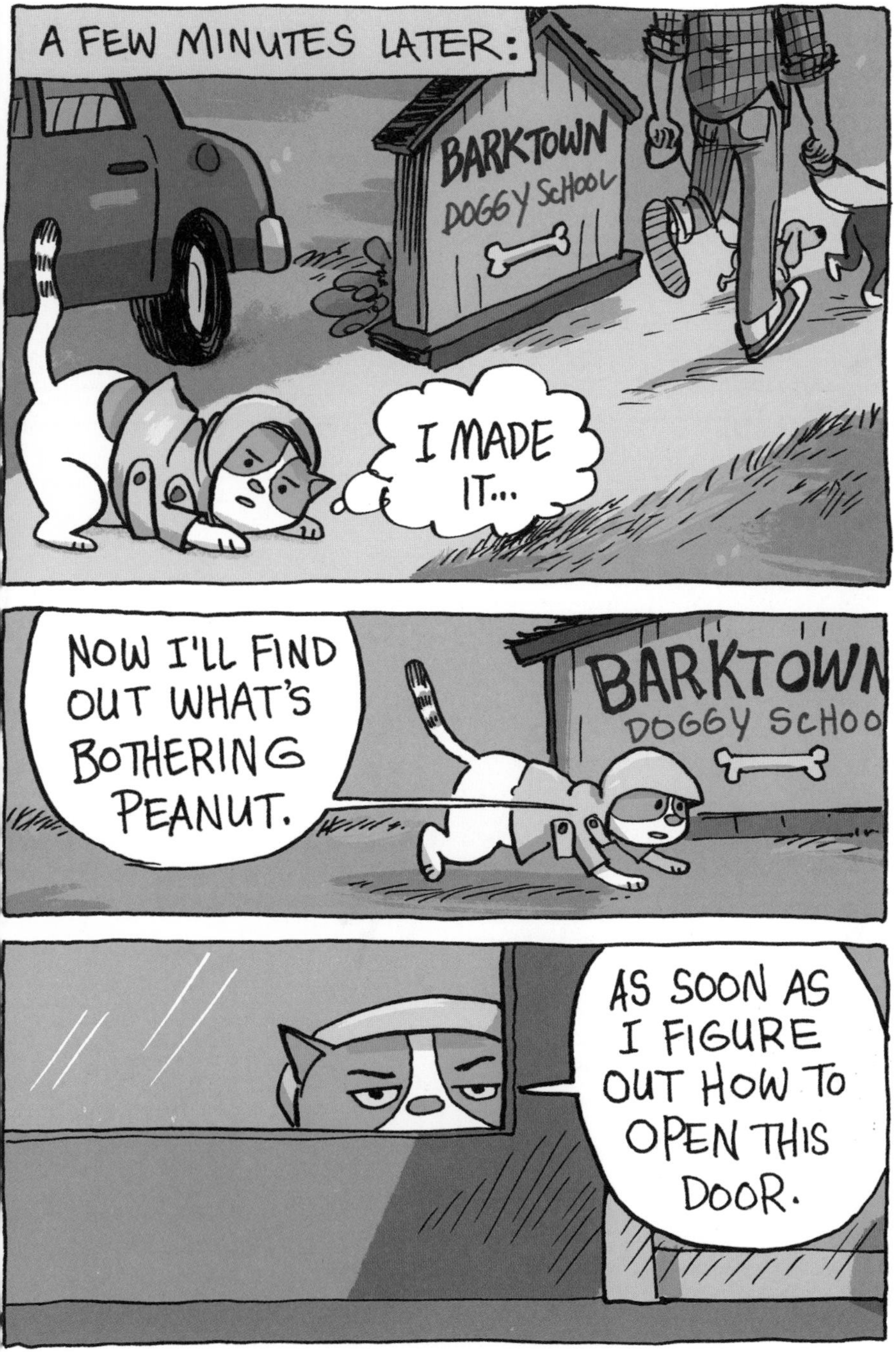
A FEW MINUTES LATER:
BARKTOWN DOGGY SCHOOL
I MADE IT...
NOW I'LL FIND OUT WHAT'S BOTHERING PEANUT.
BARKTOWN DOGGY SCHOO
AS SOON AS I FIGURE OUT HOW TO OPEN THIS DOOR.

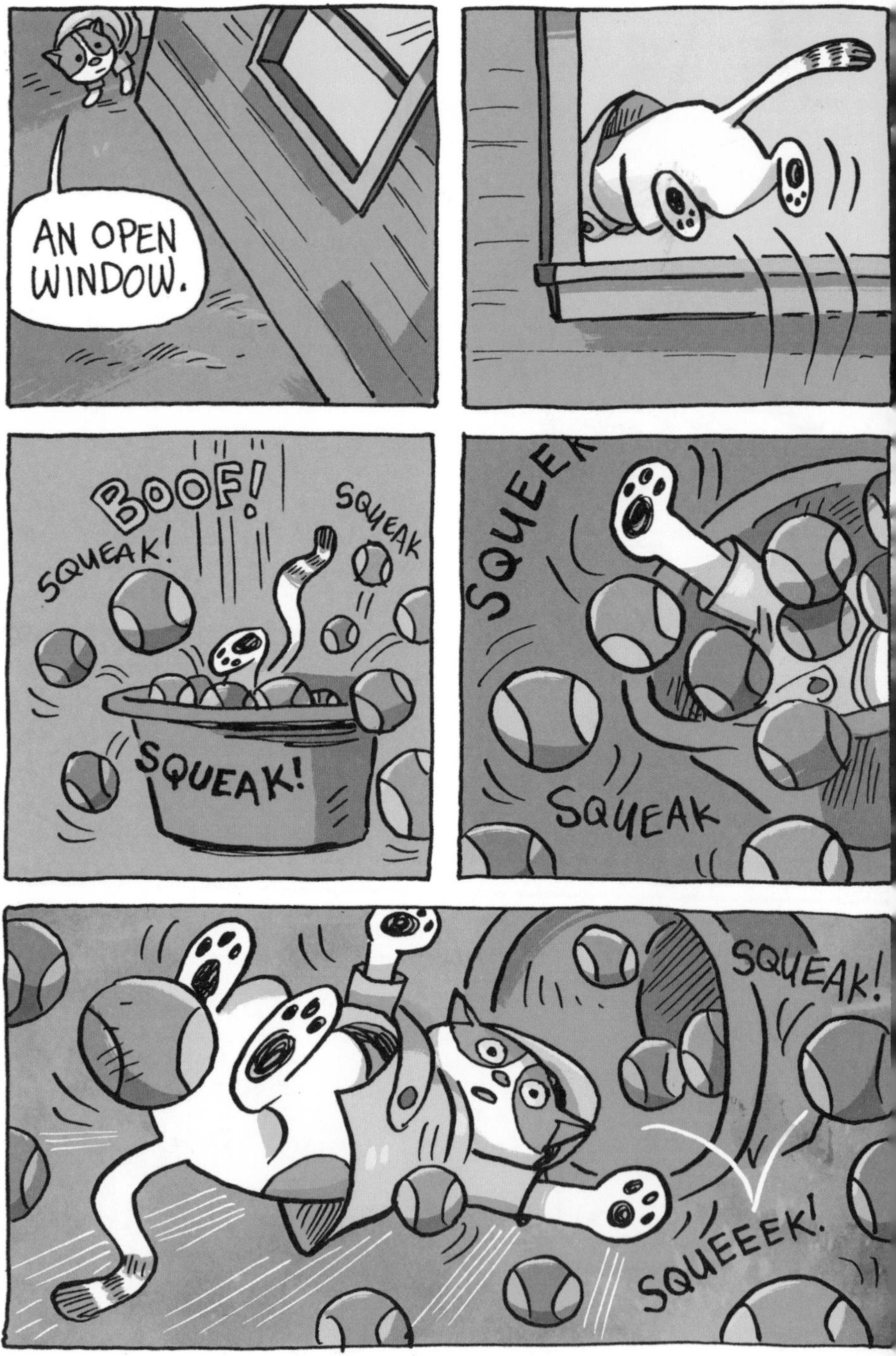
AN OPEN WINDOW.
BOOF!
SQUEAK!
SQUEAK
SQUEAK!
SQUEEK
SQUEAK
SQUEAK!
SQUEEEEK!

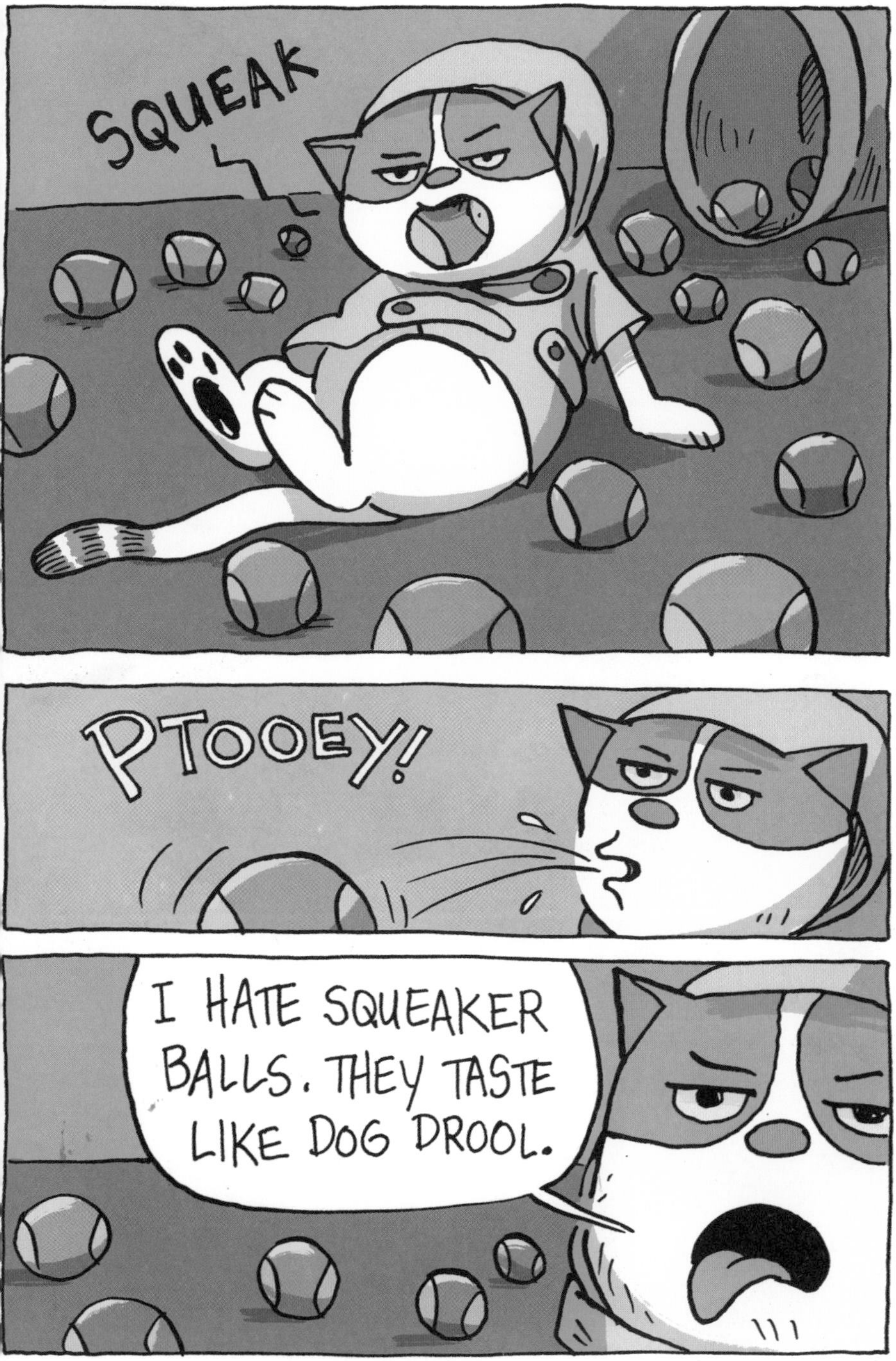
SQUEAK
PTOOEY!
I HATE SQUEAKER BALLS. THEY TASTE LIKE DOG DROOL.

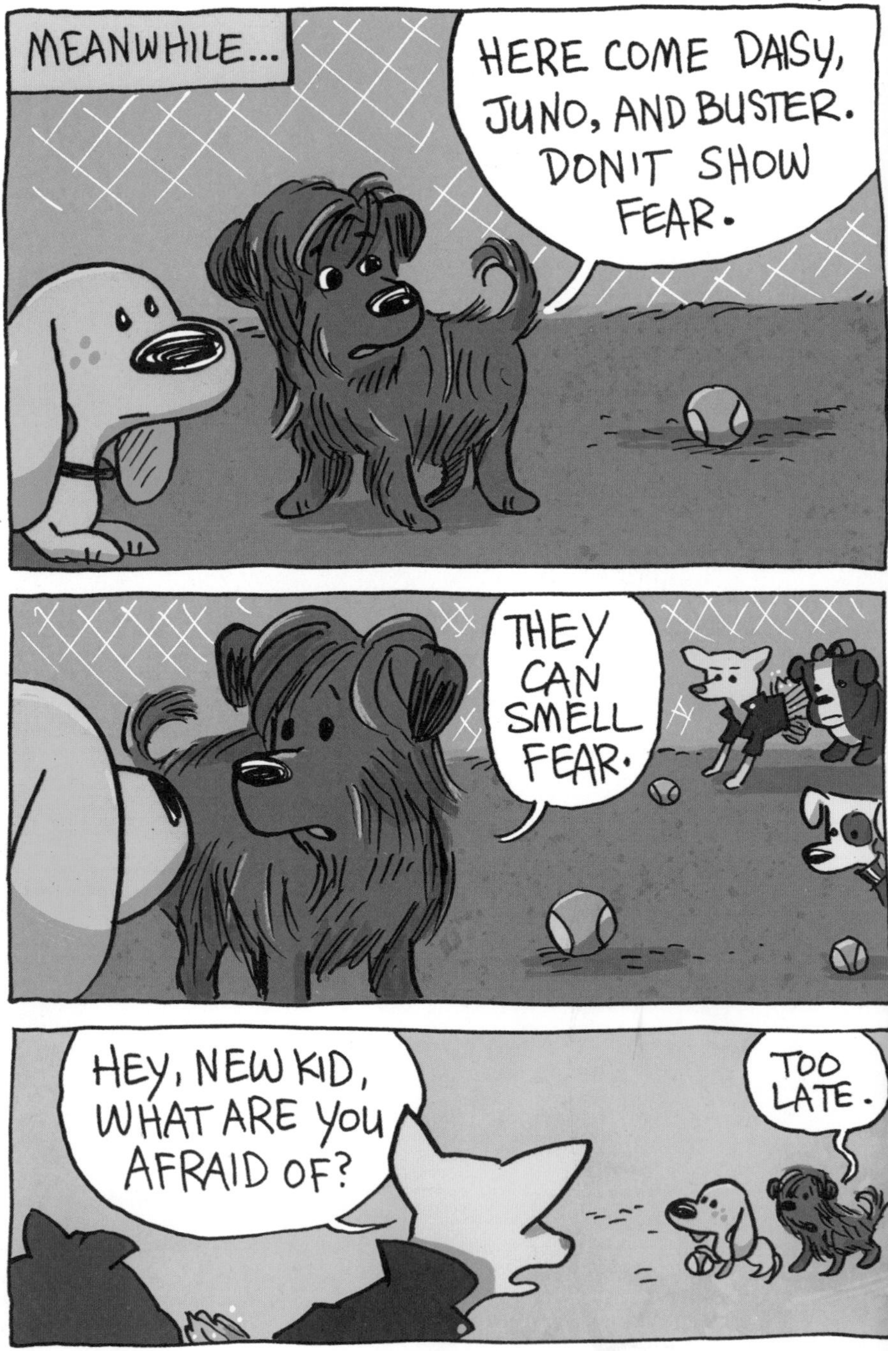
MEANWHILE...
HERE COME DAISY, JUNO, AND BUSTER. DON'T SHOW FEAR.
THEY CAN SMELL FEAR.
HEY, NEW KID, WHAT ARE YOU AFRAID OF?
TOO LATE.

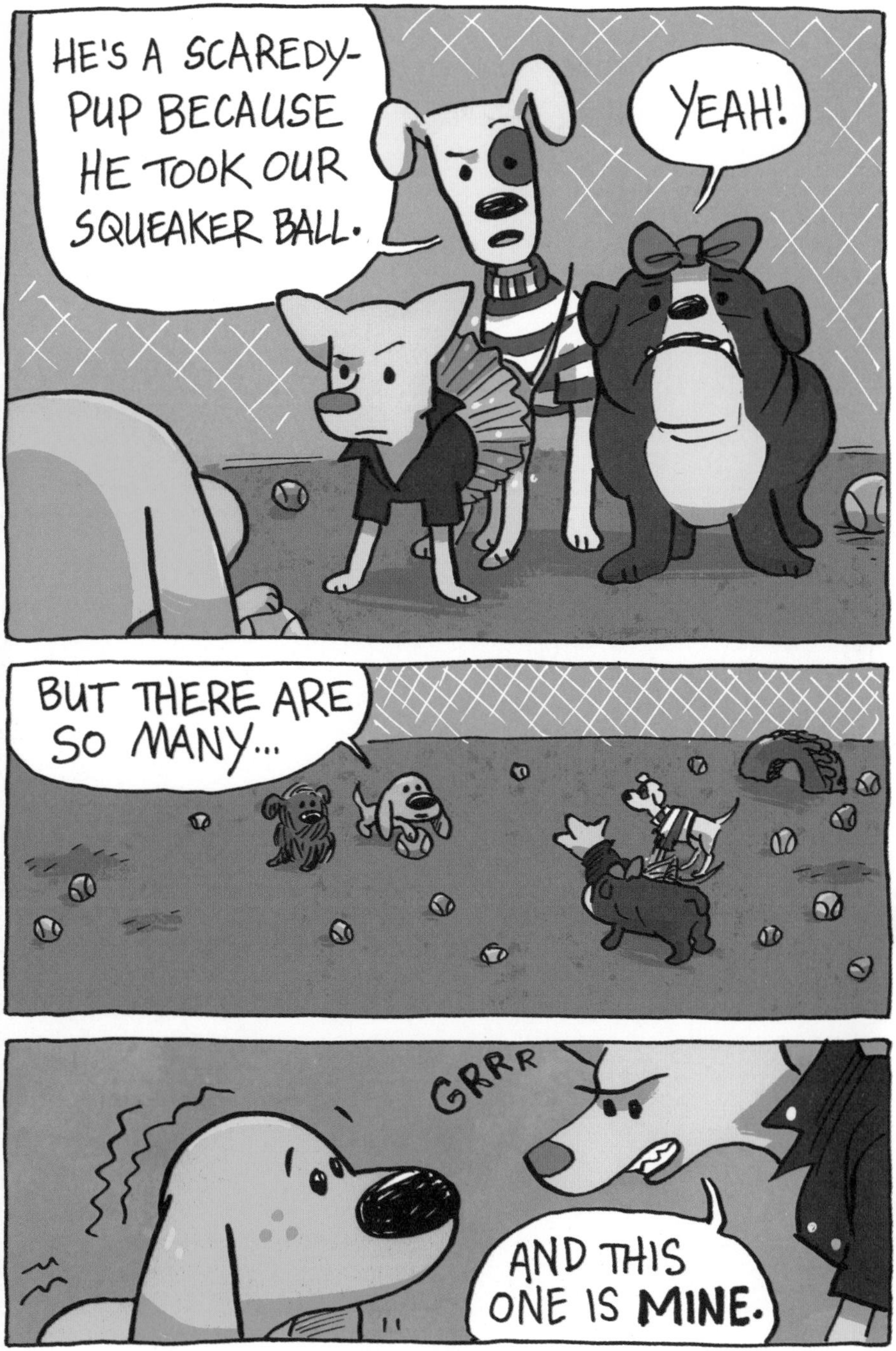
HE'S A SCAREDY-PUP BECAUSE HE TOOK OUR SQUEAKER BALL.
YEAH!
BUT THERE ARE SO MANY...
GRRR
AND THIS ONE IS **MINE.**

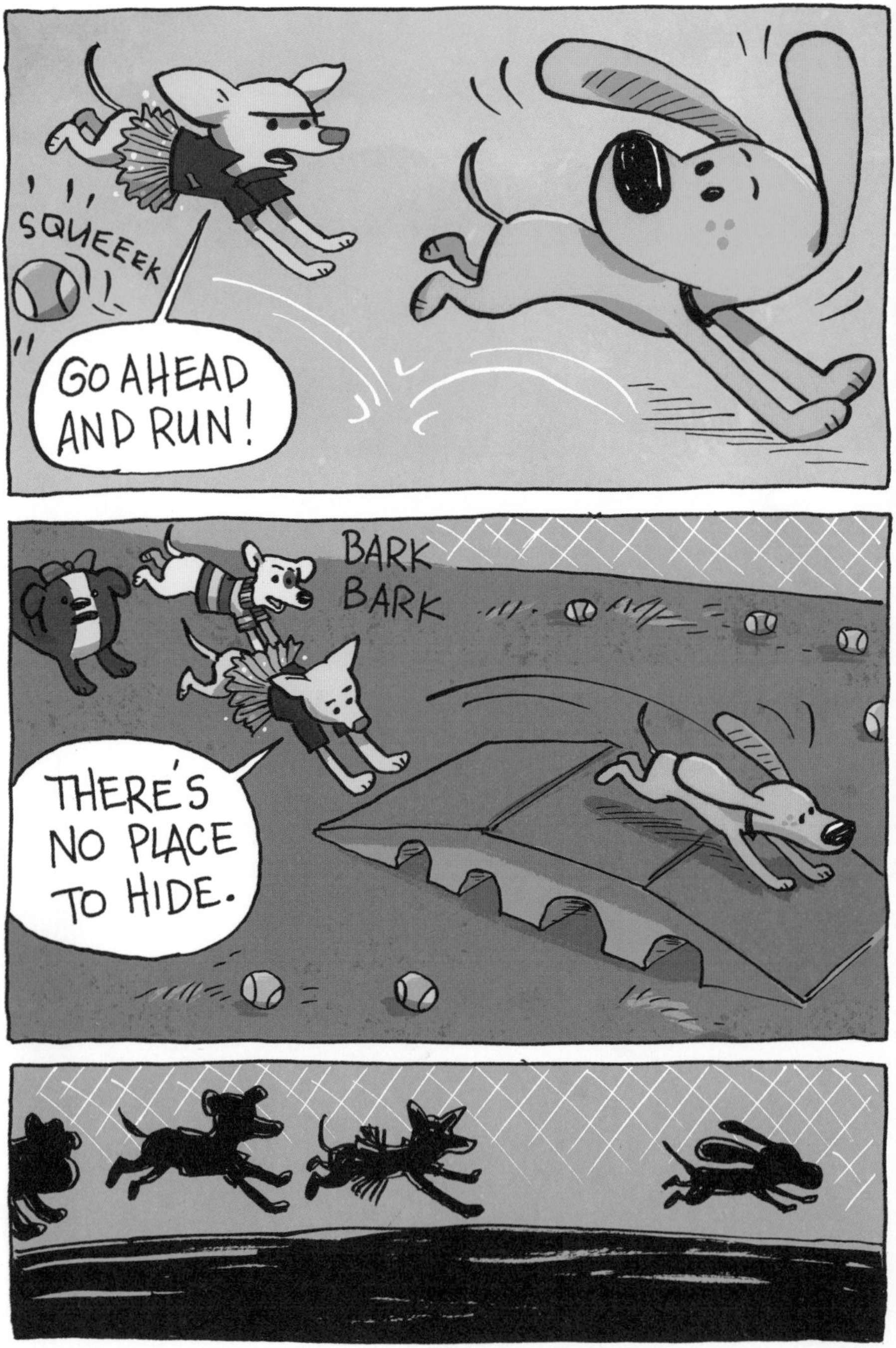
SQUEEEEK
GO AHEAD AND RUN!
BARK BARK
THERE'S NO PLACE TO HIDE.

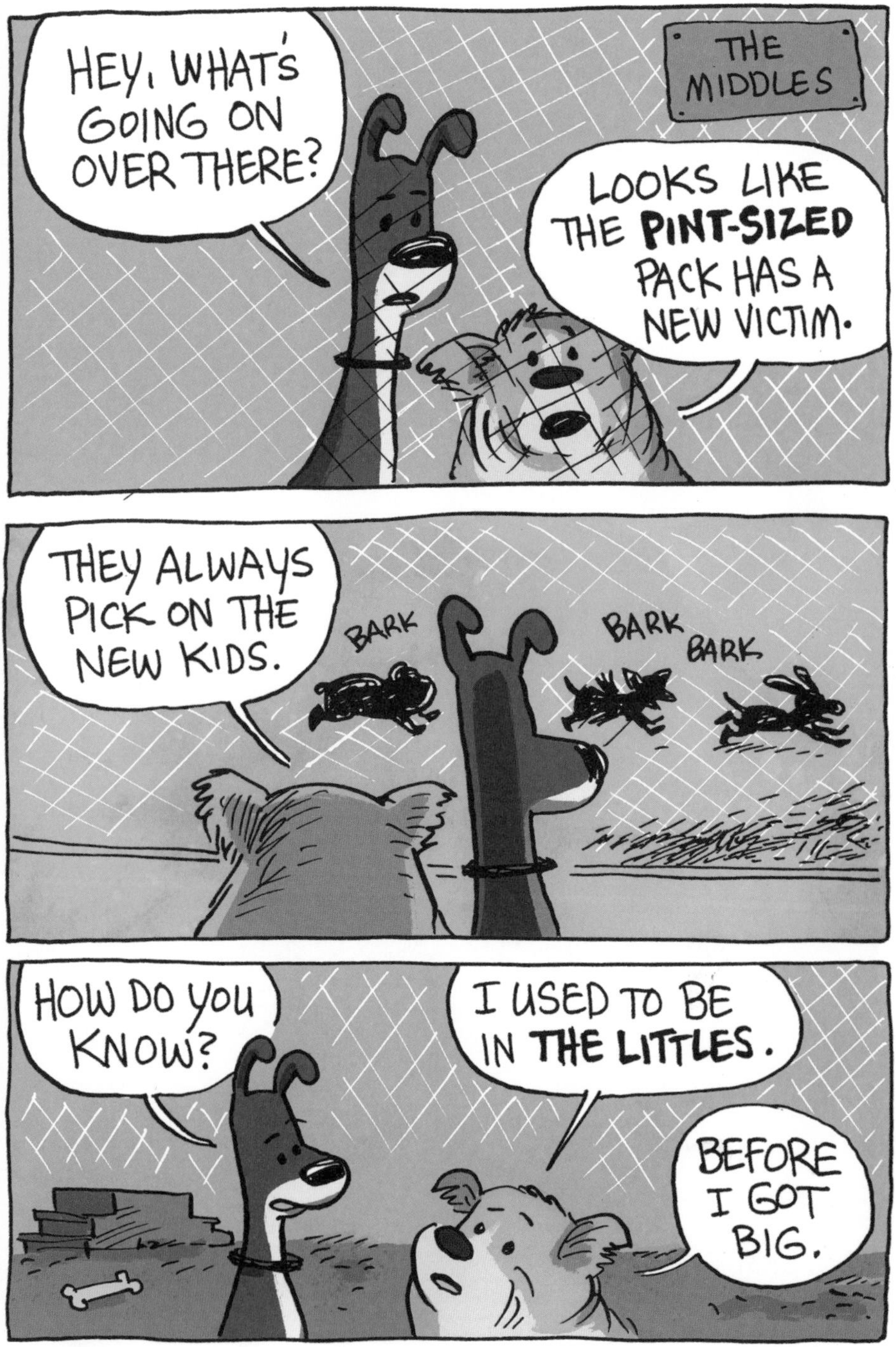
THE MIDDLES
HEY, WHAT'S GOING ON OVER THERE?
LOOKS LIKE THE **PINT-SIZED** PACK HAS A NEW VICTIM.
THEY ALWAYS PICK ON THE NEW KIDS.
BARK
BARK
BARK
HOW DO YOU KNOW?
I USED TO BE IN **THE LITTLES**.
BEFORE I GOT BIG.

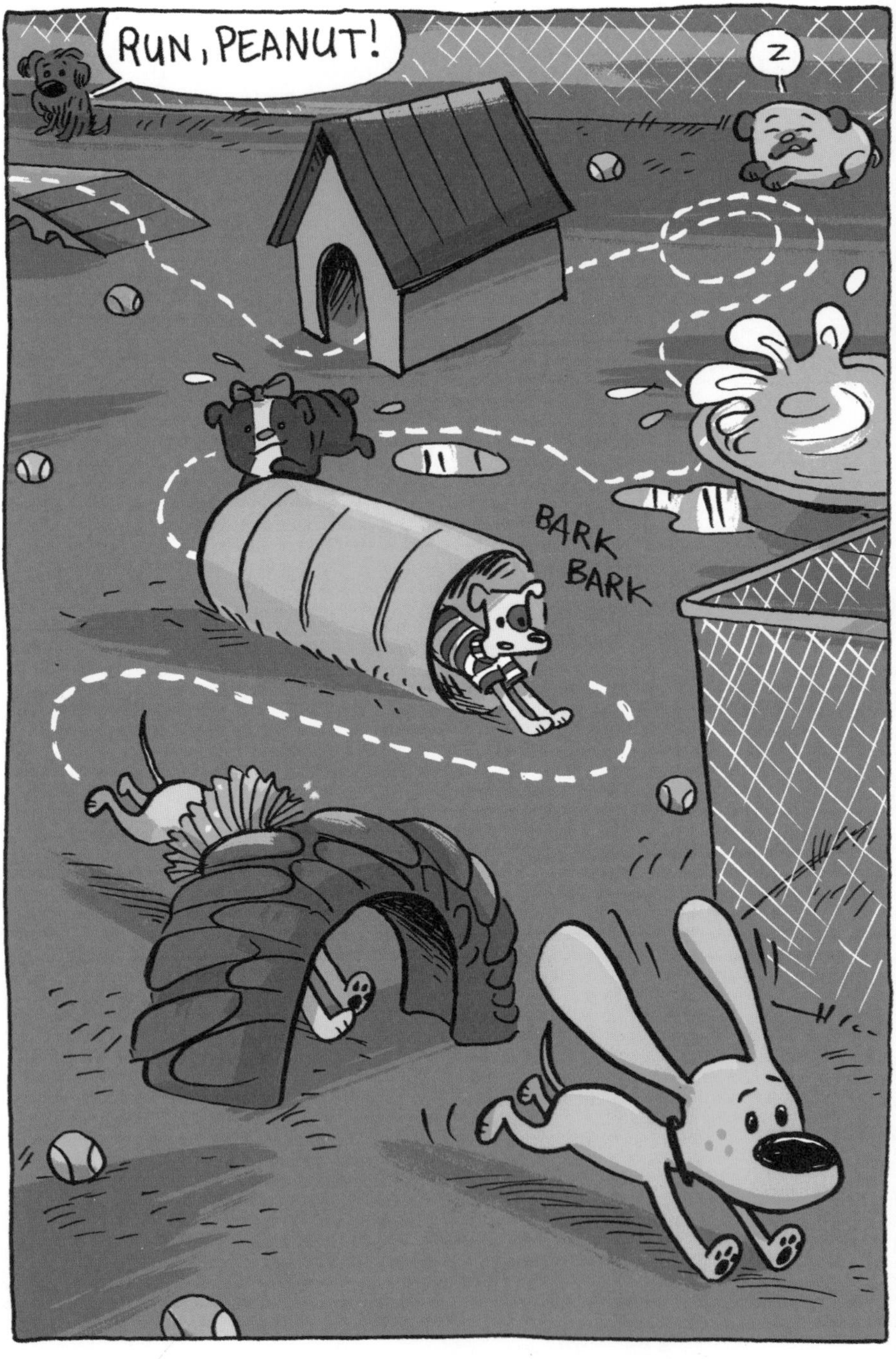
RUN, PEANUT!
Z
BARK
BARK

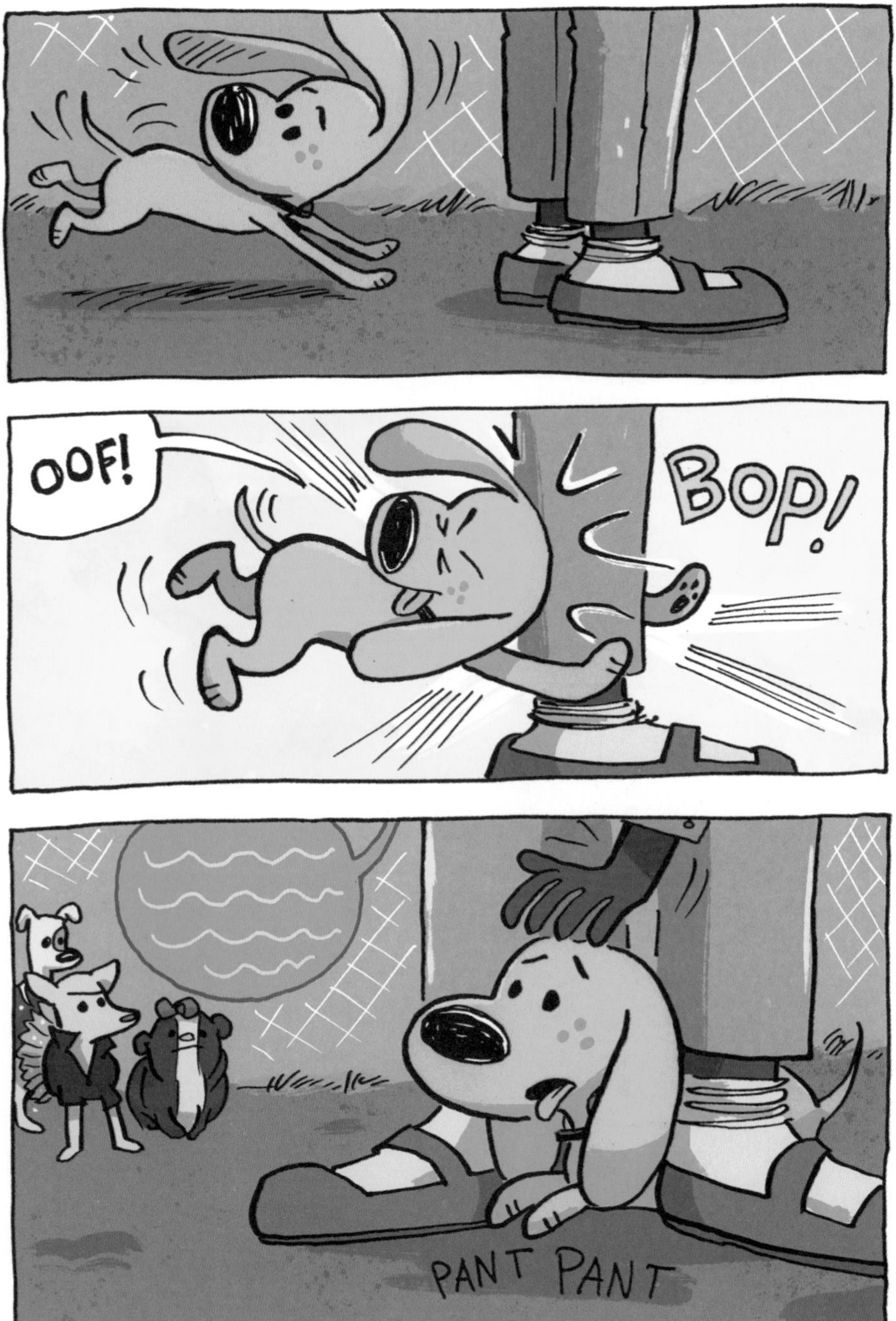
OOF!
BOP!
PANT PANT

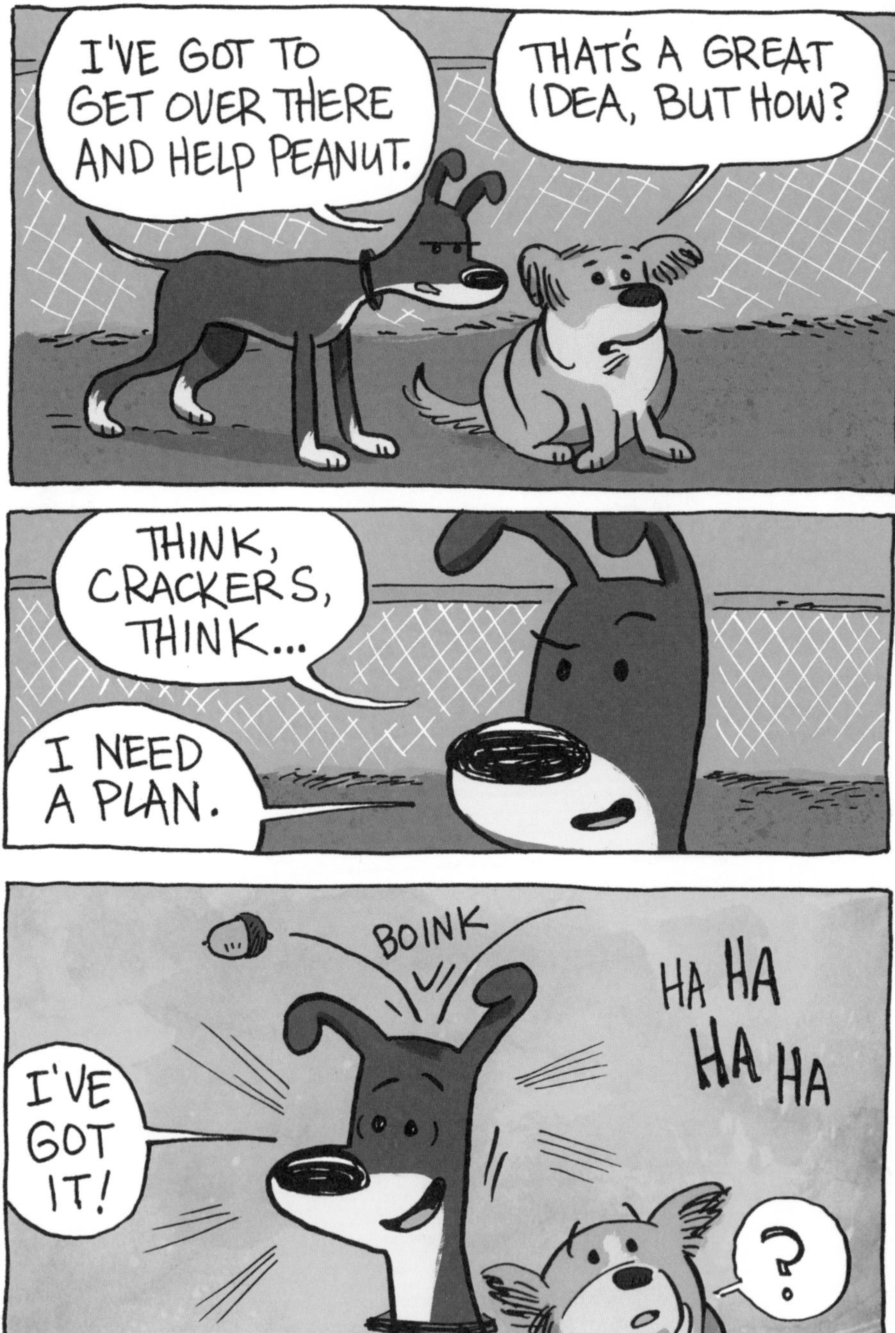
I'VE GOT TO GET OVER THERE AND HELP PEANUT.
THAT'S A GREAT IDEA, BUT HOW?
THINK, CRACKERS, THINK...
I NEED A PLAN.
BOINK
HA HA HA HA
I'VE GOT IT!
?

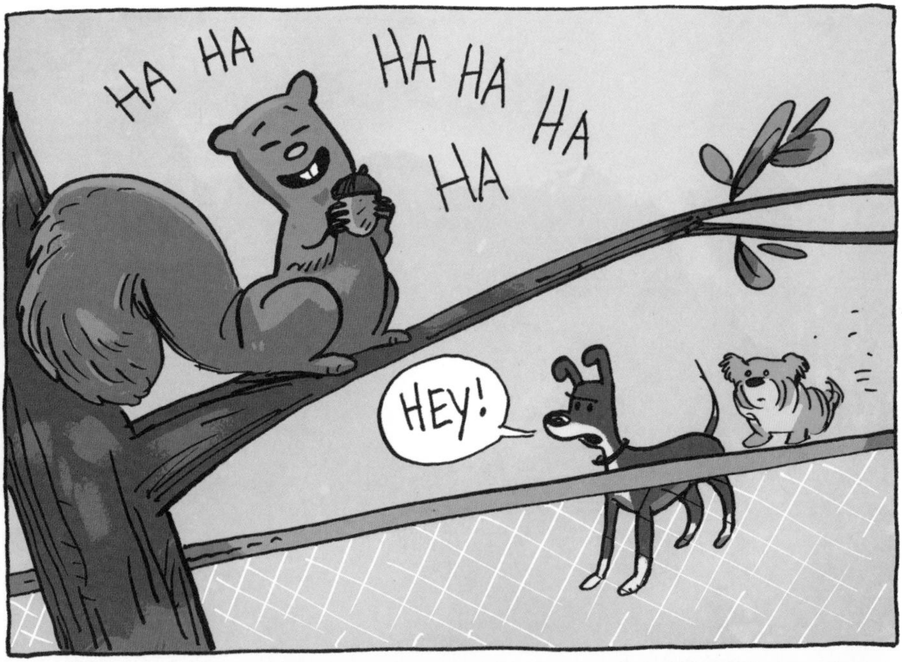
HA HA
HA HA HA
HA
HEY!

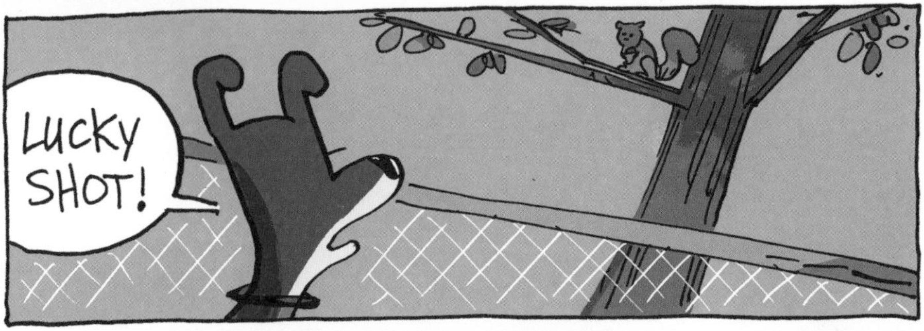
LUCKY SHOT!

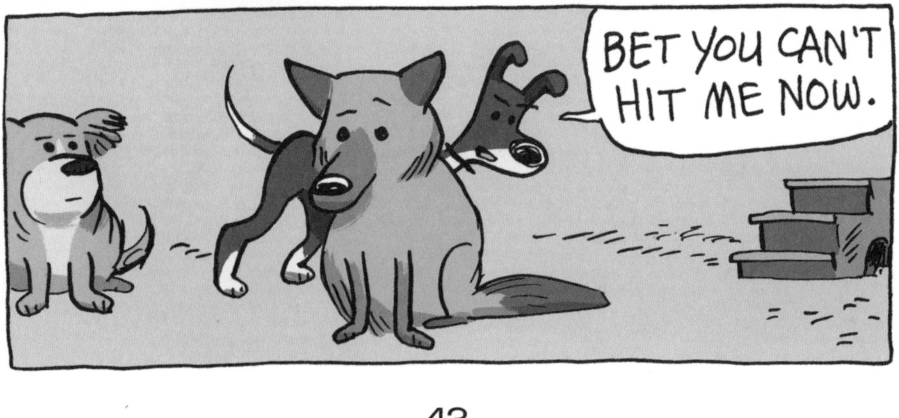
BET YOU CAN'T HIT ME NOW.

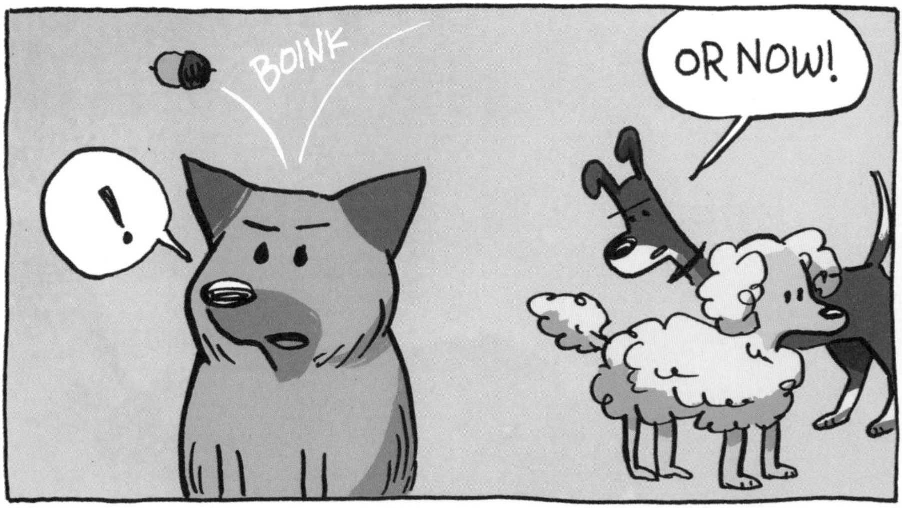
BOINK
!
OR NOW!

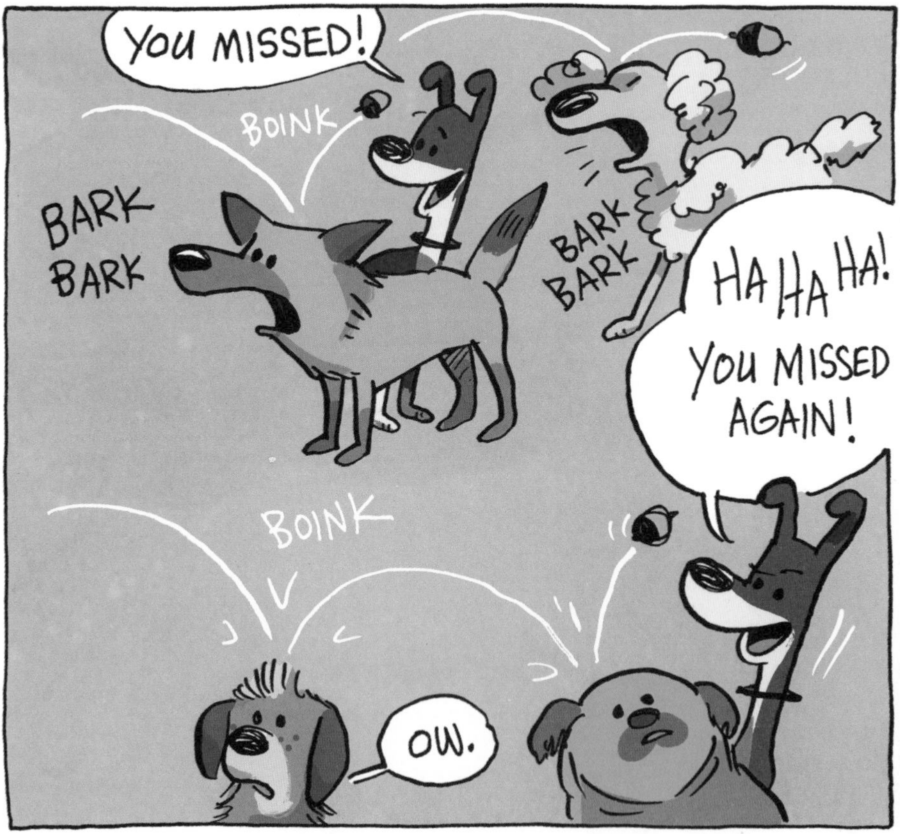
YOU MISSED!
BOINK
BARK
BARK
BARK
BARK
HA HA HA!
YOU MISSED AGAIN!
BOINK
OW.

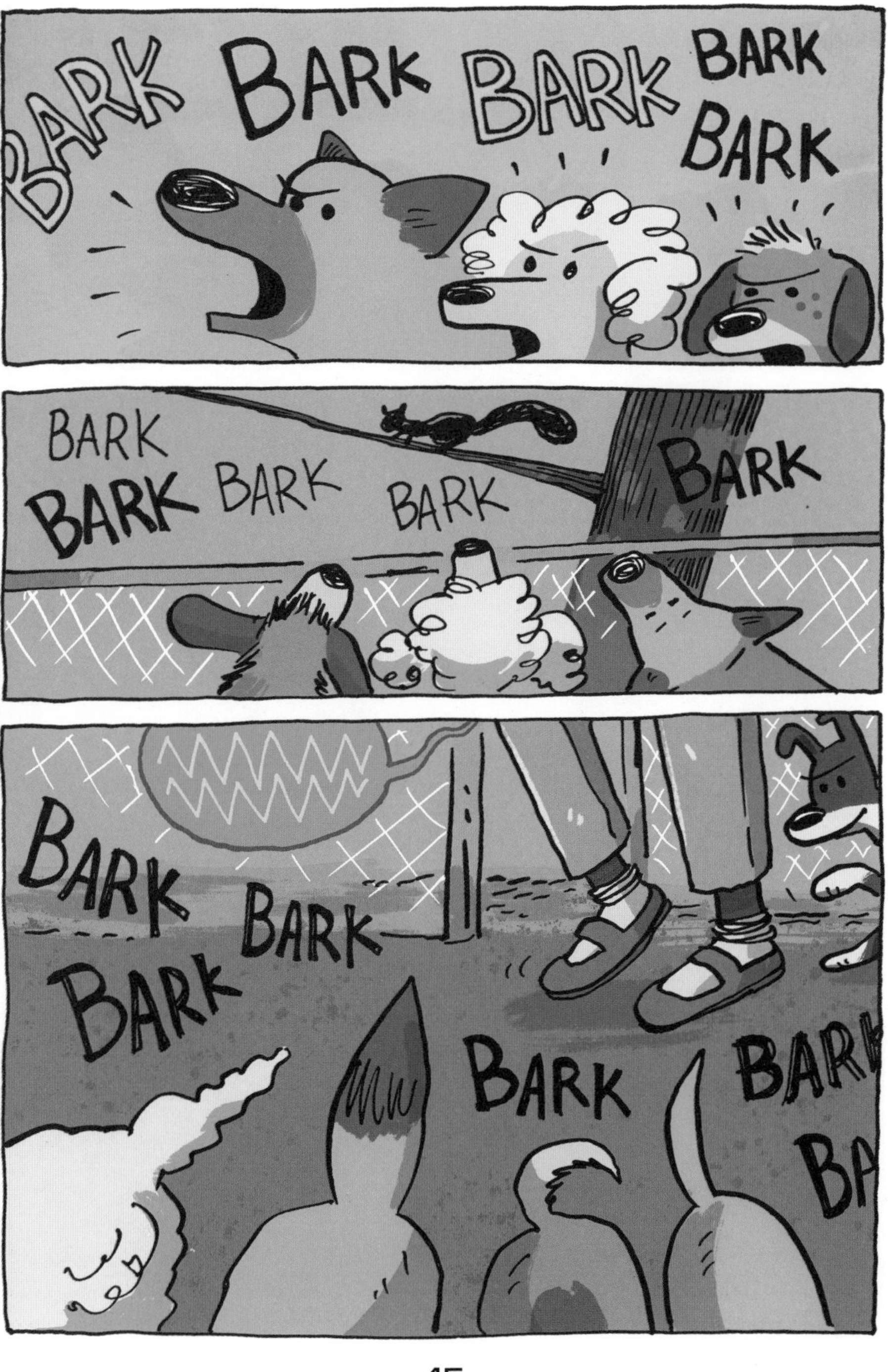
BARK
BARK
BARK
BARK
BARK
BARK
BARK
BARK
BARK
BARK
BARK
BARK
BARK
BARK
BAR
BA

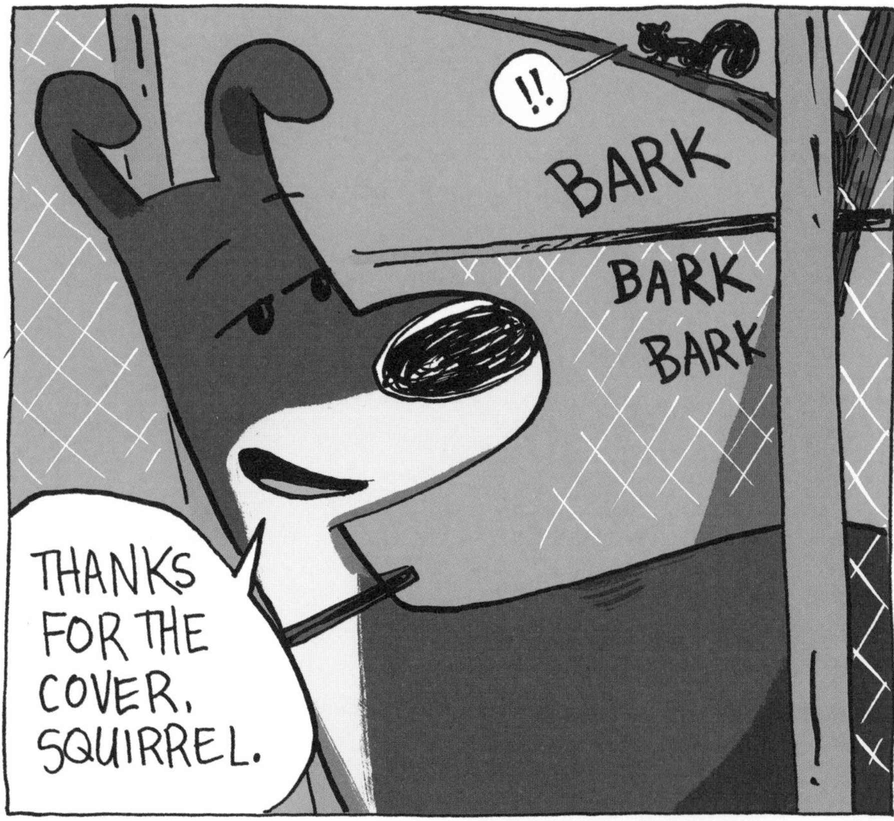
!!
BARK
BARK
BARK
THANKS FOR THE COVER, SQUIRREL.

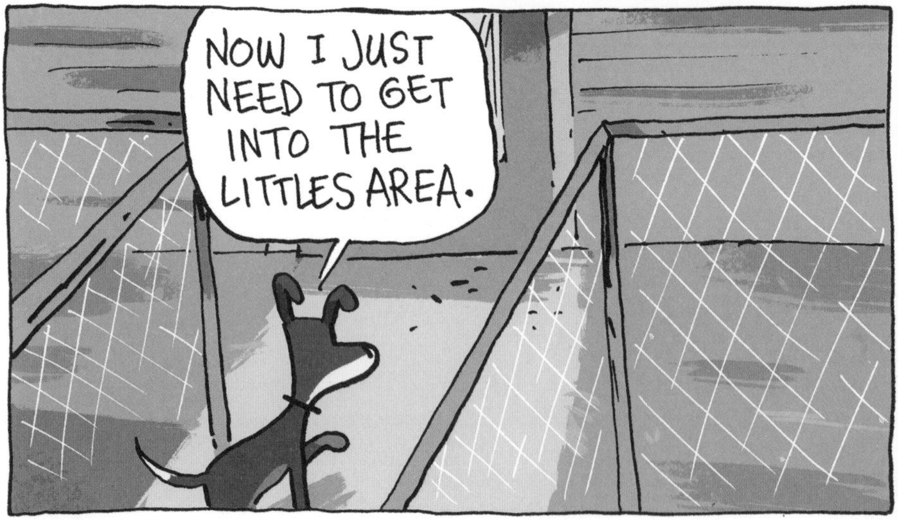
NOW I JUST NEED TO GET INTO THE LITTLES AREA.

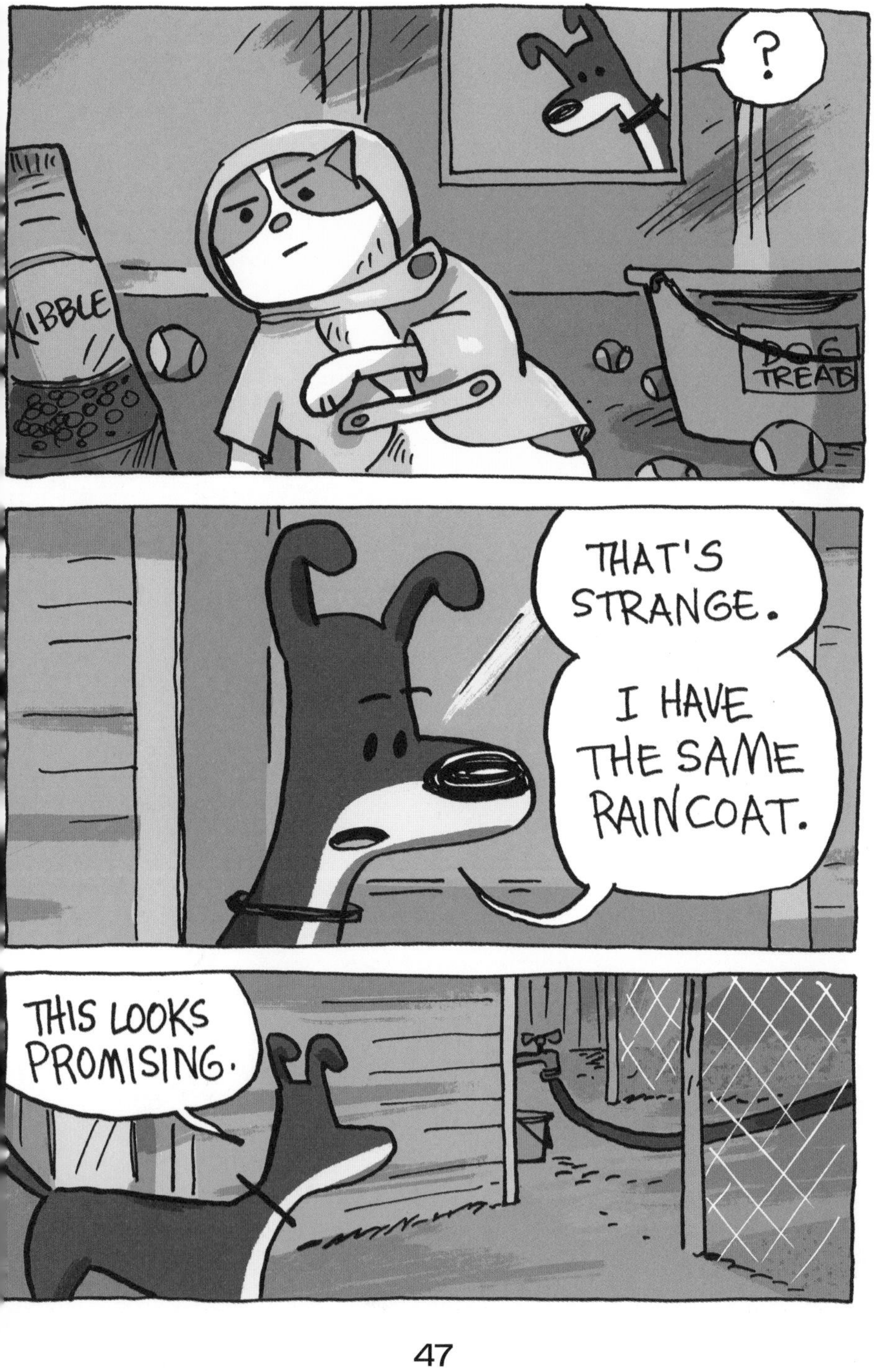
KIBBLE
?
DOG TREAT
THAT'S STRANGE.
I HAVE THE SAME RAINCOAT.
THIS LOOKS PROMISING.

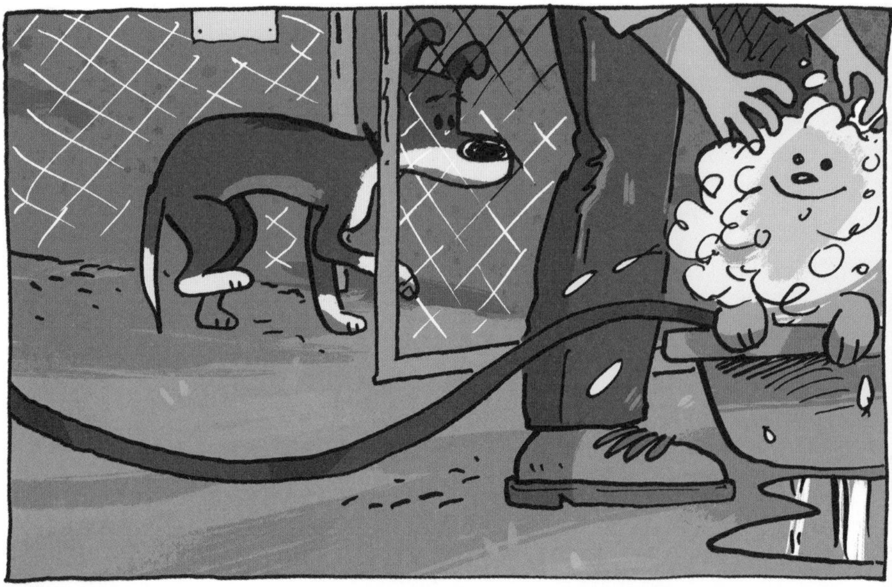

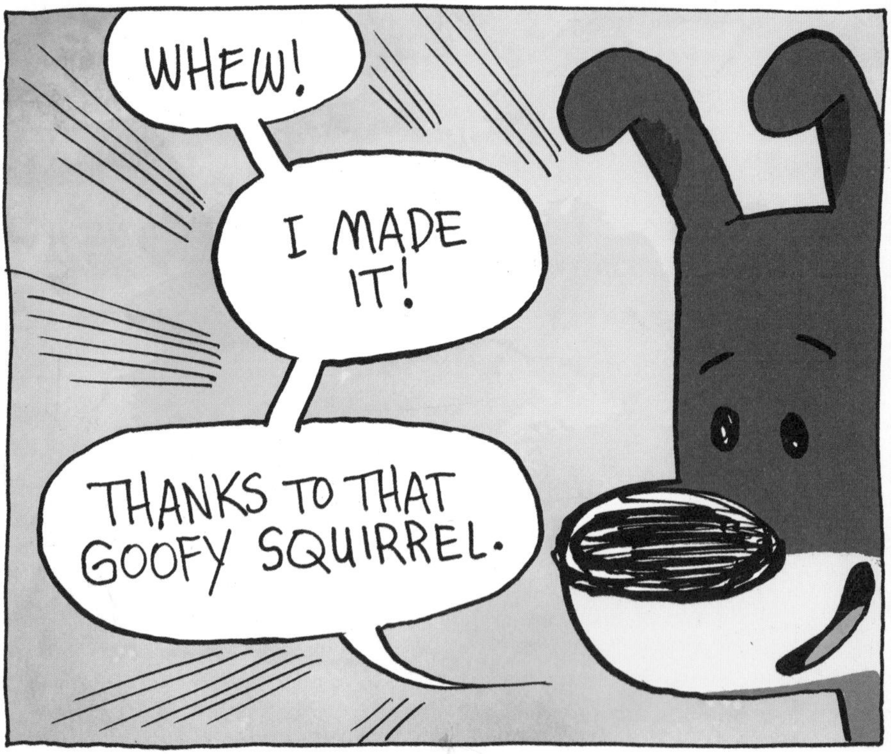
WHEW!
I MADE IT!
THANKS TO THAT GOOFY SQUIRREL.

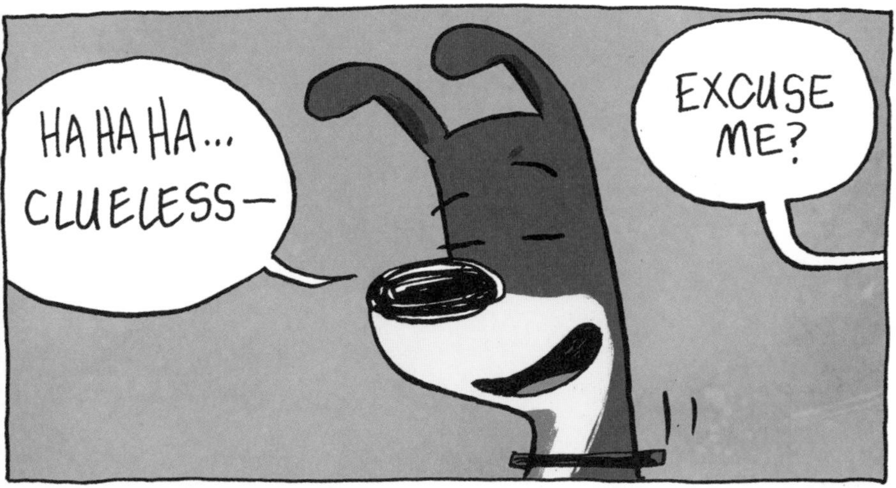
HA HA HA...
CLUELESS—
EXCUSE ME?

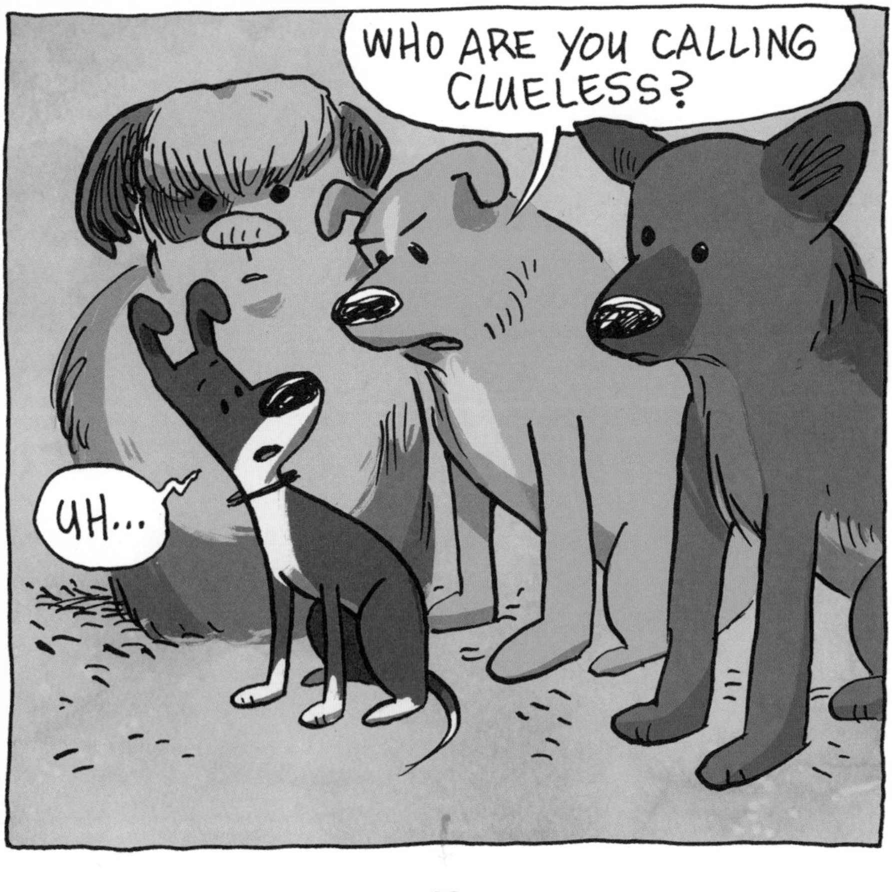
WHO ARE YOU CALLING CLUELESS?
UH...

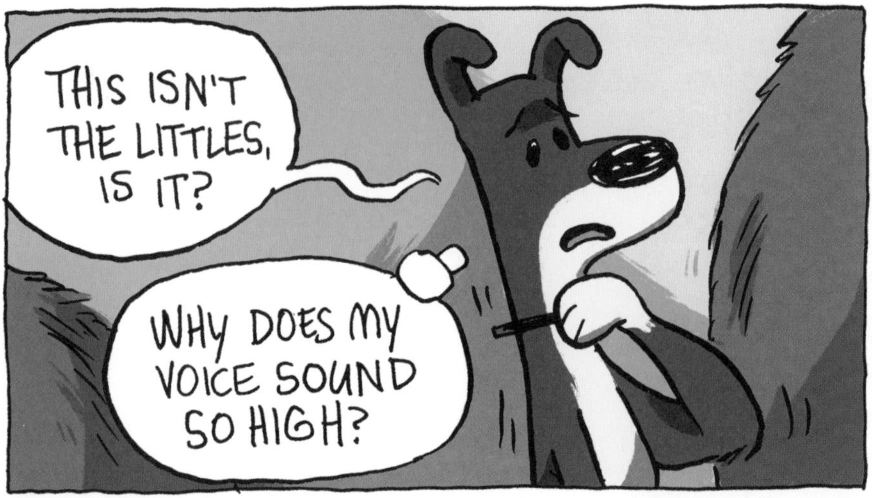
THIS ISN'T THE LITTLES, IS IT?
WHY DOES MY VOICE SOUND SO HIGH?

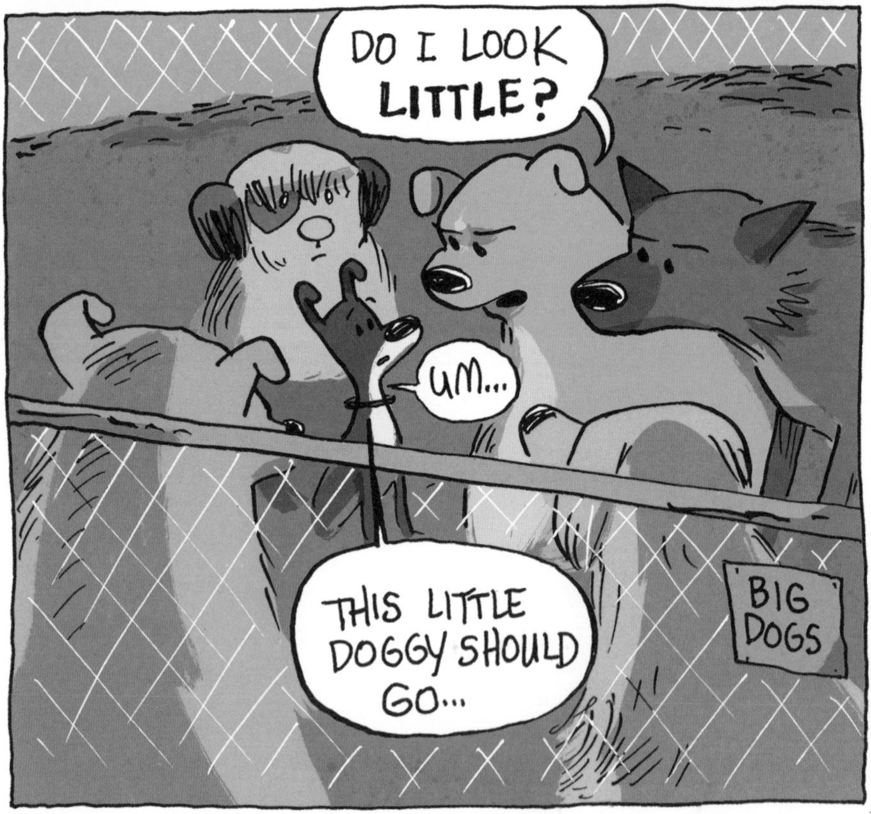
DO I LOOK LITTLE?
UM...
THIS LITTLE DOGGY SHOULD GO...
BIG DOGS

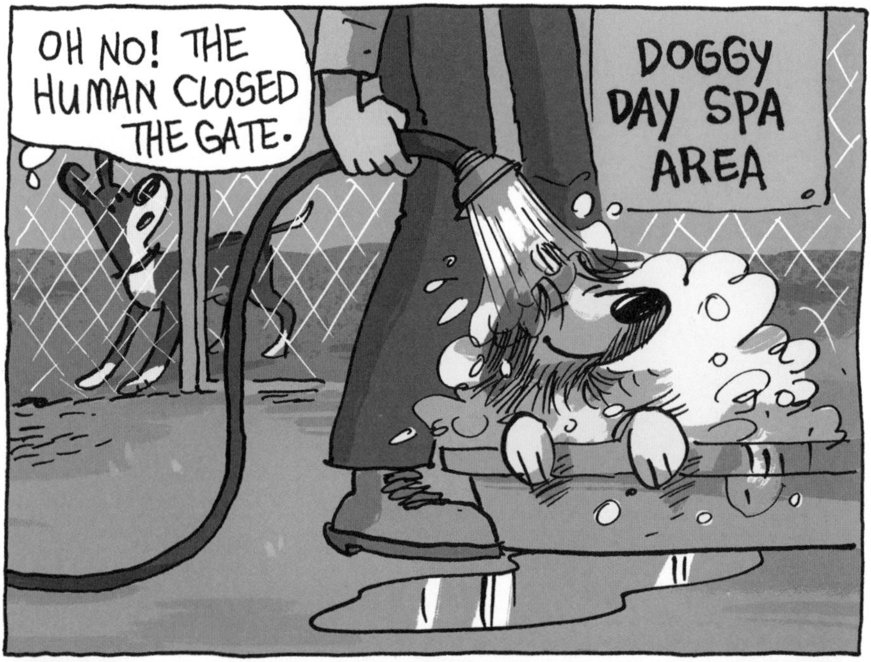
OH NO! THE HUMAN CLOSED THE GATE.
DOGGY DAY SPA AREA

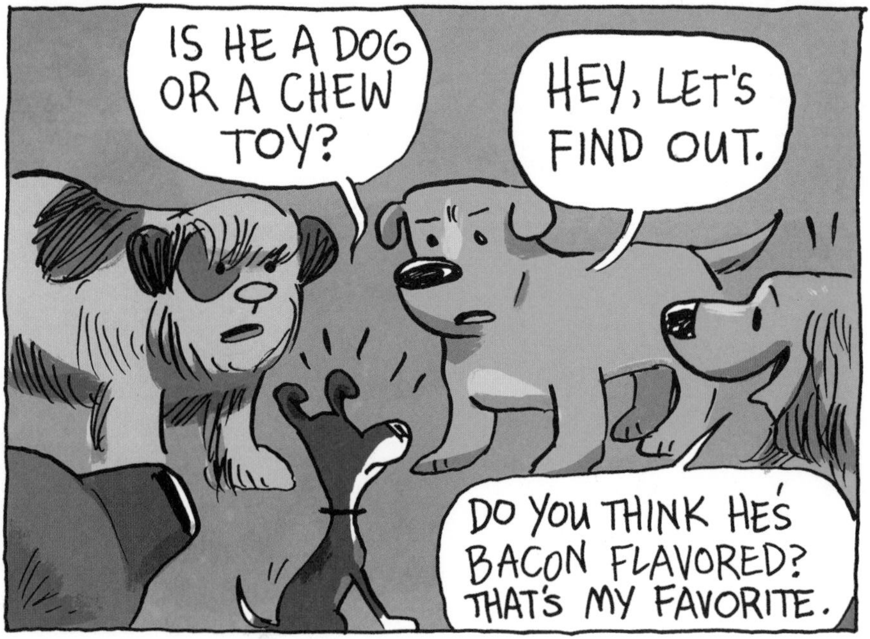
IS HE A DOG OR A CHEW TOY?
HEY, LET'S FIND OUT.
DO YOU THINK HE'S BACON FLAVORED? THAT'S MY FAVORITE.

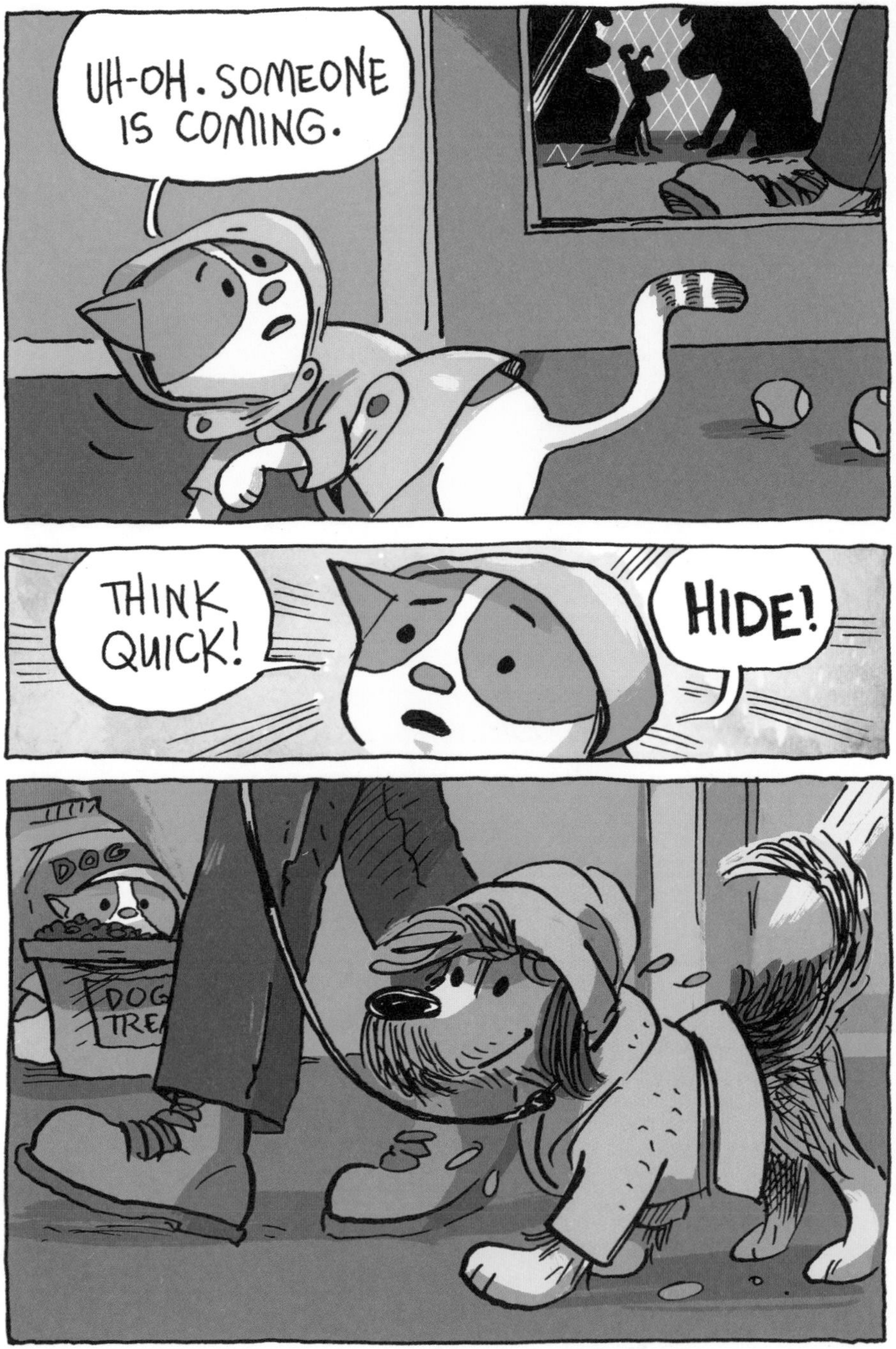
UH-OH. SOMEONE IS COMING.
THINK QUICK!
HIDE!
DOG
DOG TREA

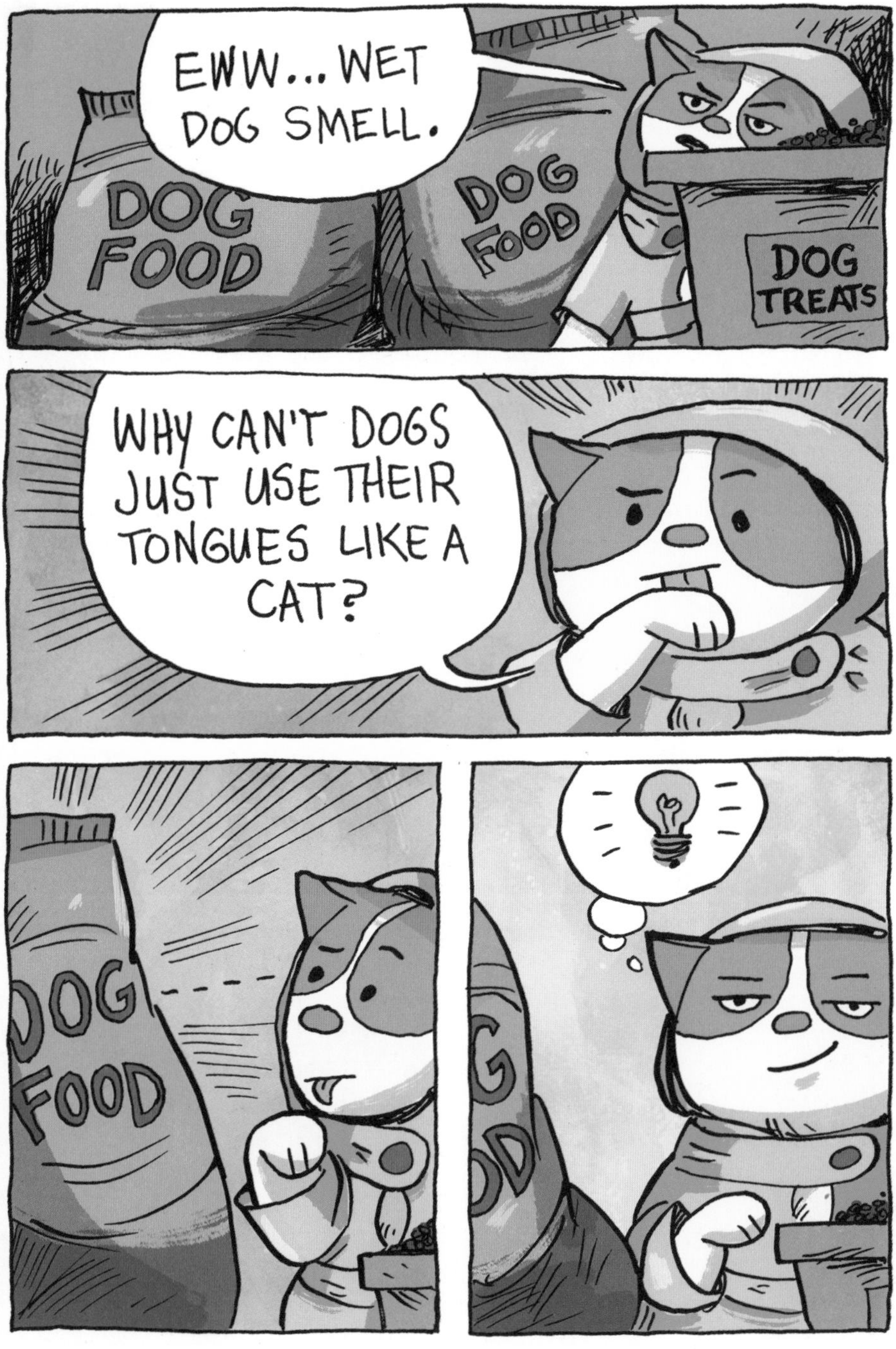
EWW... WET DOG SMELL.
DOG FOOD
DOG FOOD
DOG TREATS
WHY CAN'T DOGS JUST USE THEIR TONGUES LIKE A CAT?
FOOD

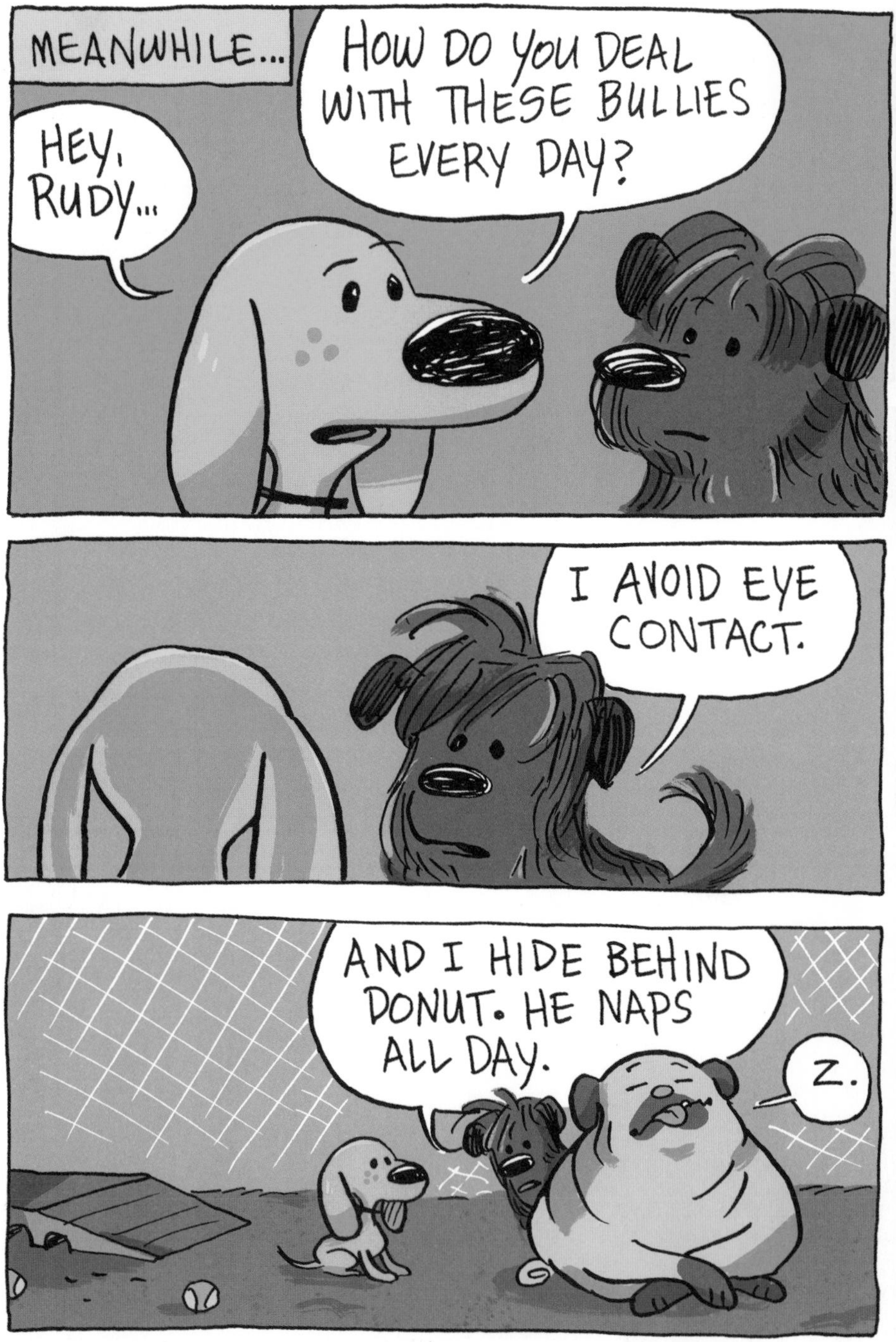
MEANWHILE...
HEY, RUDY...
HOW DO YOU DEAL WITH THESE BULLIES EVERY DAY?
I AVOID EYE CONTACT.
AND I HIDE BEHIND DONUT. HE NAPS ALL DAY.
Z.

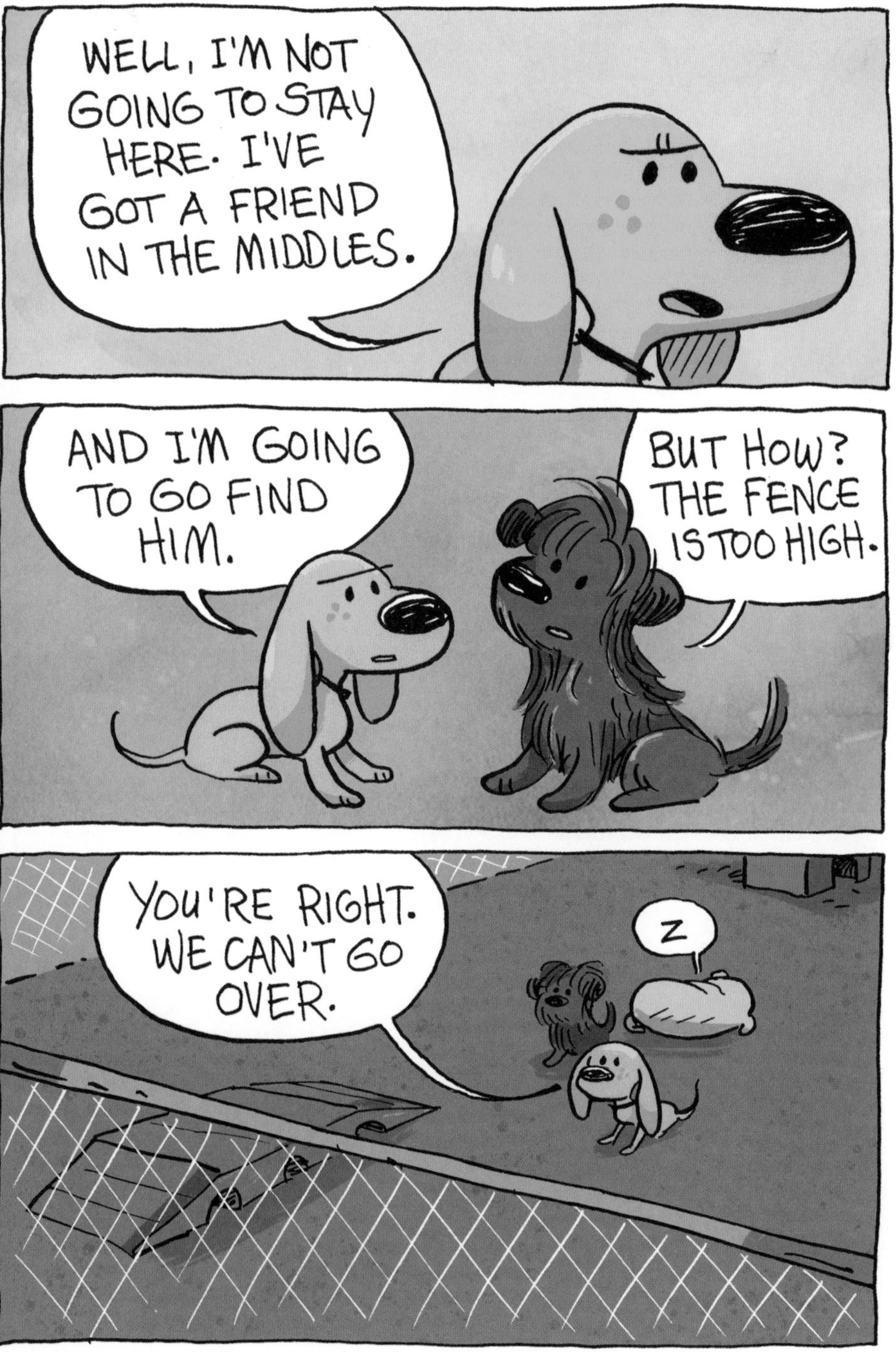
WELL, I'M NOT GOING TO STAY HERE. I'VE GOT A FRIEND IN THE MIDDLES.
AND I'M GOING TO GO FIND HIM.
BUT HOW? THE FENCE IS TOO HIGH.
YOU'RE RIGHT. WE CAN'T GO OVER.
Z

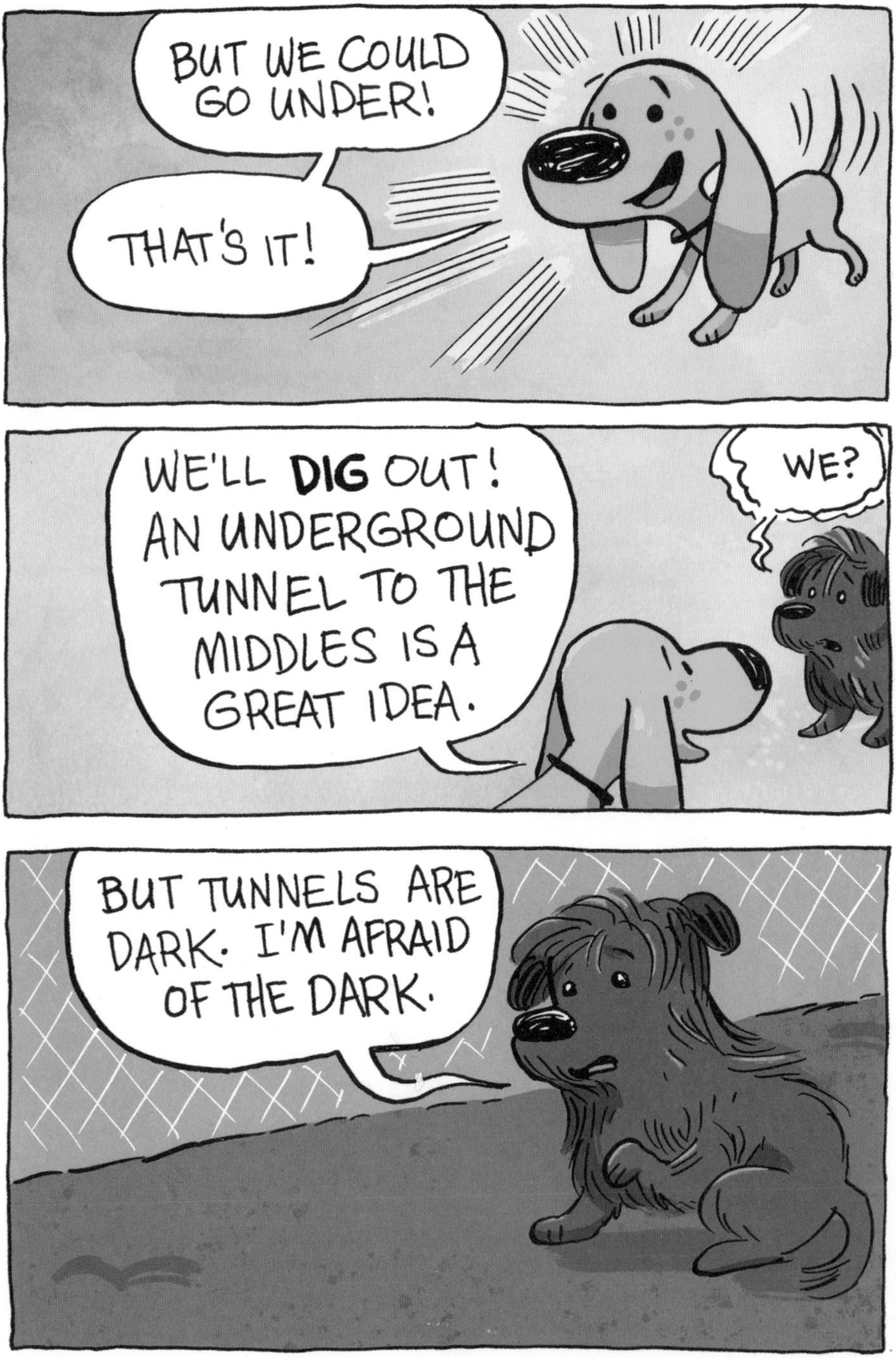
BUT WE COULD GO UNDER!
THAT'S IT!
WE'LL **DIG** OUT! AN UNDERGROUND TUNNEL TO THE MIDDLES IS A GREAT IDEA.
WE?
BUT TUNNELS ARE DARK. I'M AFRAID OF THE DARK.

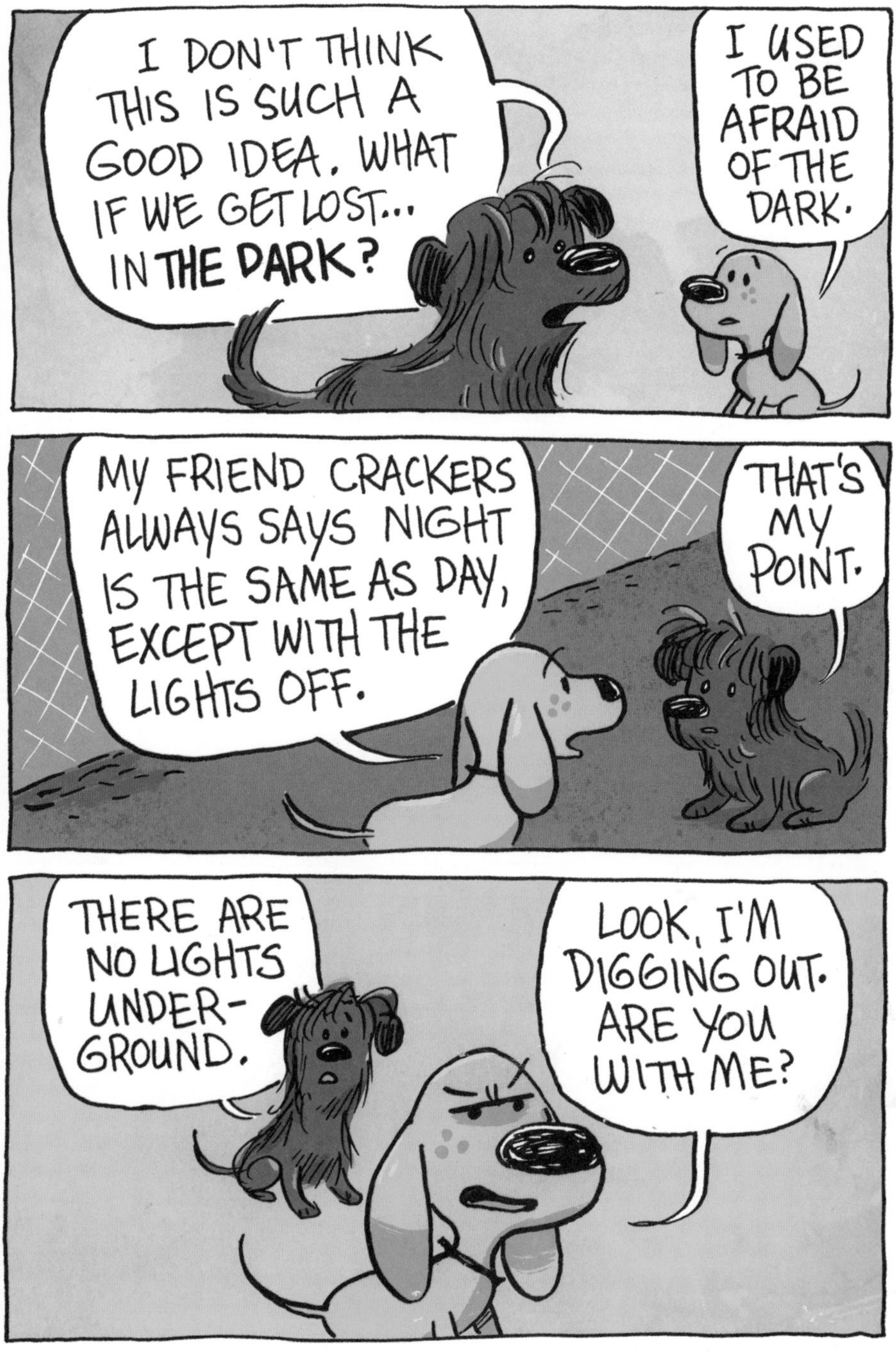
I DON'T THINK THIS IS SUCH A GOOD IDEA. WHAT IF WE GET LOST... IN THE DARK?
I USED TO BE AFRAID OF THE DARK.
MY FRIEND CRACKERS ALWAYS SAYS NIGHT IS THE SAME AS DAY, EXCEPT WITH THE LIGHTS OFF.
THAT'S MY POINT.
THERE ARE NO LIGHTS UNDER-GROUND.
LOOK, I'M DIGGING OUT. ARE YOU WITH ME?

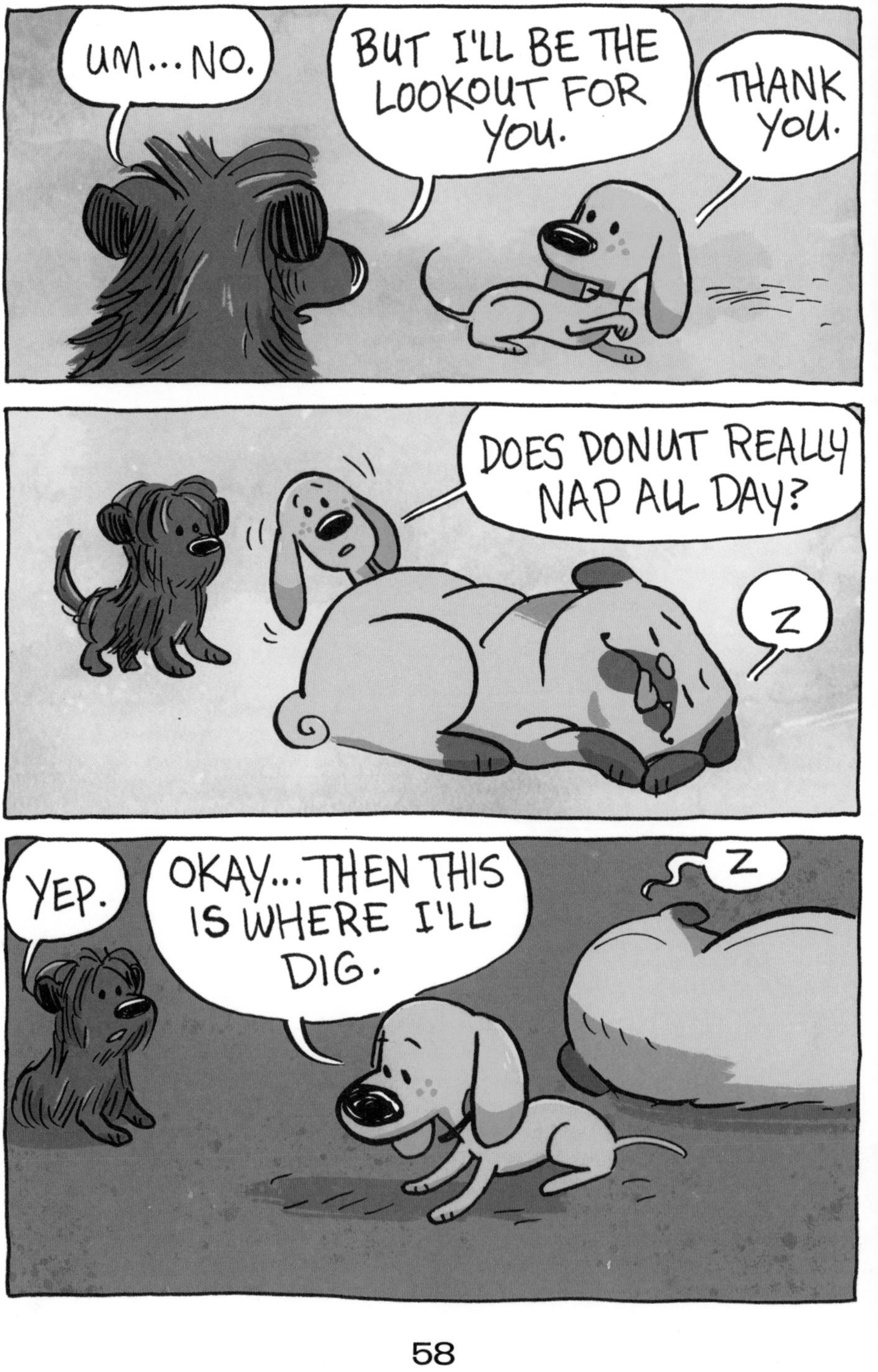
UM...NO.
BUT I'LL BE THE LOOKOUT FOR YOU.
THANK YOU.
DOES DONUT REALLY NAP ALL DAY?
Z
YEP.
OKAY...THEN THIS IS WHERE I'LL DIG.
Z

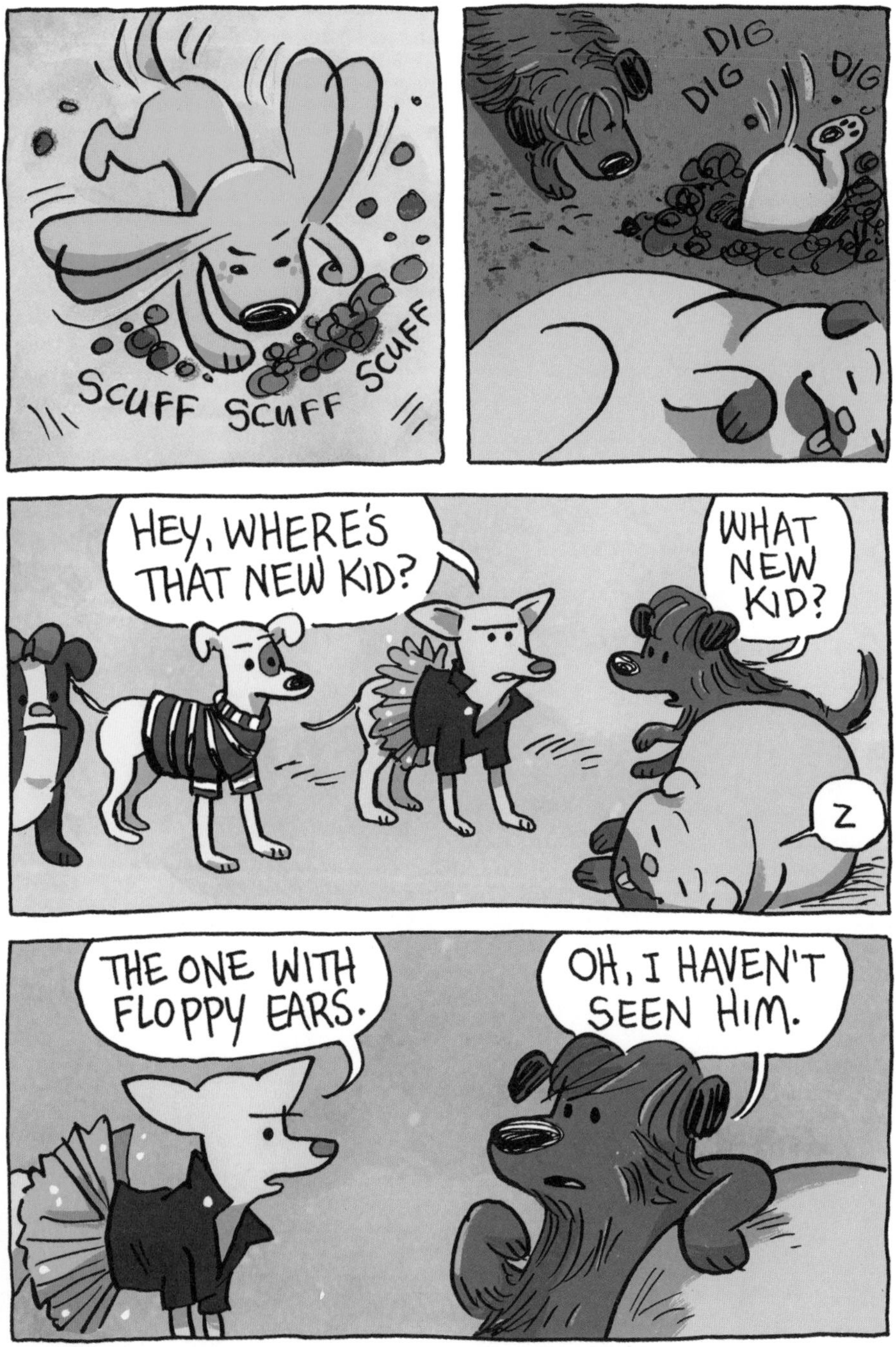
SCUFF SCUFF SCUFF
DIG DIG DIG
HEY, WHERE'S THAT NEW KID?
WHAT NEW KID?
Z
THE ONE WITH FLOPPY EARS.
OH, I HAVEN'T SEEN HIM.

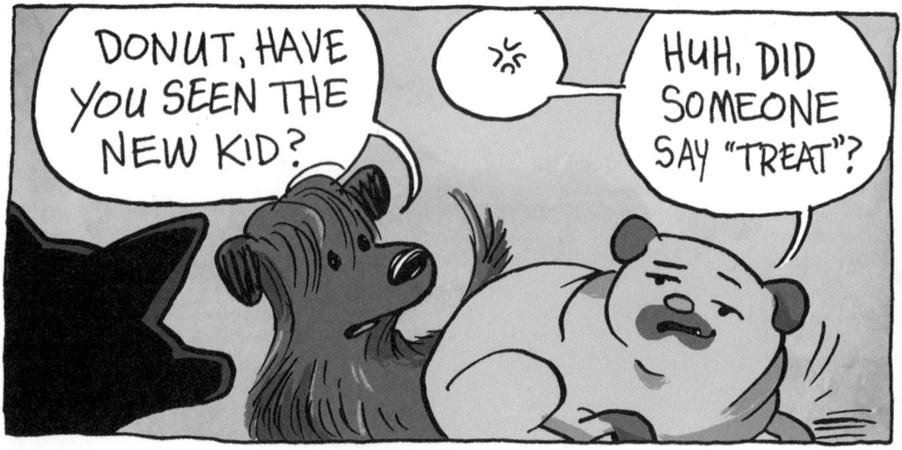
DONUT, HAVE YOU SEEN THE NEW KID?
HUH, DID SOMEONE SAY "TREAT"?

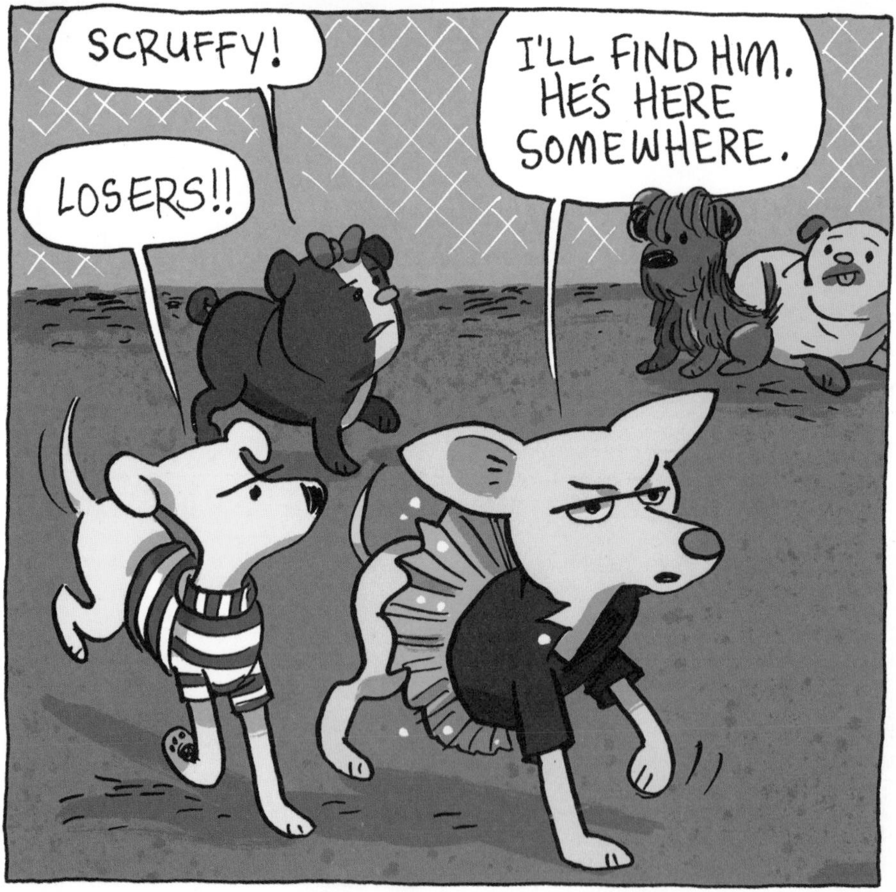
SCRUFFY!
LOSERS!!
I'LL FIND HIM. HE'S HERE SOMEWHERE.

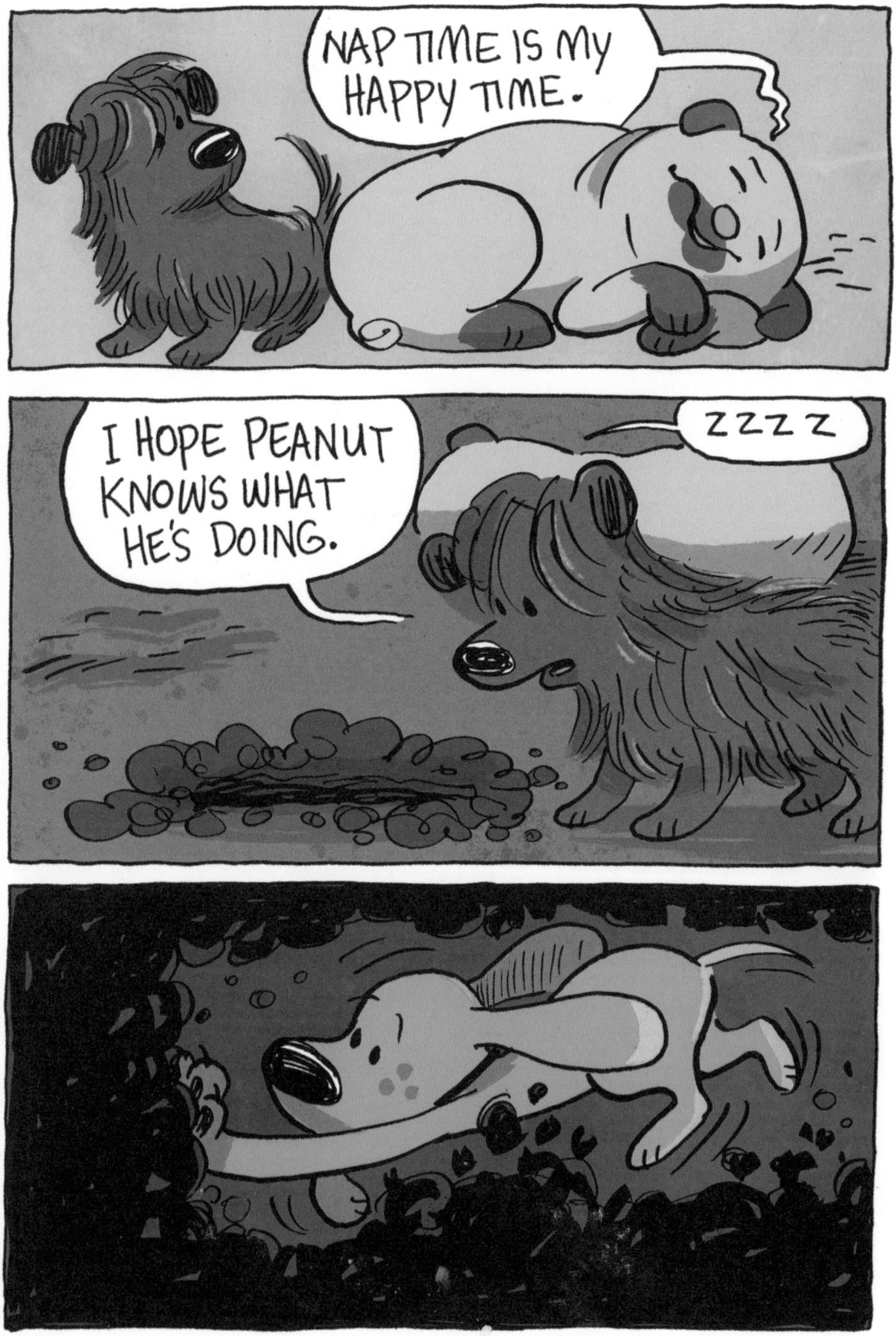
NAP TIME IS MY HAPPY TIME.
I HOPE PEANUT KNOWS WHAT HE'S DOING.
ZZZZ

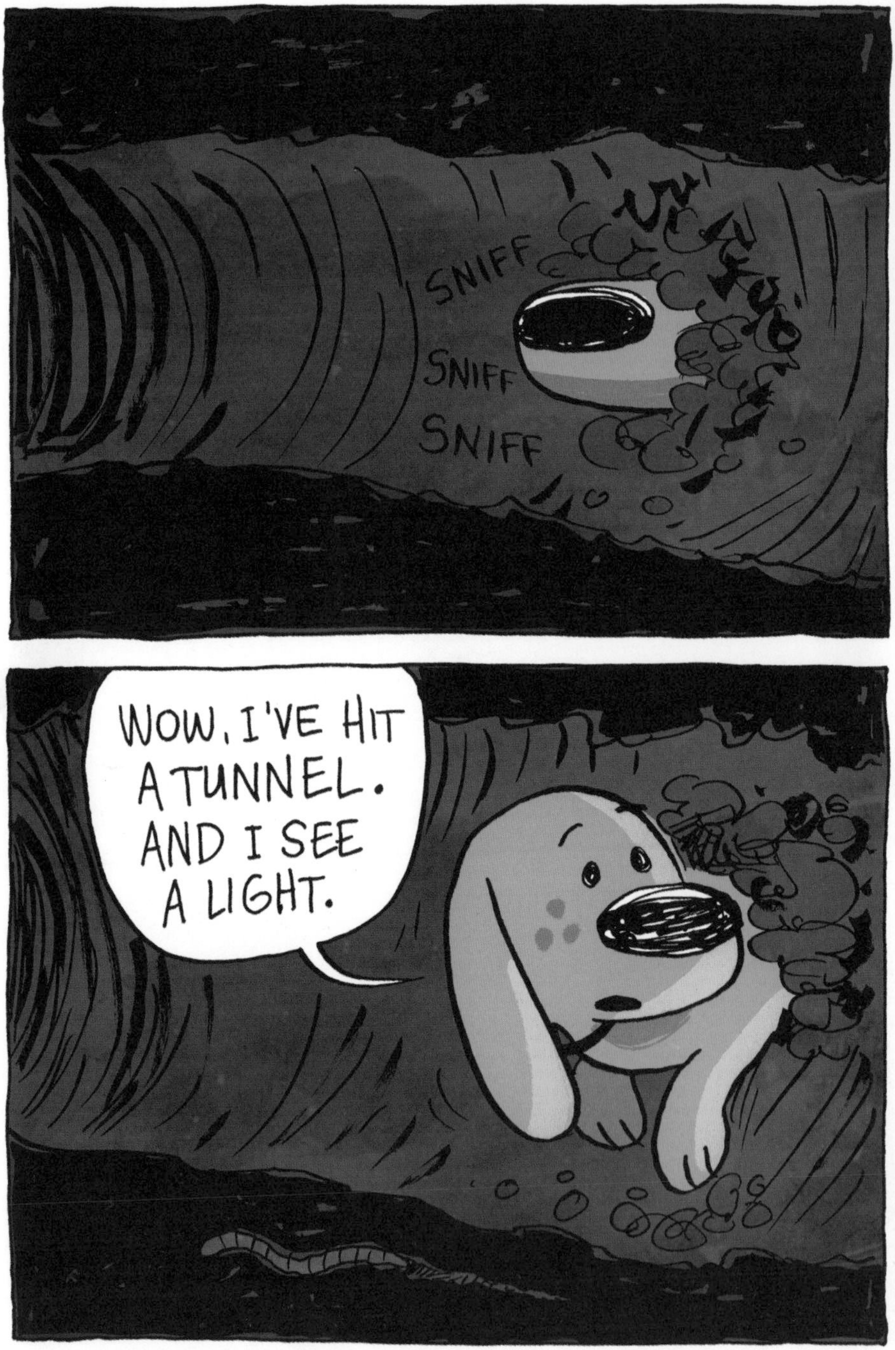
SNIFF
SNIFF
SNIFF
WOW, I'VE HIT A TUNNEL. AND I SEE A LIGHT.

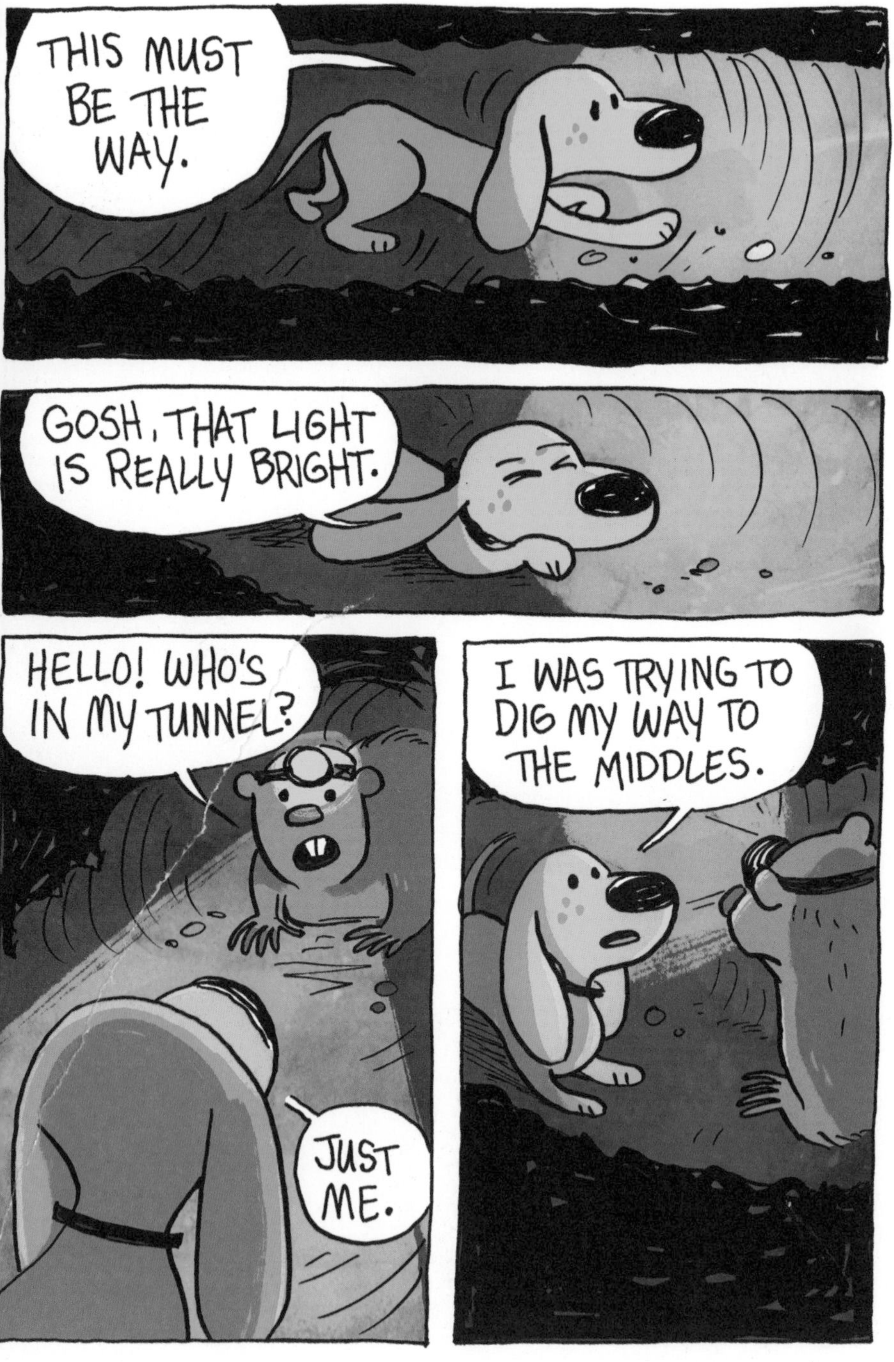
THIS MUST BE THE WAY.
GOSH, THAT LIGHT IS REALLY BRIGHT.
HELLO! WHO'S IN MY TUNNEL?
JUST ME.
I WAS TRYING TO DIG MY WAY TO THE MIDDLES.

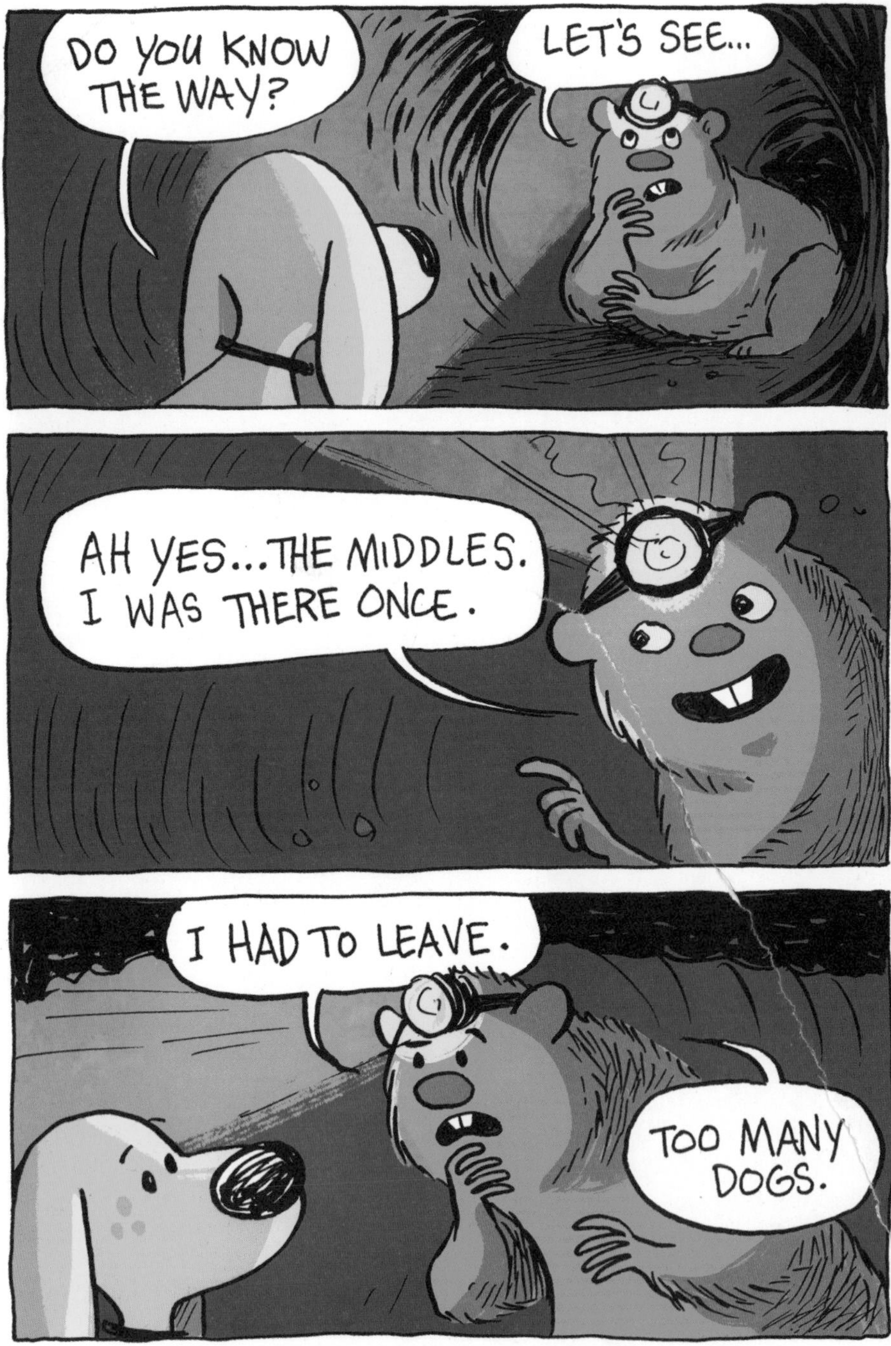
DO YOU KNOW THE WAY?
LET'S SEE...
AH YES...THE MIDDLES. I WAS THERE ONCE.
I HAD TO LEAVE.
TOO MANY DOGS.

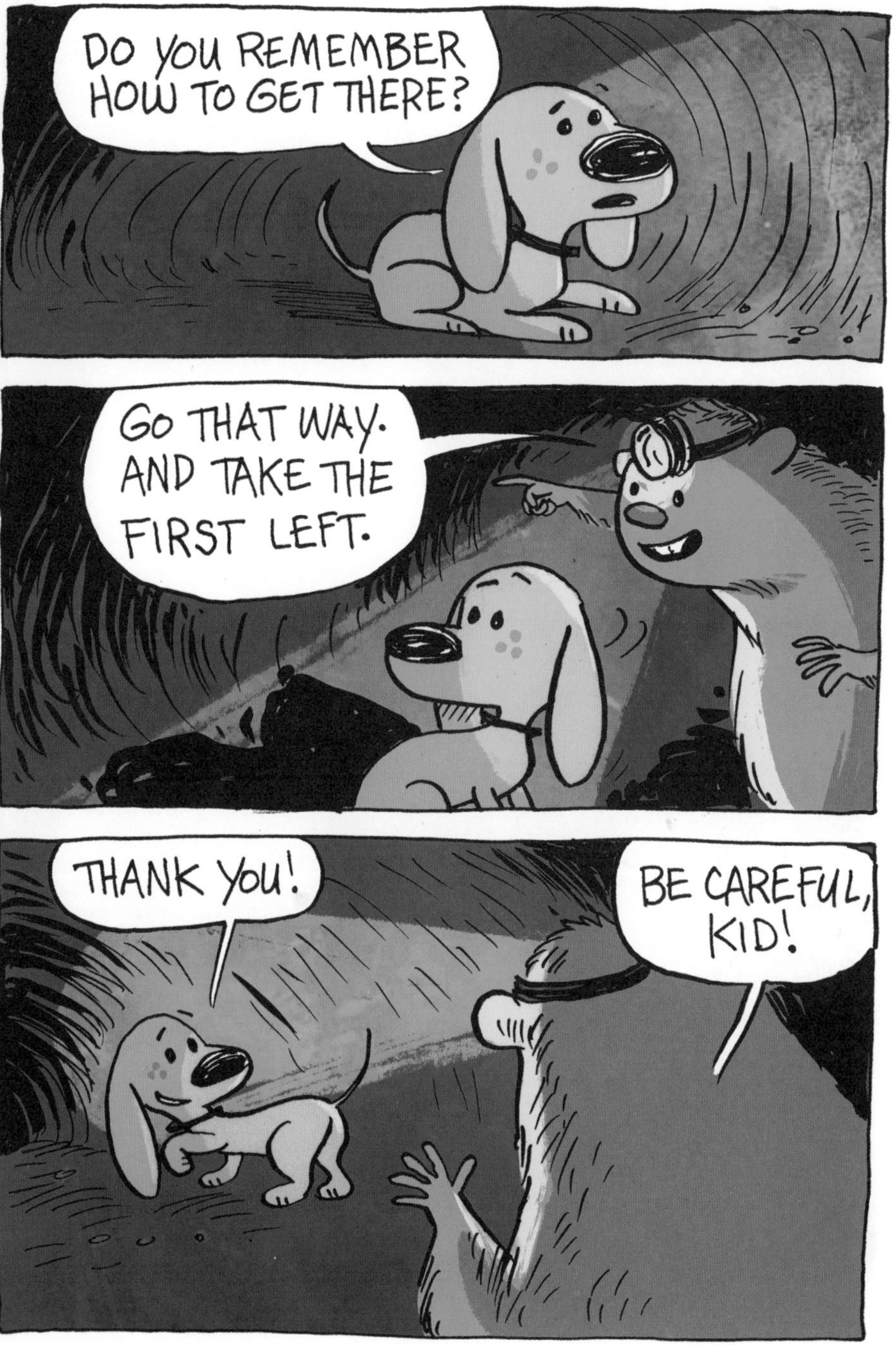
DO YOU REMEMBER HOW TO GET THERE?
GO THAT WAY. AND TAKE THE FIRST LEFT.
THANK YOU!
BE CAREFUL, KID!

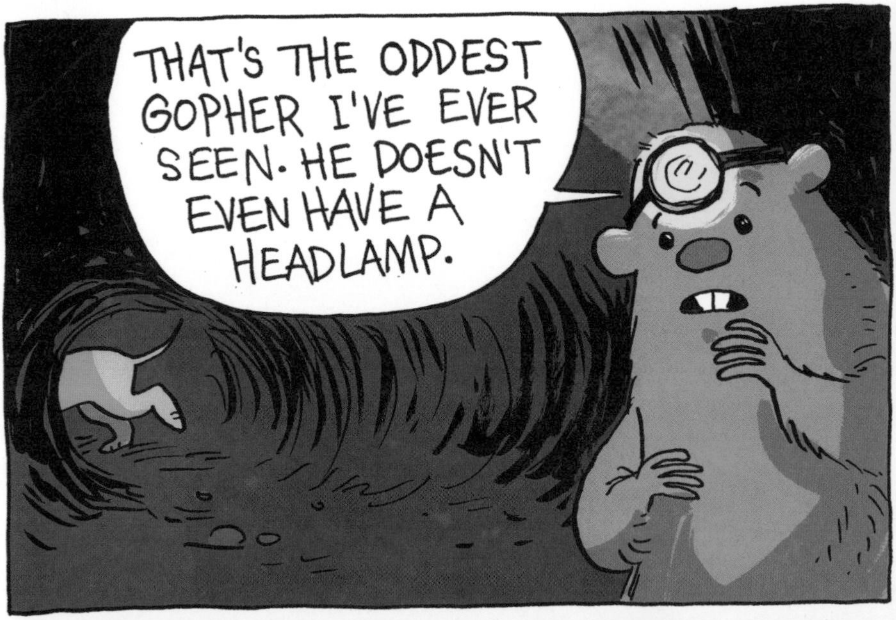
THAT'S THE ODDEST GOPHER I'VE EVER SEEN. HE DOESN'T EVEN HAVE A HEADLAMP.

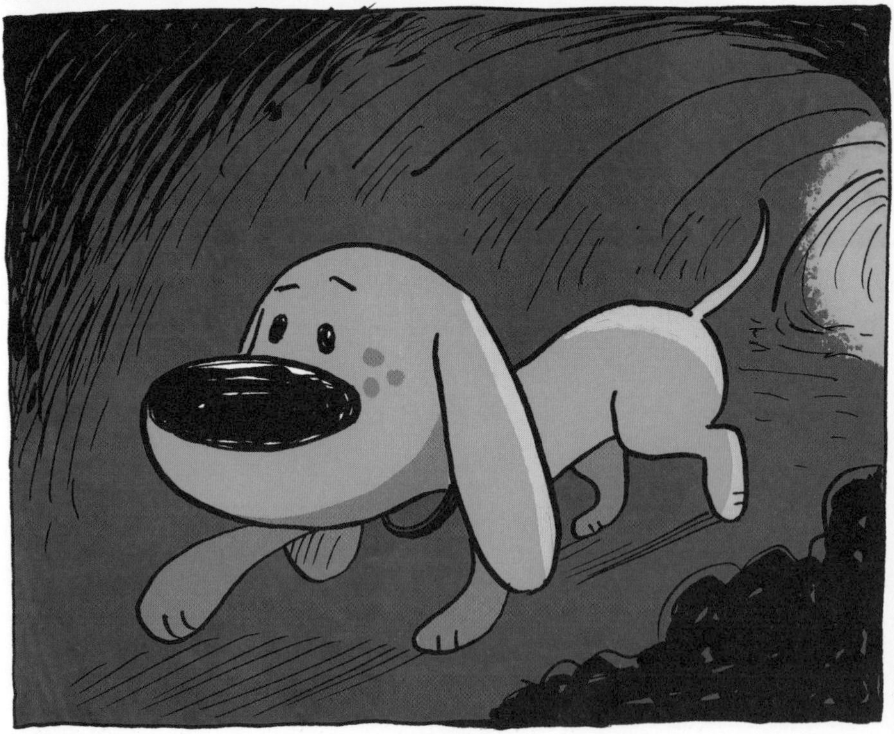

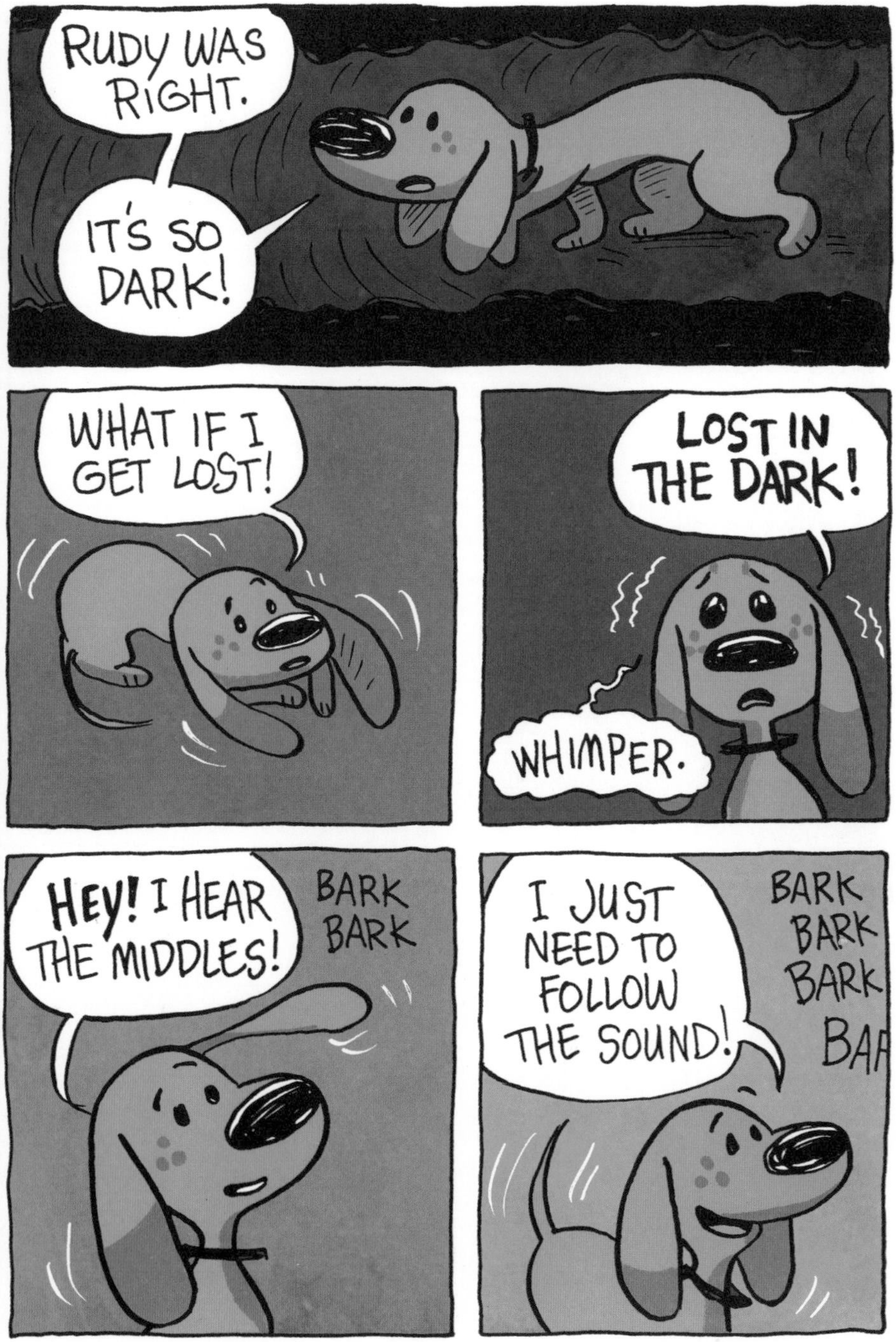
RUDY WAS RIGHT.
IT'S SO DARK!
WHAT IF I GET LOST!
LOST IN THE DARK!
WHIMPER.
HEY! I HEAR THE MIDDLES!
BARK BARK
I JUST NEED TO FOLLOW THE SOUND!
BARK BARK BARK

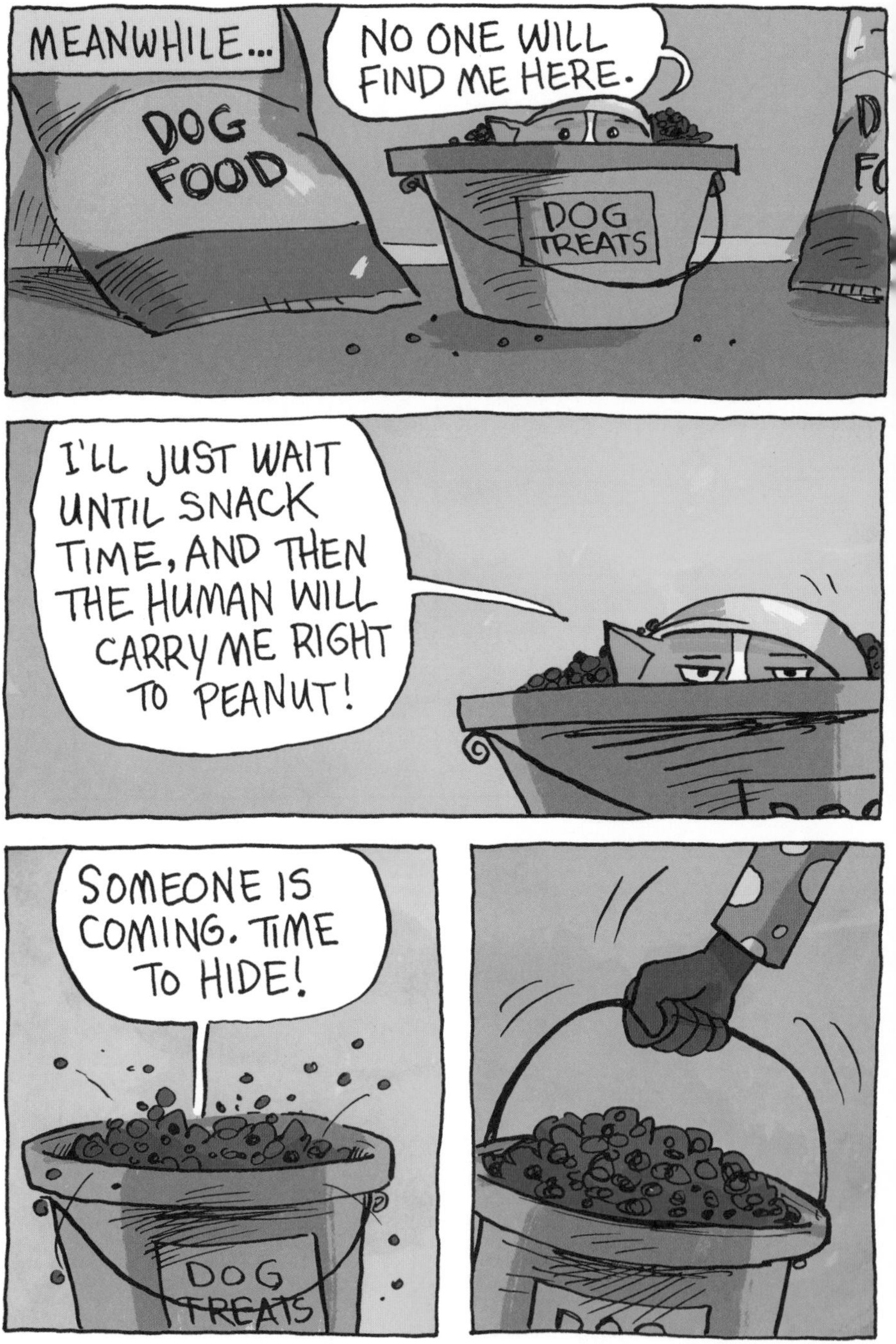
MEANWHILE...
NO ONE WILL FIND ME HERE.
DOG FOOD
DOG TREATS
I'LL JUST WAIT UNTIL SNACK TIME, AND THEN THE HUMAN WILL CARRY ME RIGHT TO PEANUT!
SOMEONE IS COMING. TIME TO HIDE!
DOG TREATS

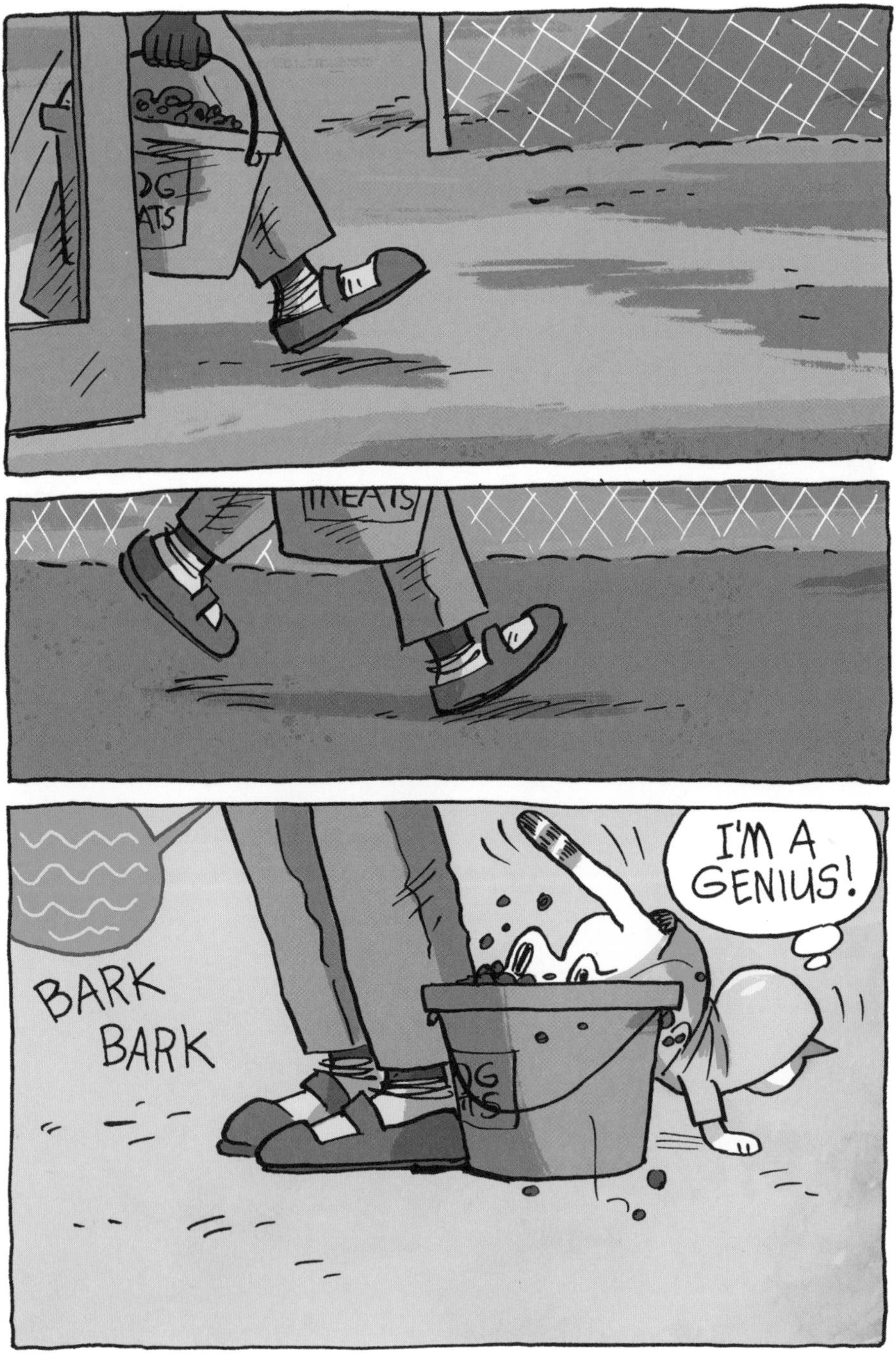
TREATS
BARK
BARK
I'M A GENIUS!

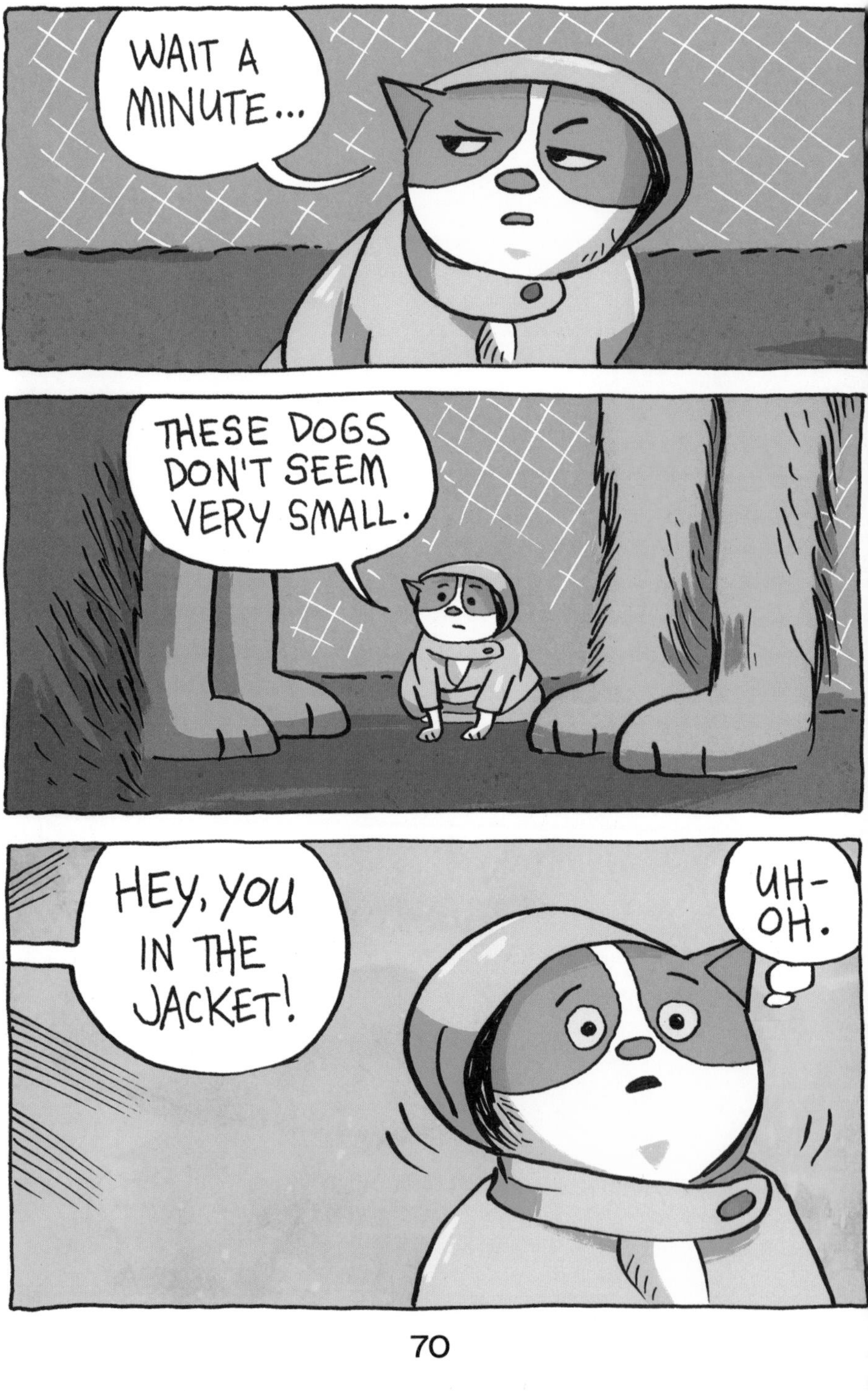
WAIT A MINUTE...
THESE DOGS DON'T SEEM VERY SMALL.
HEY, YOU IN THE JACKET!
UH-OH.

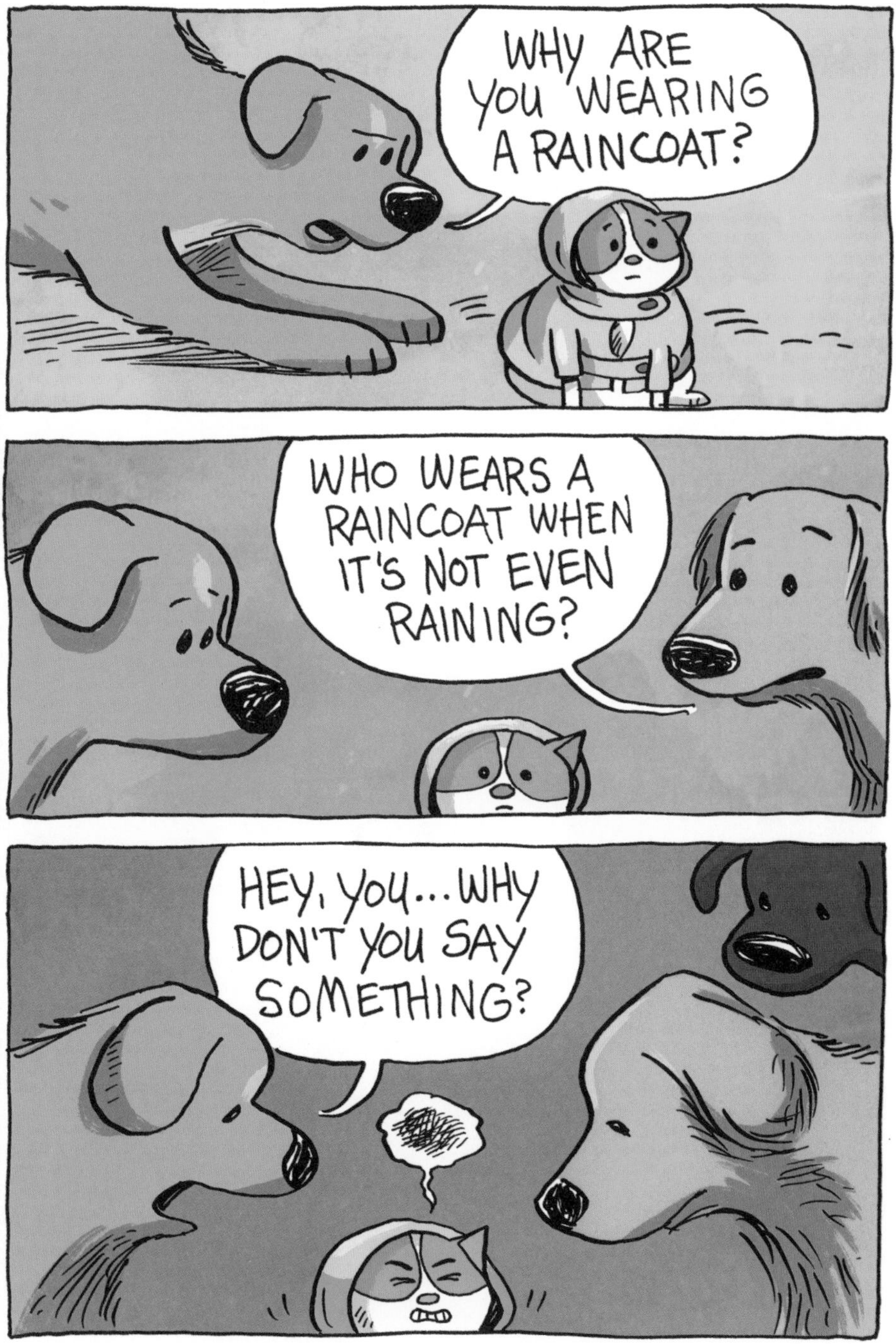
WHY ARE YOU WEARING A RAINCOAT?
WHO WEARS A RAINCOAT WHEN IT'S NOT EVEN RAINING?
HEY, YOU... WHY DON'T YOU SAY SOMETHING?

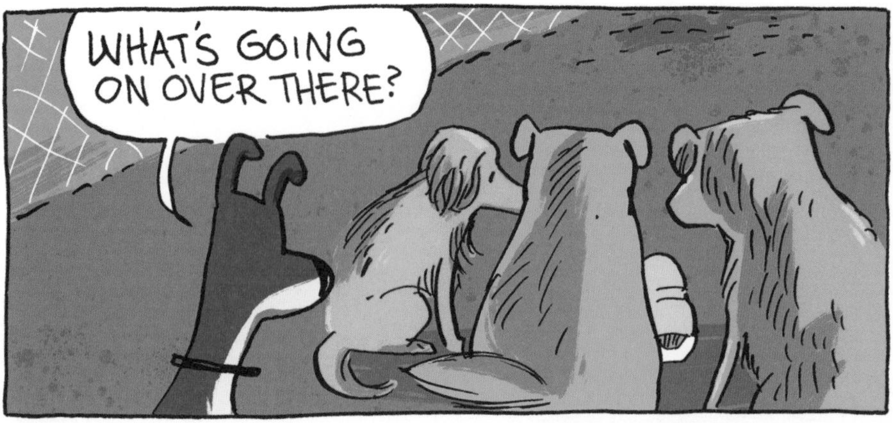
WHAT'S GOING ON OVER THERE?

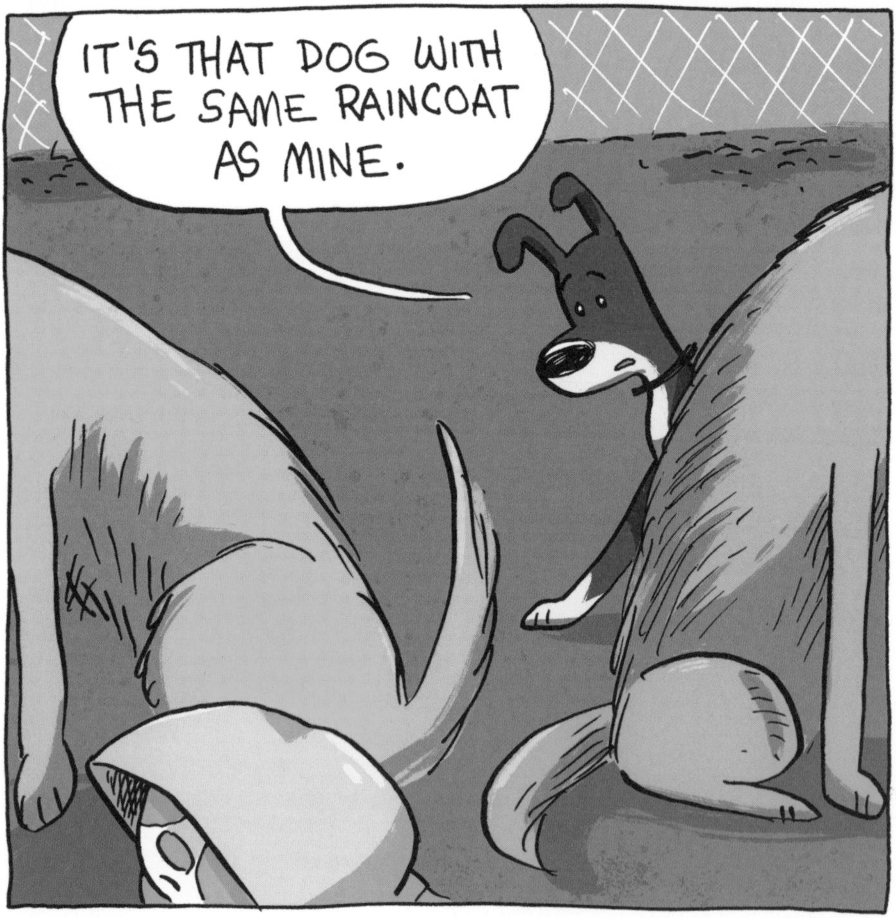
IT'S THAT DOG WITH THE SAME RAINCOAT AS MINE.

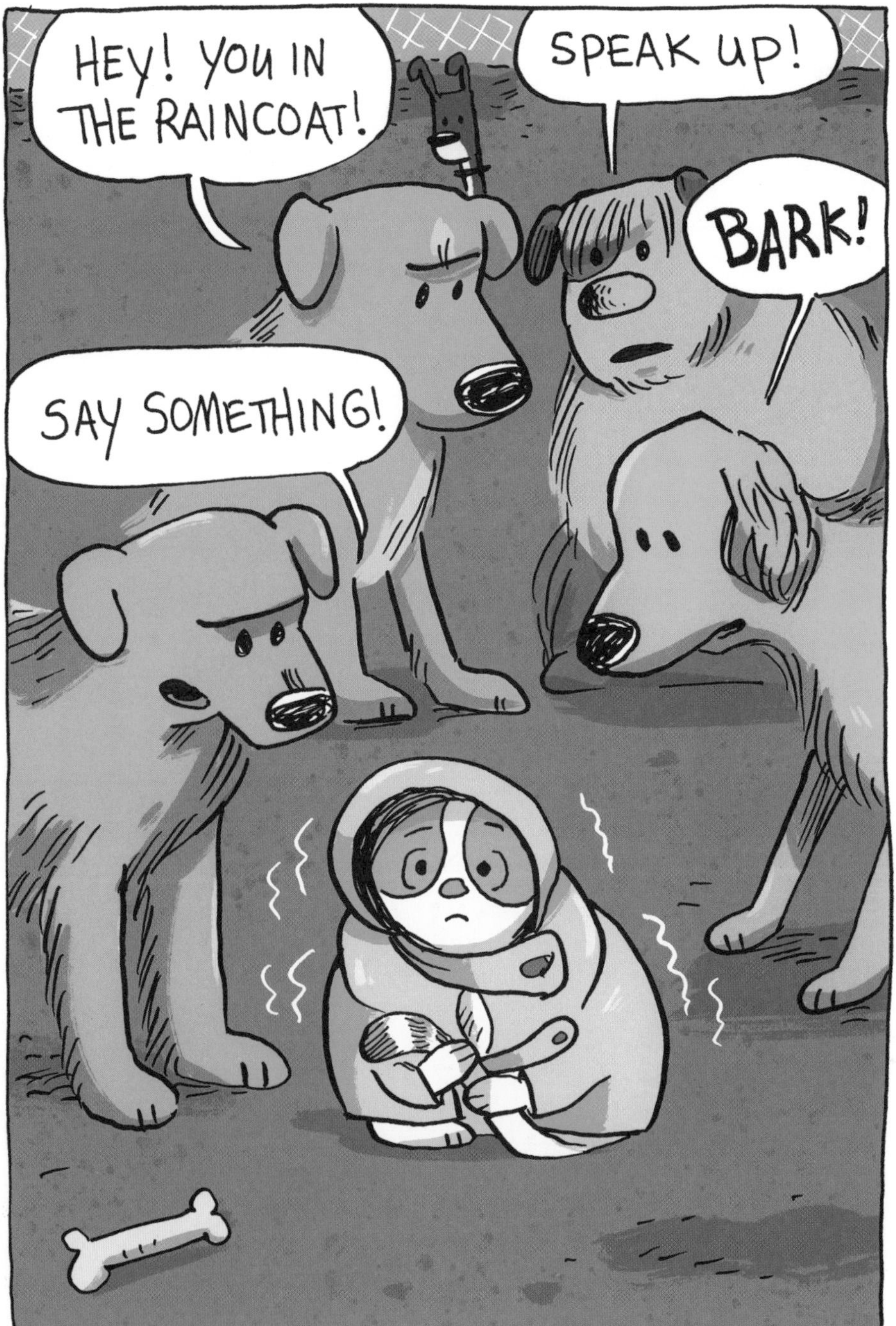
HEY! YOU IN THE RAINCOAT!
SPEAK UP!
BARK!
SAY SOMETHING!

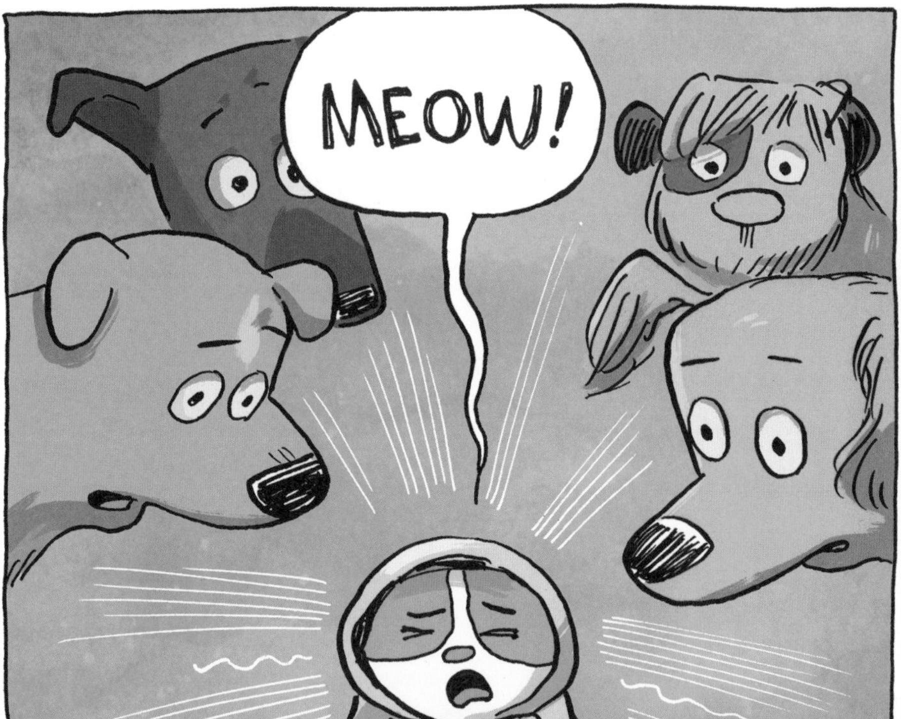
MEOW!

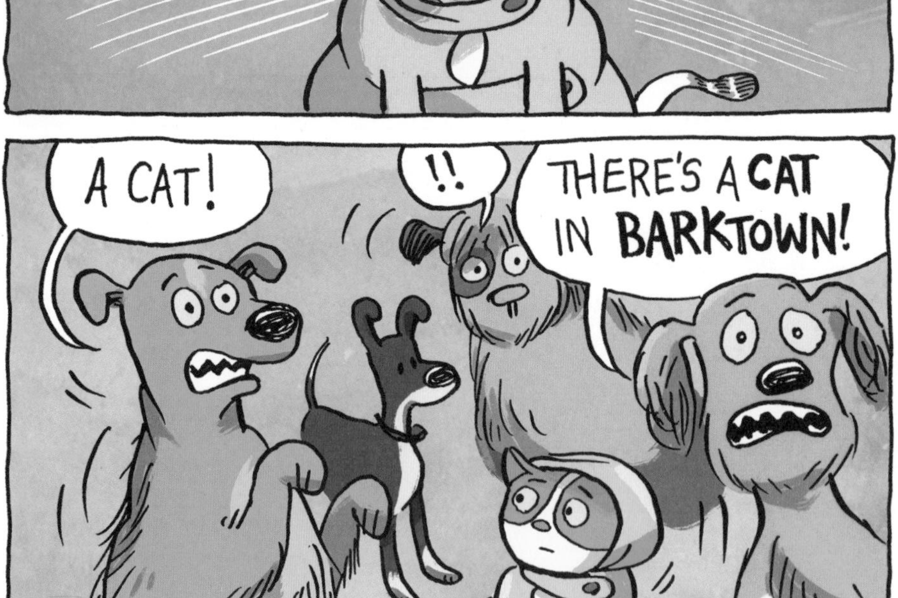
A CAT!
!!
THERE'S A CAT IN BARKTOWN!

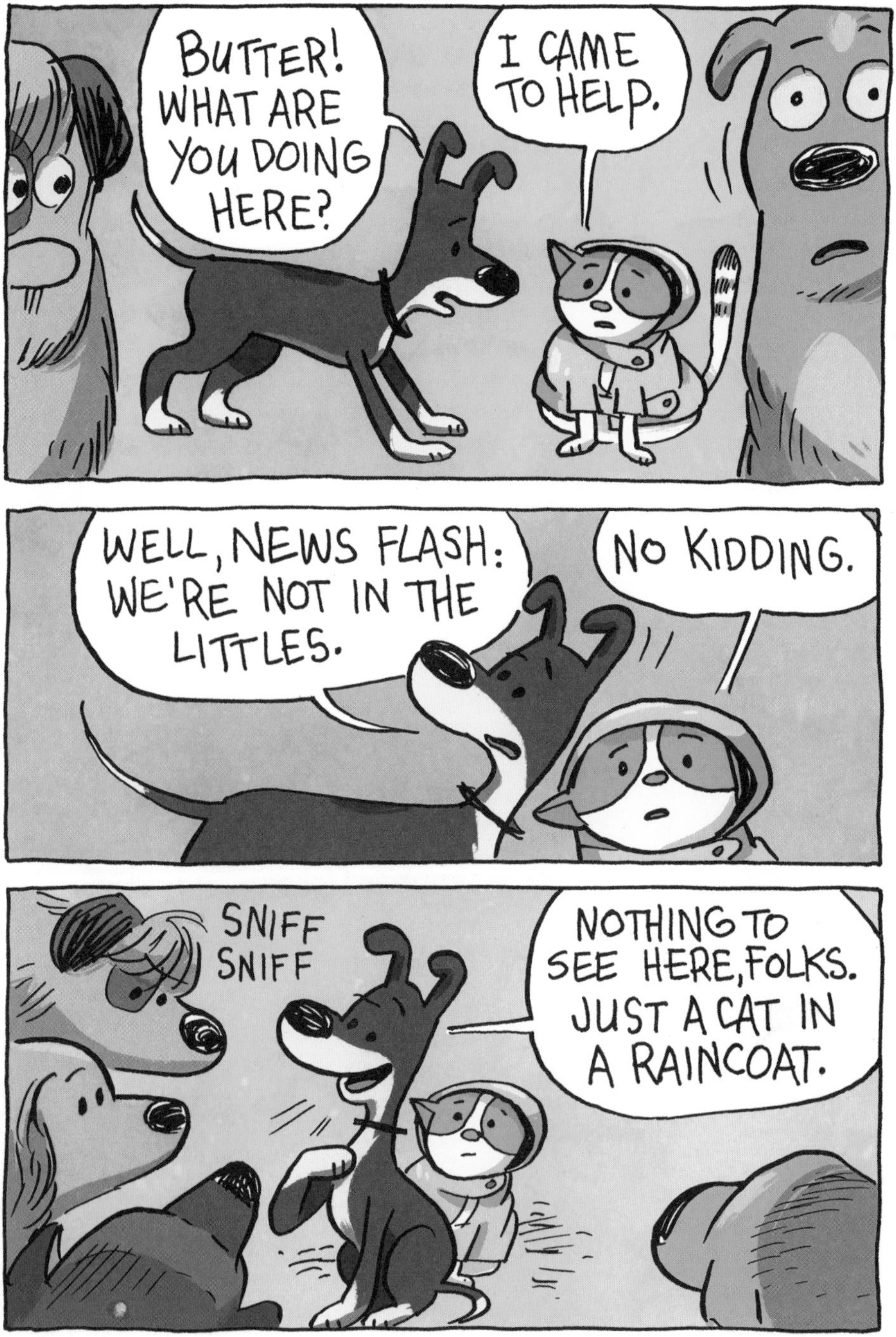
BUTTER! WHAT ARE YOU DOING HERE?
I CAME TO HELP.
WELL, NEWS FLASH: WE'RE NOT IN THE LITTLES.
NO KIDDING.
SNIFF SNIFF
NOTHING TO SEE HERE, FOLKS. JUST A CAT IN A RAINCOAT.

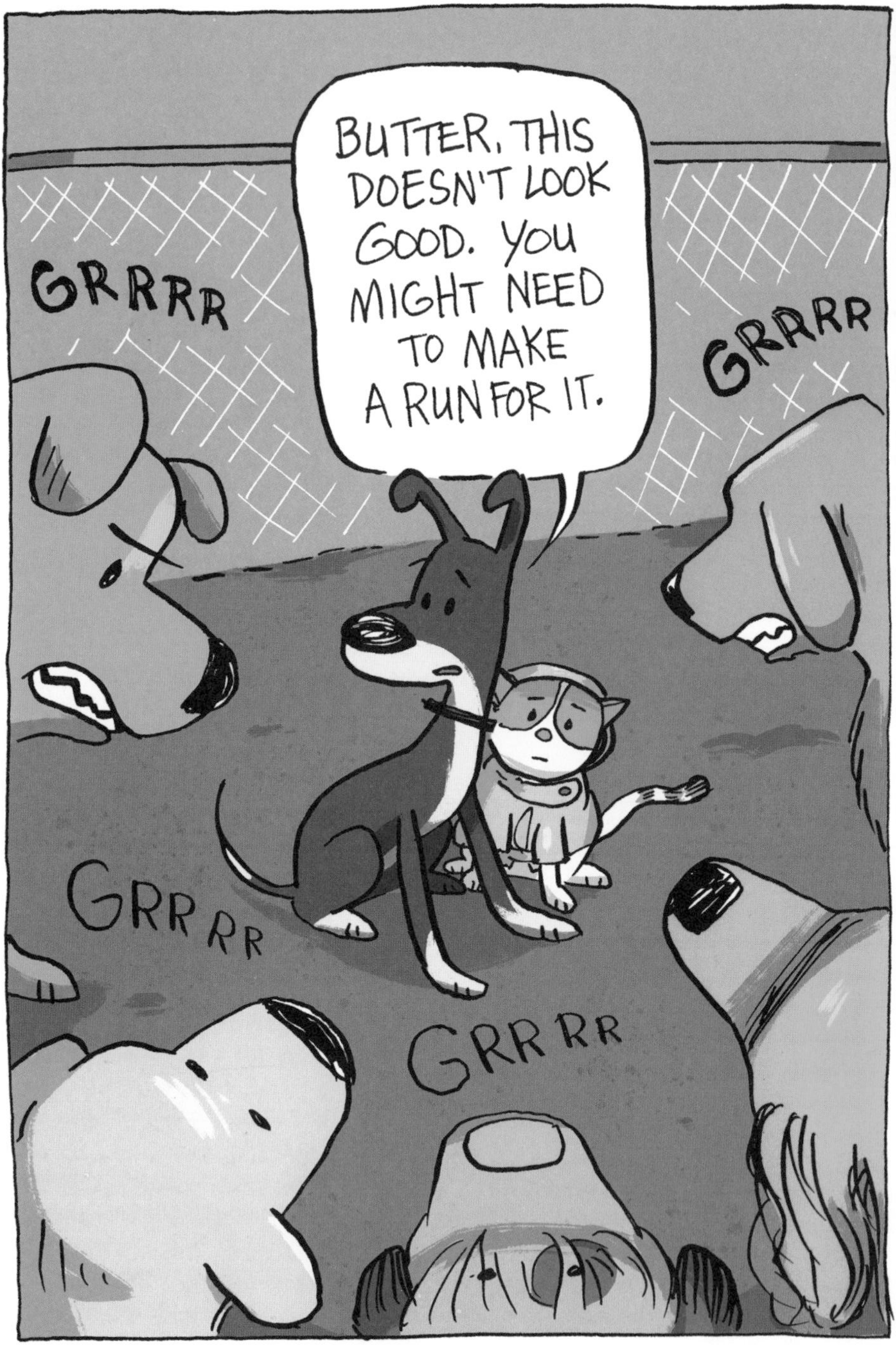
BUTTER, THIS DOESN'T LOOK GOOD. YOU MIGHT NEED TO MAKE A RUN FOR IT.
GRRRR
GRRRR
GRRRR
GRRRR

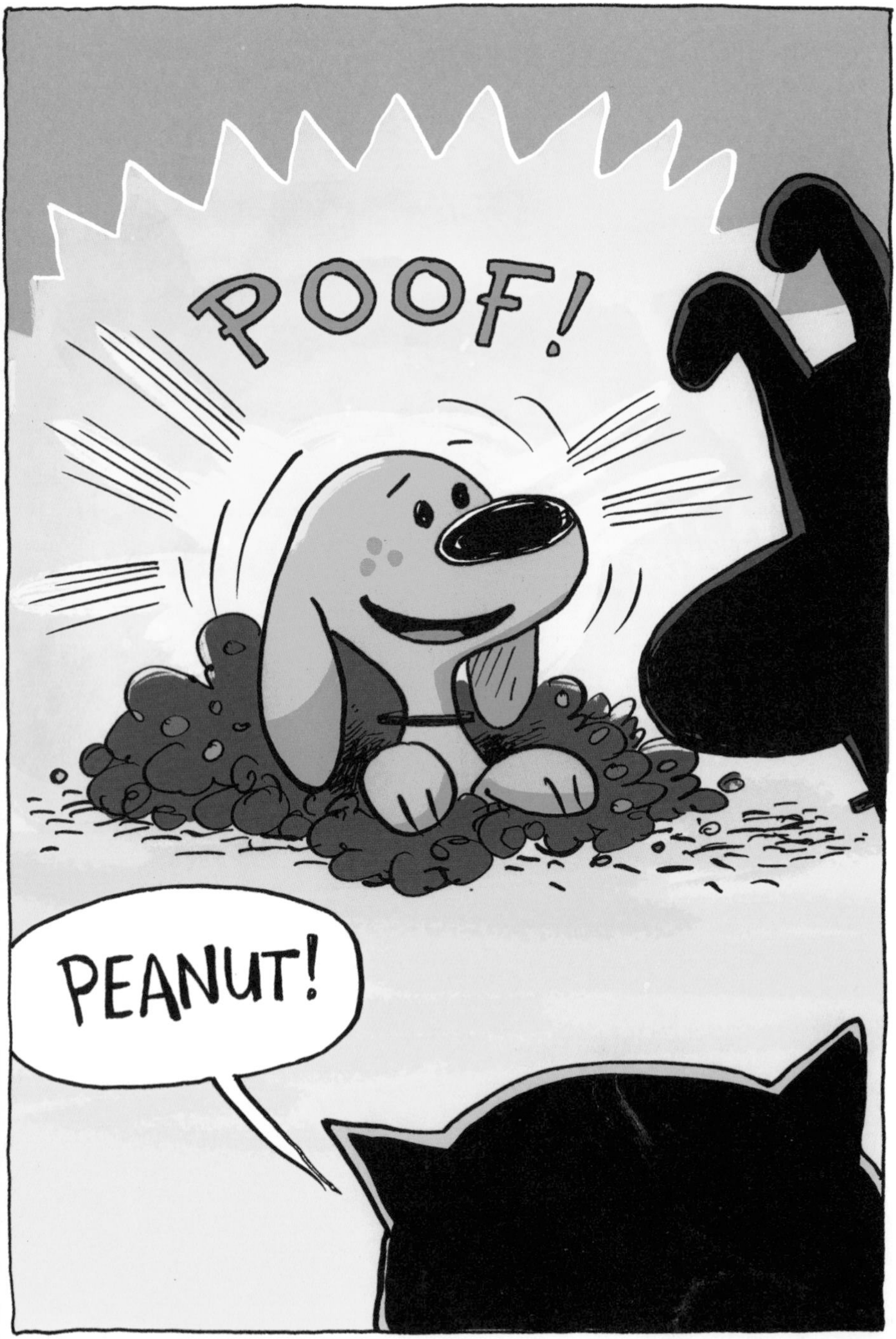
POOF!
PEANUT!

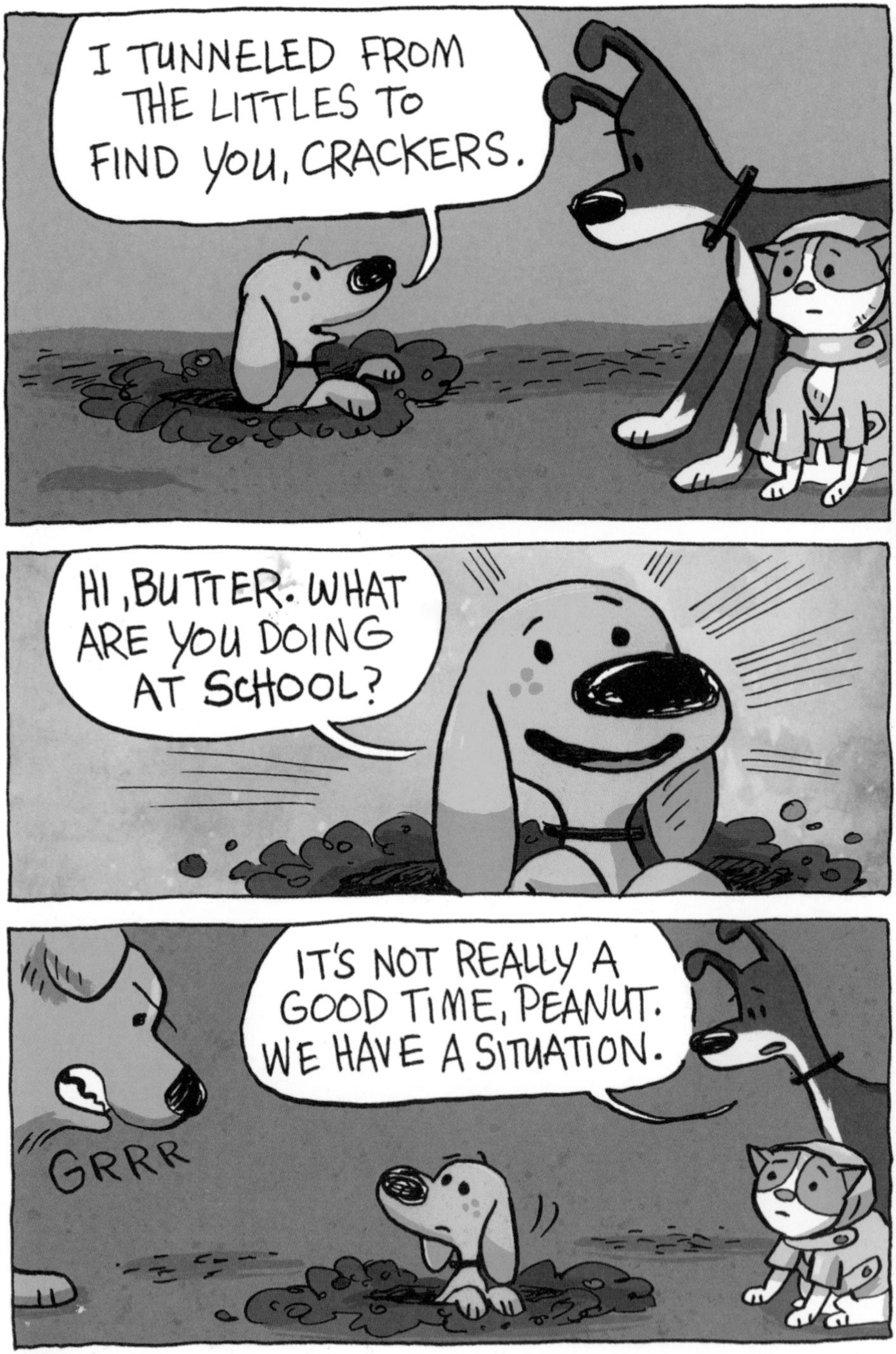
I TUNNELED FROM THE LITTLES TO FIND YOU, CRACKERS.
HI, BUTTER. WHAT ARE YOU DOING AT SCHOOL?
IT'S NOT REALLY A GOOD TIME, PEANUT. WE HAVE A SITUATION.
GRRR

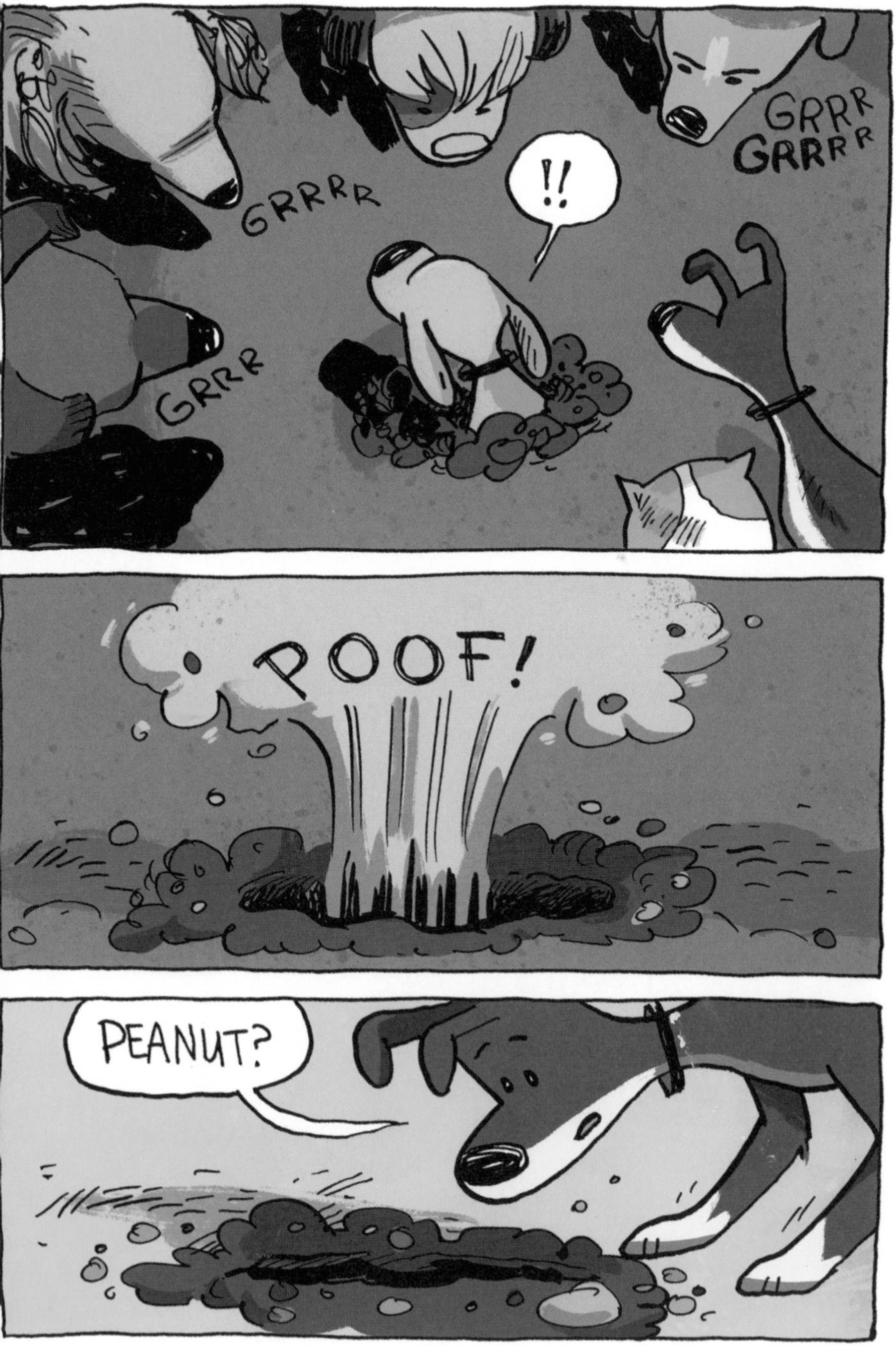
GRRR
GRRRR
!!
GRRRR
GRRRR
GRRR
POOF!
PEANUT?

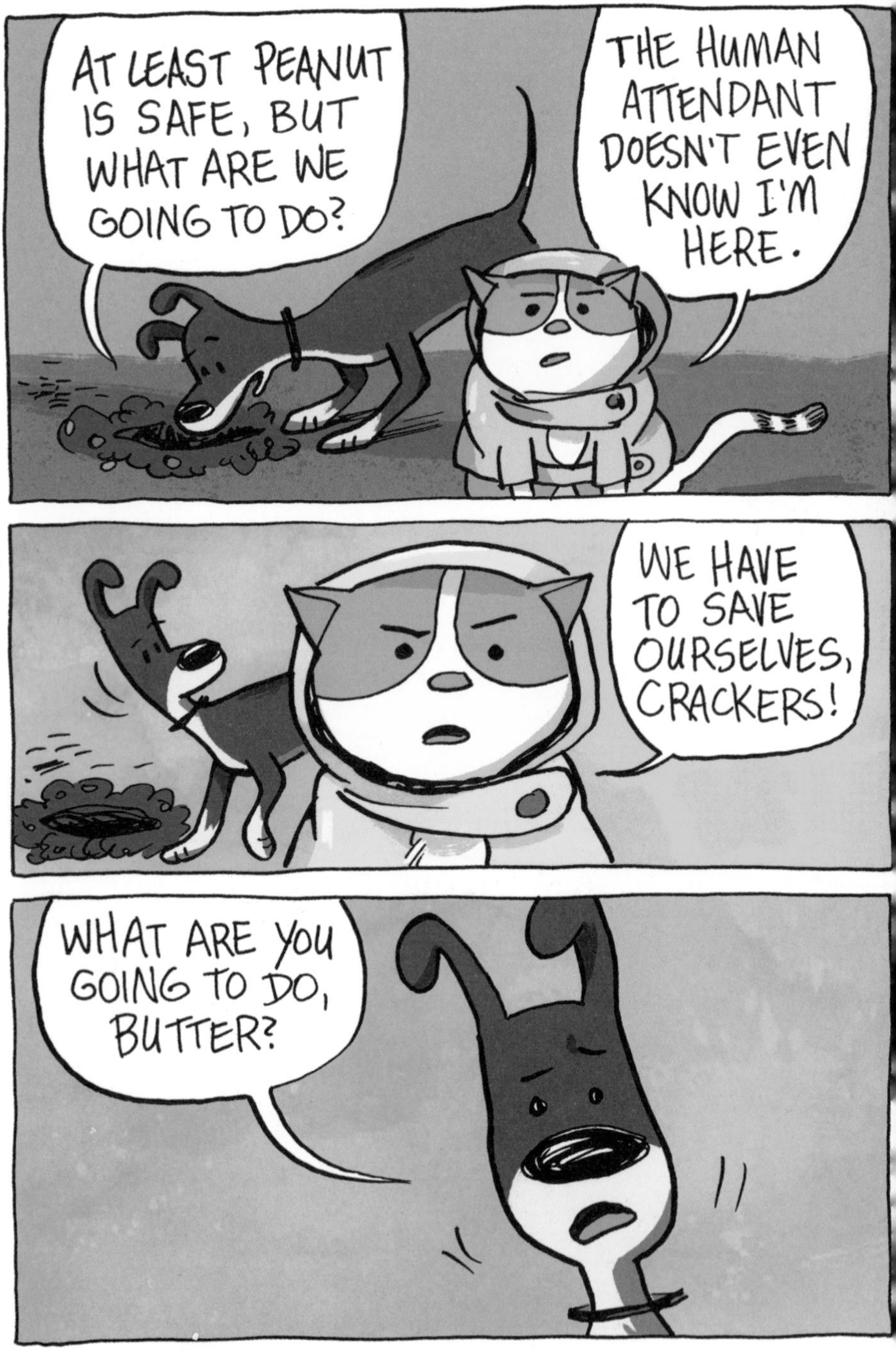
AT LEAST PEANUT IS SAFE, BUT WHAT ARE WE GOING TO DO?
THE HUMAN ATTENDANT DOESN'T EVEN KNOW I'M HERE.
WE HAVE TO SAVE OURSELVES, CRACKERS!
WHAT ARE YOU GOING TO DO, BUTTER?

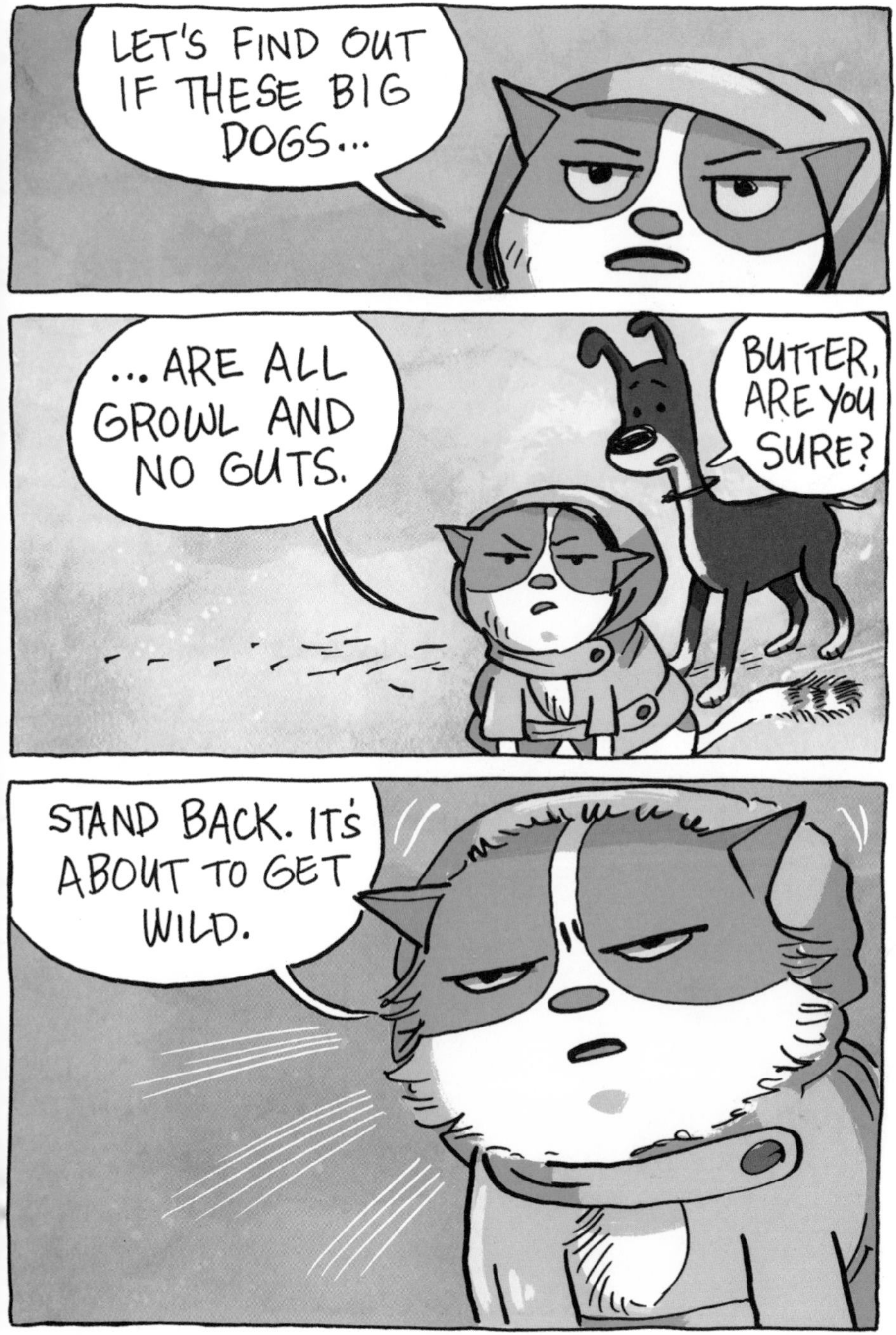
LET'S FIND OUT IF THESE BIG DOGS...
... ARE ALL GROWL AND NO GUTS.
BUTTER, ARE YOU SURE?
STAND BACK. IT'S ABOUT TO GET WILD.

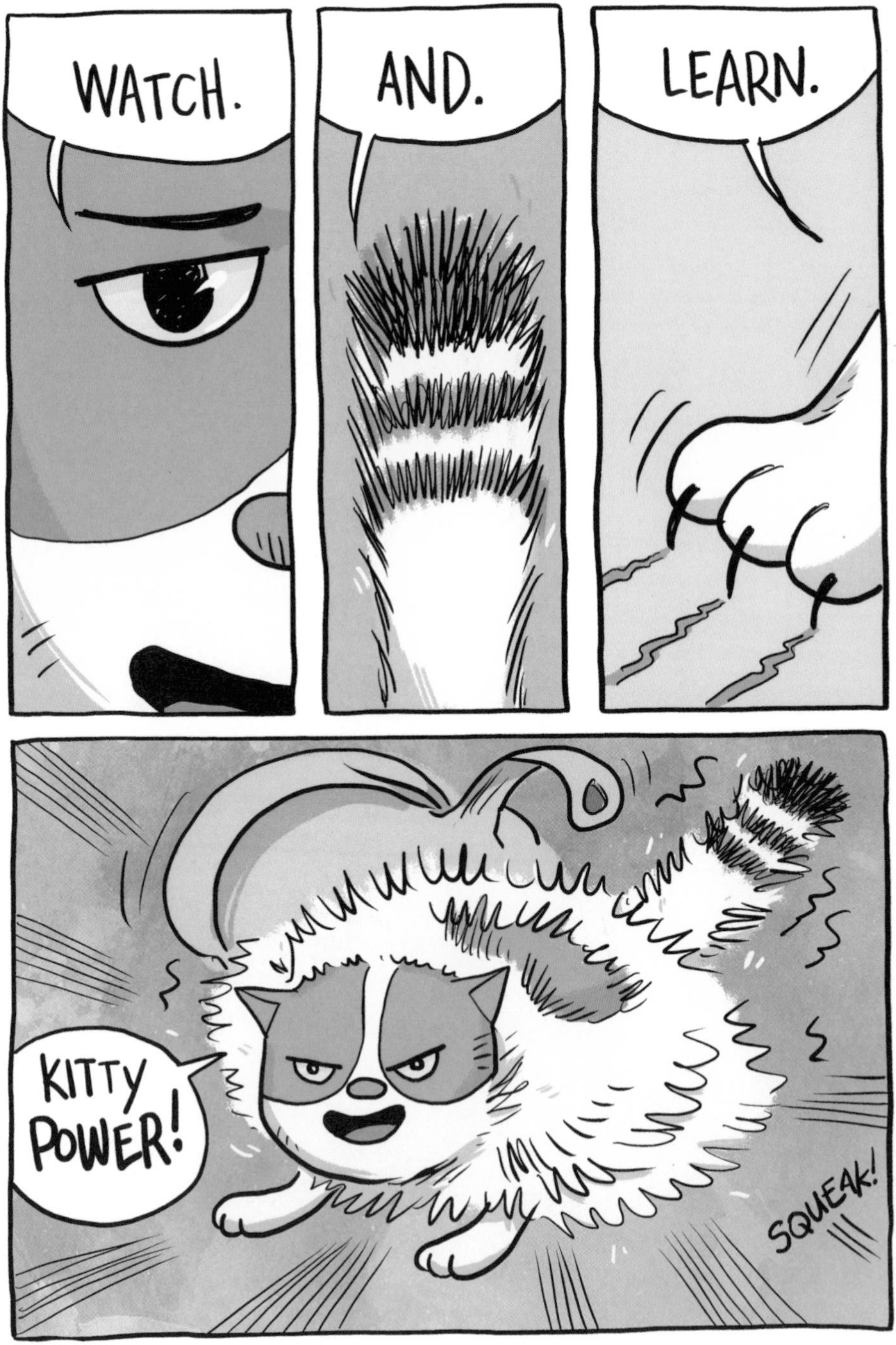
WATCH.
AND.
LEARN.
KITTY POWER!
SQUEAK!

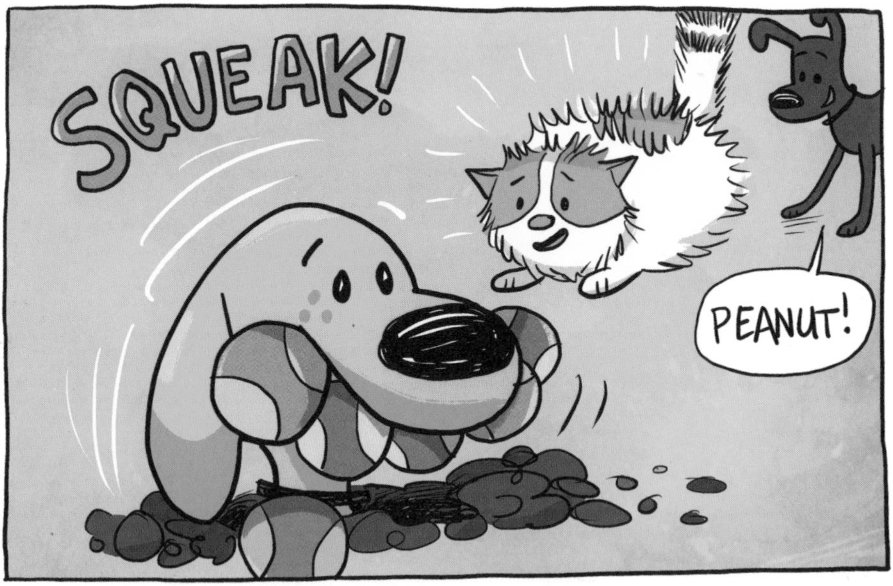
SQUEAK!
PEANUT!

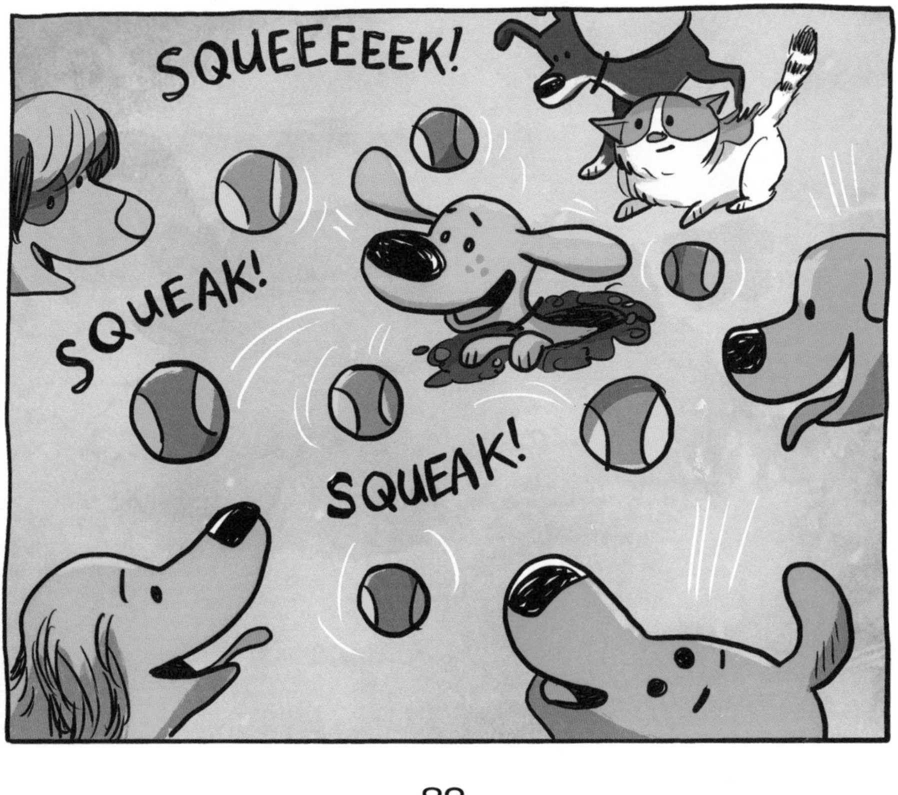
SQUEEEEEEK!
SQUEAK!
SQUEAK!

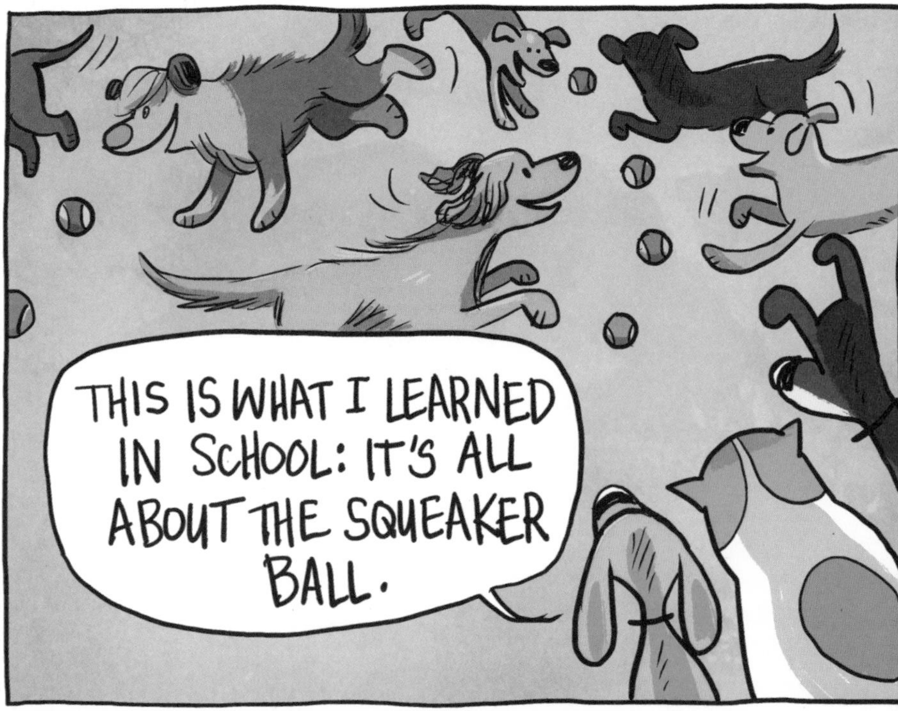
THIS IS WHAT I LEARNED IN SCHOOL: IT'S ALL ABOUT THE SQUEAKER BALL.

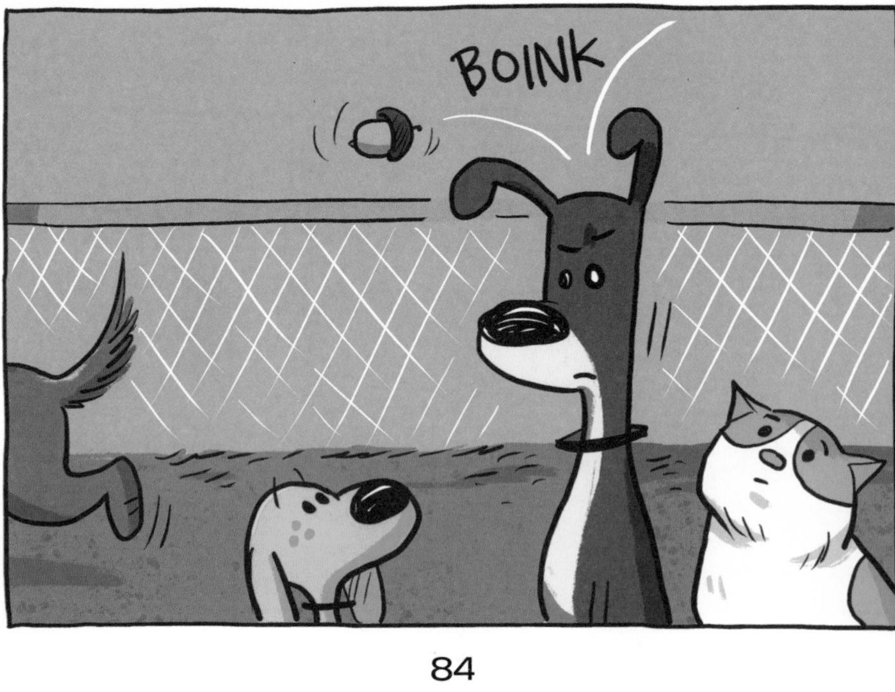
BOINK

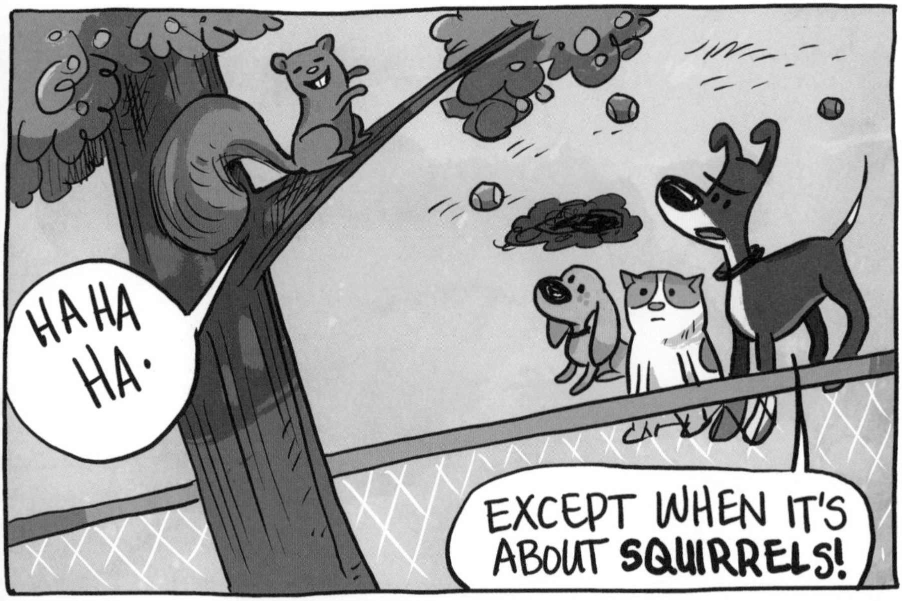
HAHA HA.
EXCEPT WHEN IT'S ABOUT **SQUIRRELS!**

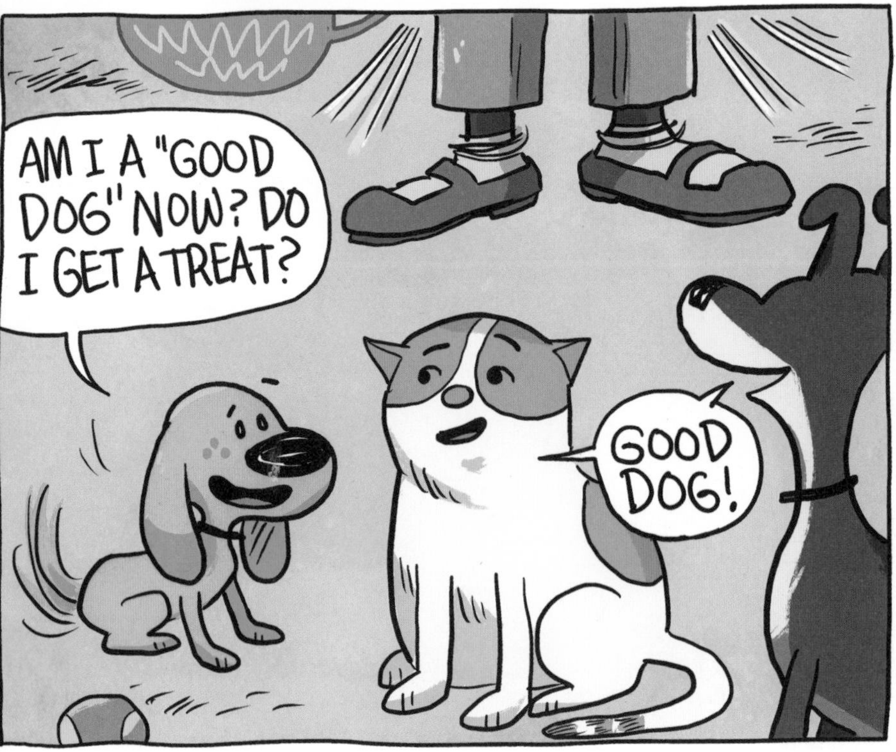
AM I A "GOOD DOG" NOW? DO I GET A TREAT?
GOOD DOG!

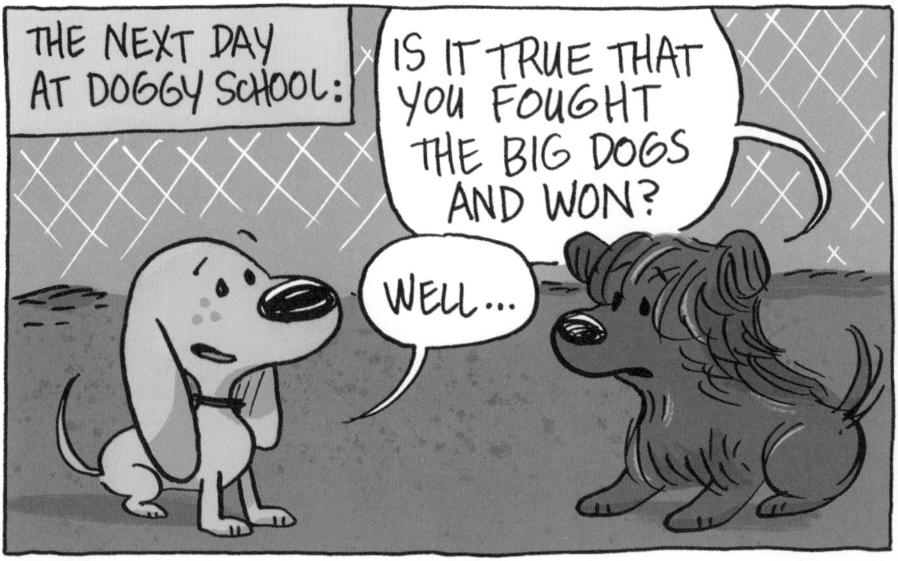
THE NEXT DAY AT DOGGY SCHOOL:
IS IT TRUE THAT YOU FOUGHT THE BIG DOGS AND WON?
WELL...

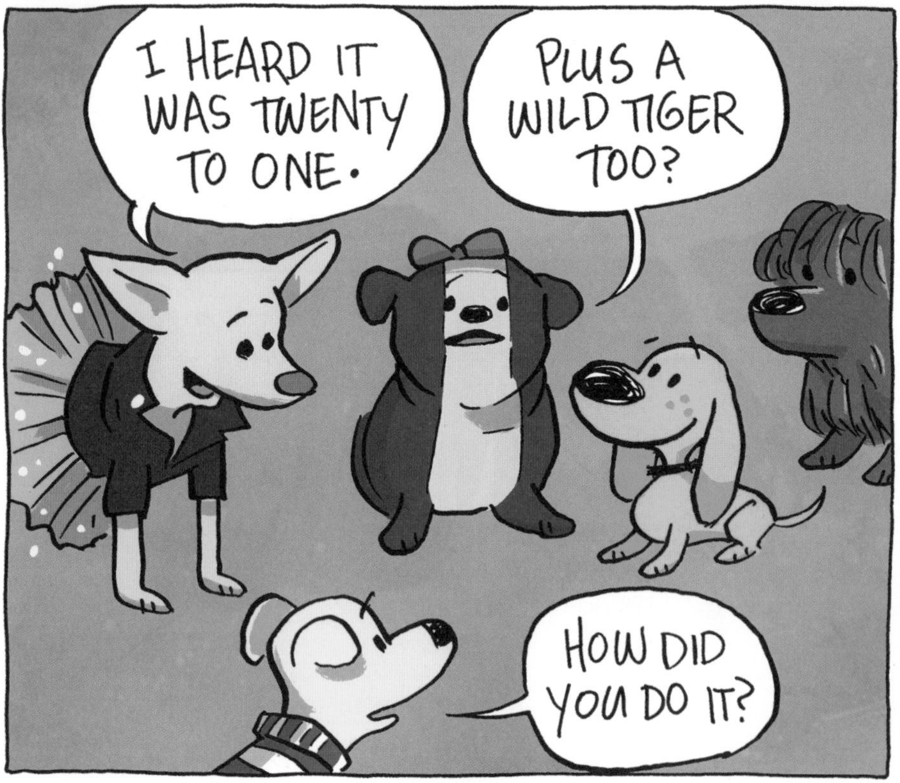
I HEARD IT WAS TWENTY TO ONE.
PLUS A WILD TIGER TOO?
HOW DID YOU DO IT?

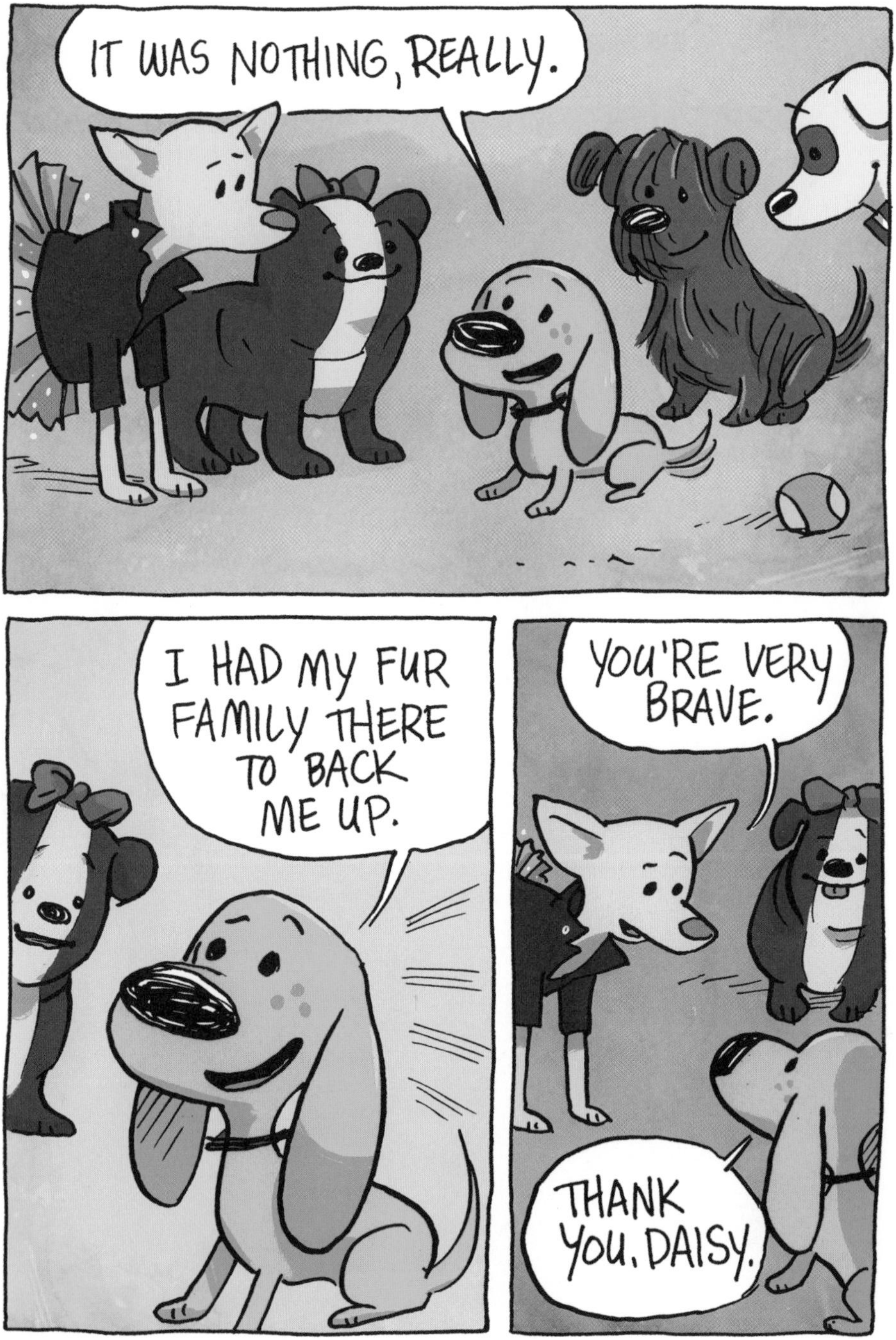
IT WAS NOTHING, REALLY.
I HAD MY FUR FAMILY THERE TO BACK ME UP.
YOU'RE VERY BRAVE.
THANK YOU, DAISY.

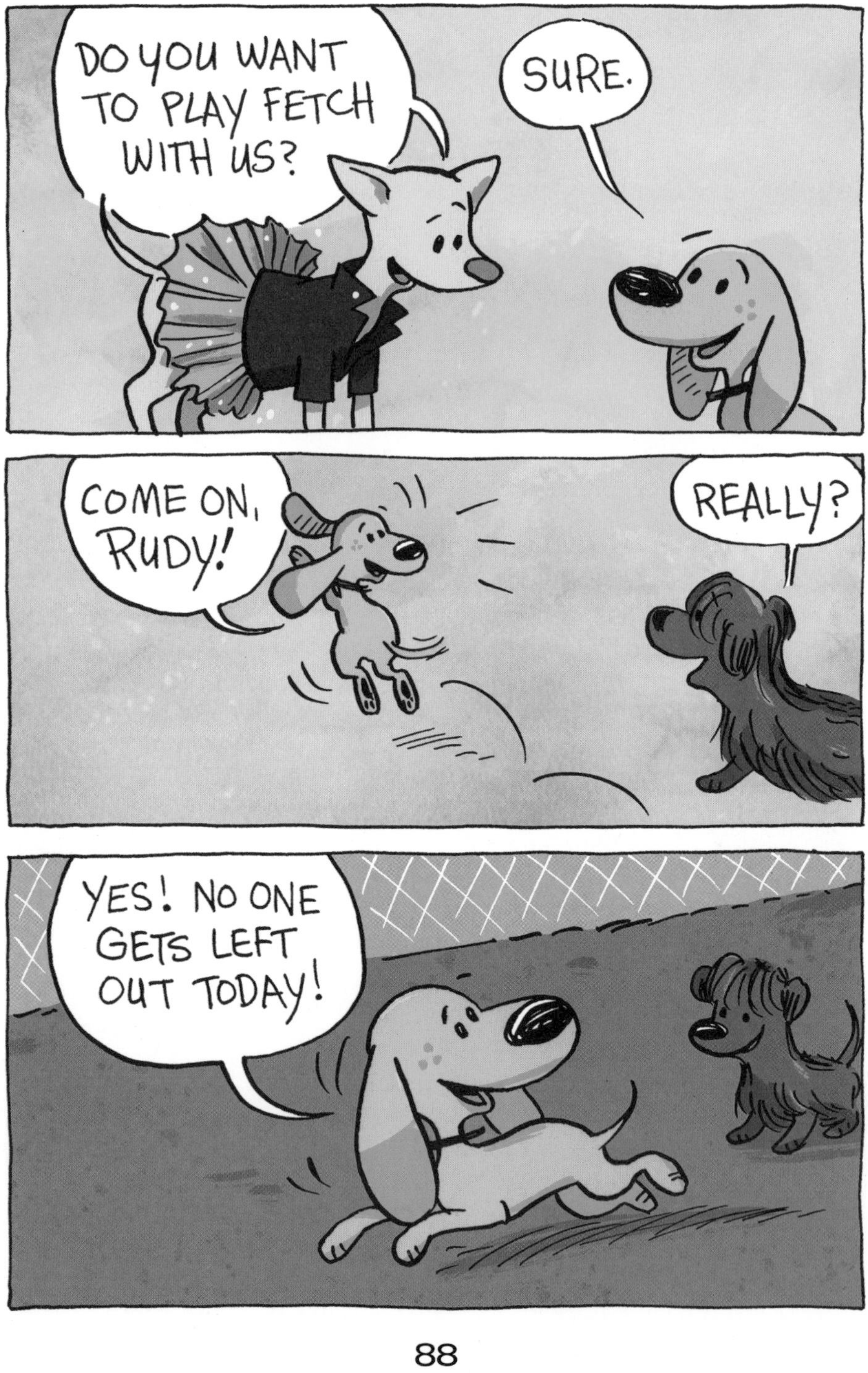
DO YOU WANT TO PLAY FETCH WITH US?
SURE.
COME ON, RUDY!
REALLY?
YES! NO ONE GETS LEFT OUT TODAY!

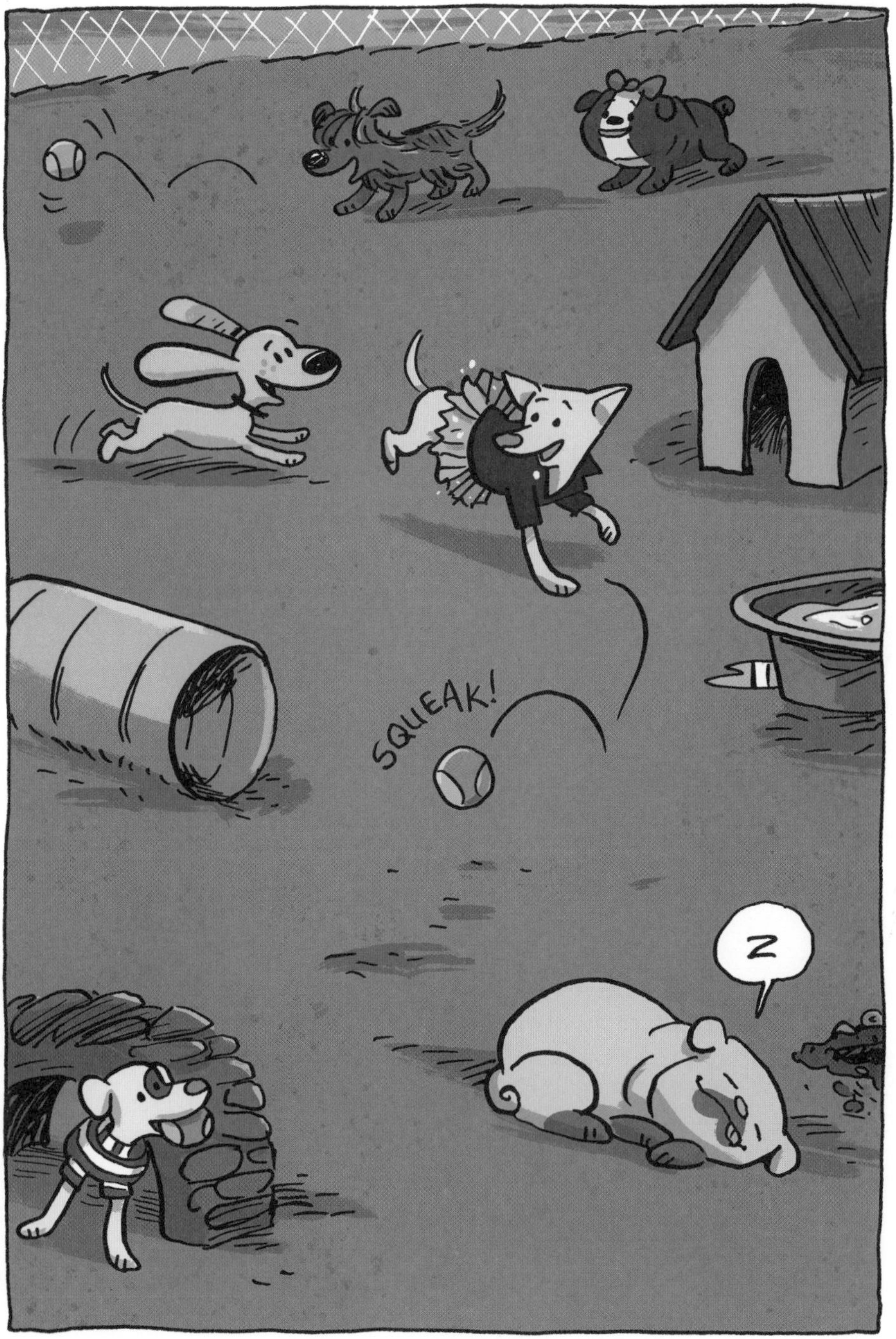
SQUEAK!
Z

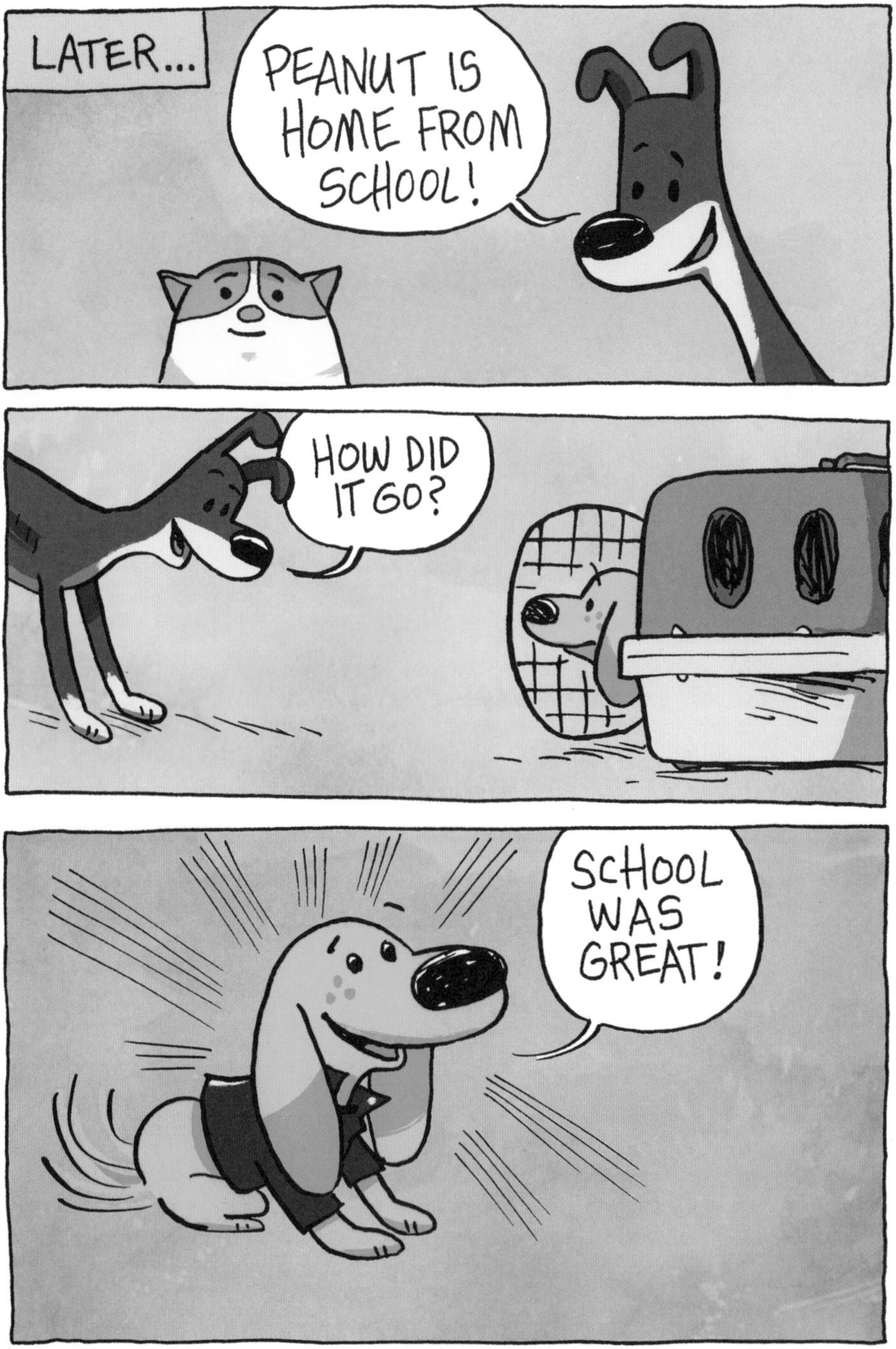
LATER...
PEANUT IS HOME FROM SCHOOL!
HOW DID IT GO?
SCHOOL WAS GREAT!

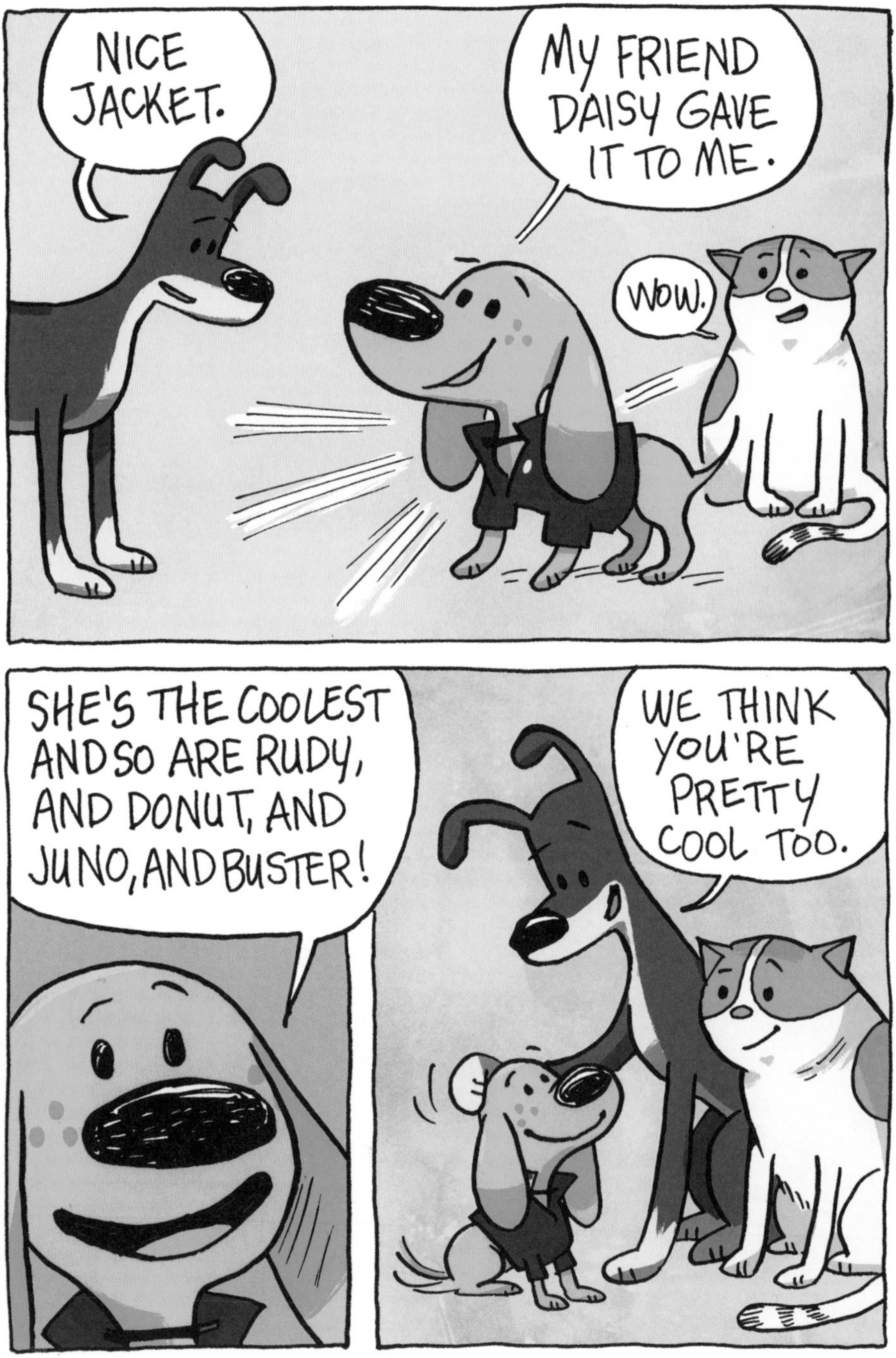
NICE JACKET.
MY FRIEND DAISY GAVE IT TO ME.
WOW.
SHE'S THE COOLEST AND SO ARE RUDY, AND DONUT, AND JUNO, AND BUSTER!
WE THINK YOU'RE PRETTY COOL TOO.

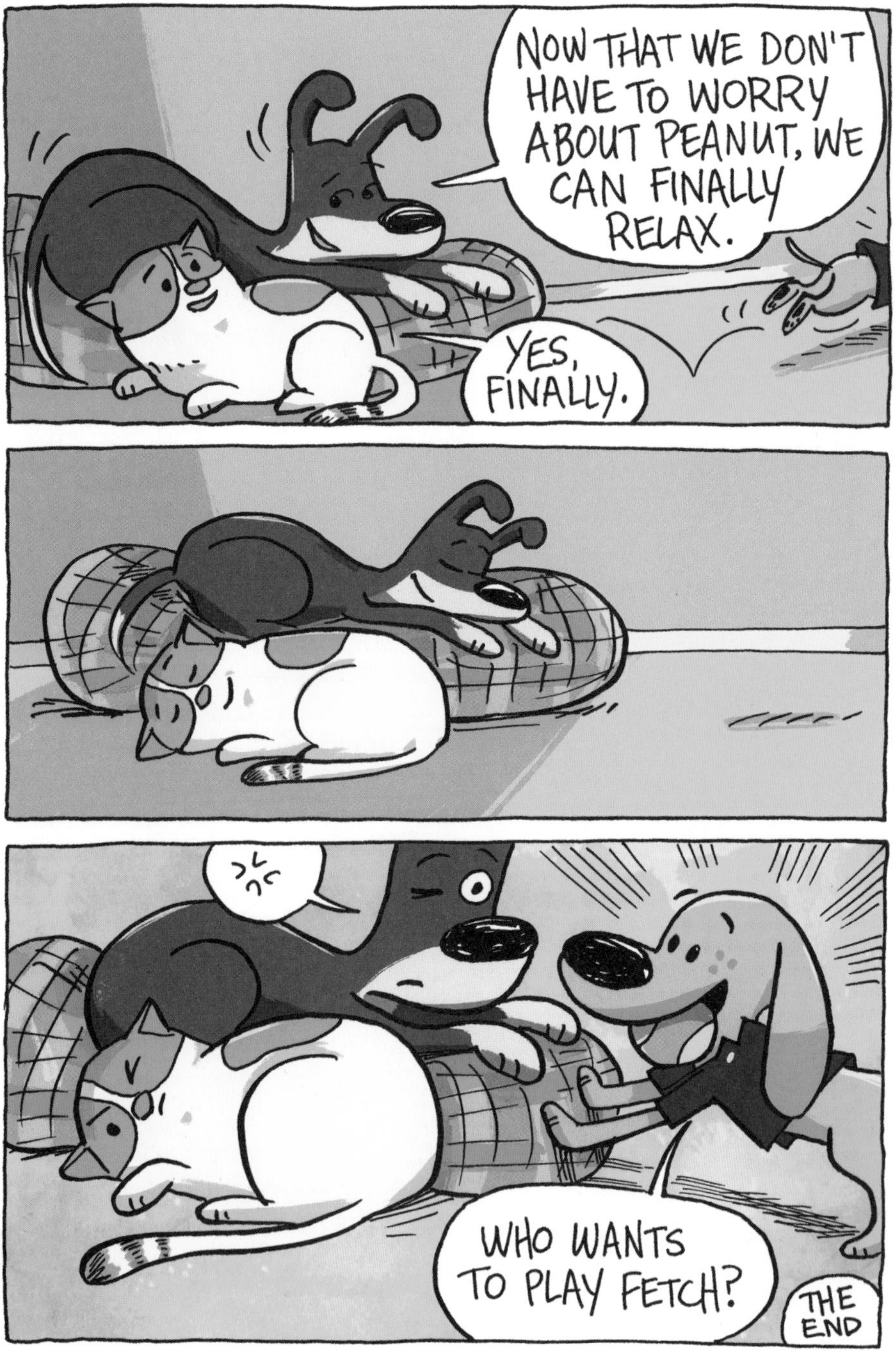
NOW THAT WE DON'T HAVE TO WORRY ABOUT PEANUT, WE CAN FINALLY RELAX.
YES, FINALLY.
WHO WANTS TO PLAY FETCH?
THE END

MEET **PAIGE BRADDOCK**

I started drawing comics when I was seven years old. Wiggins, Mississippi, the town I grew up in, was very small. Wiggins didn't have a comic shop or a bookstore. Mostly, I learned about comics by reading the Sunday funnies in the newspaper. My favorite characters to draw were Snoopy, Popeye, and Beetle Bailey. It wasn't long before I started creating my own characters. *Captain Lightning* was the first comics story I wrote and drew. It starred a very clumsy superhero whose cape was always getting snagged on fences and bushes.

Comics have always been one of my favorite things. I majored in illustration in college at the University of Tennessee and later worked as an illustrator for several newspapers. Then I got my dream job: working with Charles M. Schulz at his studio in California. He was the creator of Charlie Brown, Snoopy, and the whole *Peanuts* gang. It's funny how things work out sometimes. Snoopy was one of my all-time favorite characters and now I get to work with him every day.

I've always loved to draw dogs, but when our pet Buddy Barker came to live with us, I started drawing dogs even more often. Buddy was one of the main inspirations for the Peanut, Butter, & Crackers series. Of course, I can't leave out our cat, Otis—who once ate a *whole stick* of butter—and when we added our little dachshund, Charlie, to the mix, we really did have puppy problems!

It's important as artists and writers to figure out what inspires us and to make that part of our story—and *everybody* has a story to tell!

ACKNOWLEDGMENTS

I'd like to offer special thanks to the colorist for this book, Kat Efird. Her color work is amazing and I feel lucky that she was able to collaborate with me on this series. A big thank-you goes out to my editor, Sheila Keenan, and the team at Viking: Meriam Metoui, Jim Hoover, and Lucia Baez. My wife, Evelyn, was a great sounding board for ideas; her sense of humor inspires me to be funnier. And lastly, I'd like to mention Almost Home Doggie Day Care in Forestville, California. Thank you for always taking such good care of Buddy Barker and Charlie and for inspiring some of the scenes in this story.